The Warrior Rabbi

DAVID R. GROSS

David R. Gross
730 112th St. SW Everett, WA 98204
e-mail: gross1@illinois.edu
website: docdavesvoice.com
phone: 206-554-1736

ISBN: 978-1-64550-643-0

CONTENTS

One

THE WELL-TRAVELED HIGHWAY from Cordoba to Malaga follows the course of an old Roman road built over a thousand years ago. The road runs south and slightly east from Cordoba, and is a little less than two hundred kilometers in length. Under normal circumstances, it is an easy eight-day trip on foot.

Before leaving Cordoba, our small group of emigrants inquired every traveler we could find about the most recent information about attacks on the roads by outlaw Berber bands. We needed to know where the attacks occurred so we could avoid those areas.

We left Cordoba walking northeast on the road to Montoro, opposite to the direction of Malaga. Two days later, we were on a little-traveled road heading south and west. There were eight of us, all less than twenty-three years old, all scholars, none of us trained nor inclined to fight. In fact, none of us had weapons, except for our small eating knives. Six of us led donkeys loaded with camping equipment, provisions, and a few of our favorite books. Two of my Jewish friends were walking with backpacks,unable to afford the purchase of a donkey. I had twenty gold coins carefully concealed inside the lining, at different locations, ofmy cloak.

As we approach the Guadajoz River crossing we encountered two travelers, merchants, also leading loaded donkeys.They were on their way to Montoro.

"Did you come from Baena?" I asked.

"Yes, it is not far."

"And you did not encounter any bandits?"

"No, the road is clear.But the Berber bandits are active in the countryside west of Baena."

Our plan, once we arrived in Baena, was to make our way east then south again, skirting the eastern slopes of the SubbéticaMountains, then to continue south toward Archidona.

I was walking in the lead of our little caravan. My donkey suddenly stopped, lifted his head, pointed his ears forward, flicked those remarkable long appendages in all directions, independent of each other, then held them alertly forward again,immobile. I strained but could see nothing. My donkey'sbehavior transmitted to the other animals and to my companions.I finally realized something or someone was coming toward us.

I twisted my head in all directions, seeking a place to hide. Off to my left, maybe two hundred meters away, I spotted a gully, its banks covered with a thick stand of alders. I pointed to it and moved quickly in that direction. Donkey—that is what I named him—followed closely, his lead rope slack;there was no need to tug him. He was more aware of danger than I was.

We weaved our way through a thick grove of red-barked corkoaks, their acorns crunching under our feet and the hooves of our pack animals. The donkeys, all sensitive to our fear, did not try to snatch at one of their favorite treats; they ignored the acorns littering the ground. In less than a minute we were all crouched in the gully, standing in a thin trickle of clear water. Close to the bank, the alders grew on either side. The air was thick with the strong scentof rosemary emanating from the bushes that helped hide us.

I took a quick peek over the rim of the gully and noticed a carob tree, its fruit hanging like single,overripe bananas; nothing more. My companions and I had our hands over our donkeys' noses to keep them from braying. I didn't worry about Donkey; he would not betray me, but I keptmy hand on his nose nevertheless. A band of perhaps twenty Berbers rode slowly past, unaware of us. They were laughing and talking, loudly repeating ribald and detailed descriptions about the small village they had just raided and the endowments of the women they raped. We stayed crouched, hiding, until the sound of them was no longer audible. We waited, still hidden, another ten minutes, then emerged, deeming it safe to continue on our way.

* * *

At forty-two years of age, it is not common to become a father for the first time. My Muslim masters oftenproducedoffspring at ages much advanced of mine, but theystartedwhen they wereyoung and hadmultiple wives and concubines. My emotionssurged through my head and chest like waves crashing against a rocky shoreline during a Mediterranean storm. With each breath my chest heaved; tears filled my eyes until they rolled gently down my face into my graying beard. There was a burning in my nose up into my sinuses. My first son, Joseph,was bornthree hours before dawn on the third day of the week, the eleventh day of Tishrei 4784, of the Hebrew calendar,426 years after the Hejira, according to the reckoning of our Muslim masters, and the year 1035 according to the Christians. It was a day of wonder and rejoicing.

I watched as my wife lay with my son in the crook of her left arm, his face pressed to her breast.Blessed be God, both were both sleeping quietly, their breathing barely audible, but regular. I was truly blessed and murmured my thanks to*Adonai.*

* * *

My name is Sh'muel Ha Levi ben Yosef ibn Nagrela. In Arabic I amcalled Ishma'il ibn Nagrela. I now live happily in Granada, the citybuilt on, and around, a huge rocky hill that dominates the river valley. The top of the hill is flat,thus forming a natural fortress, with steep cliffs on three sides. The Romans used the top of this same hill to erect a fortress of stone. Those same stonesnow comprise the foundation of the current alcazaba. Although I hold an important position in the government, my house is not within the alcazaba. I reside in the Jewish community of Granada, a separate walled city within the city, known as Gharnatat-al Yahud.

Shortly after my appointment as vizier of finance, the caliph gave me the responsibility of managing the renovation and additions to the palace and to the alcazaba. The city grew because of the influx of skilled workers and laborers, followed by tradespeople to support them. I made the decision, with the approval of the caliph, that all the bricks used in the new construction should make use of the local bright-red clay. The palace and fortifications thus became known as the Red Fort. It is purposely designed as a show of culture, force, and power.

My son Joseph will be my legacy. If God wills it, he will be a better than good student and a fast learner. As soon as he is capable, I will begin his education. I will engage expert teachers in Hebrew, Arabic, Aramaic, and Ladino. When he has progressed, I will add teachers for Latin and Greek, mathematics and science. He will learn Torah and Talmud. He will need all this knowledge and more to take my place.

I am the first Jew to attain so high a position in Muslim government since Hasdai ibn Shaprut, of blessed memory, who served the caliph of Cordoba when that worthy ruled all of Andalusia. That caliph was Abd al-Rahman III, and he relied on Hasdai ibn Shaprut for many years. Abd al-Rahman III was the grandson of Abd al-Rahman, the half-Berber, half-Syrian exile who founded the Umayyad caliphate in Cordoba. The founder of that dynasty arrived in Andalusia about fifty years after the first Muslim armies came across the shortest distance from North Africa. Those forces conquered nearly all of the old Visigoth territories of Spain, known as Al-Andalus, as far north as Narbonne. Because of the long reigns and orderly successions of Abd al-Rahman's sons, grandsons, and great-grandsons, Cordoba prospered economically and culturally.

The number of Muslim soldiers and settlers that came to Andalusia were few in proportion to the existing population of the peninsula. They only represented about 1 percent of the total population. They soon discovered that Jewish communities were a source of educated, capable men who made ideal civil servants. Within a few generations, due to vigorous efforts to convert the population to Islam, the Andalusian Muslim population was considerably larger. Much of this came about when the Muslim invaders intermarried with the original Christian and pagan populations. They insisted that not only their spouses but the families of the spouses convert. Even a few Jews converted, although not many. The Muslim community was, and still is on the whole, very tolerant of the *dhimmi*, the protected "Peoples of the Book," Jews and Christians who share their Abrahamic monotheism and scripture.

The adventurous and energetic Muslim culture treasures the written word and is completely enamored of recited or read poetry. Cordoba's libraries represented both the scholarly and social wellbeing of the society. During my childhood, there were many libraries in Cordoba, housing as many as 700,000 books, all laboriously written by hand. Essential to this library culture was a paper factory in Jativa, a town near the coastal city of Valencia. Paper is significantly cheaper and more plentiful than parchment. Because of the availability of inexpensive paper, many new books were and are still published, along with copies made of classics in Arabic, Latin, Greek, and Hebrew.

There was and still is, in both the Muslim and Hebrew cultures, a positive attitude toward learning. It is considered a duty to transmit knowledge from one generation to another. I also observe that there exists a remarkable understanding of the differences in the way people learn. All of this is embodied in our wonderful culture of libraries and learning. It is an ideal setting for the migration of Jews from all over the Diaspora.

I was born in Cordoba in the Hebrew year 4654 (993). My brother, Isaac, is slightly over a year older than me. We were, and still are, keen students. To this day Isaac still has a quick, retentive mind and superior powers of reasoning. I am marginally slower than he. My father is not extremely wealthy, but he is a successful businessman. He made certain his sons studied with the best teachers available. We both studied with the renowned scholar Rabbi Hanokh and his son, Rabbi Moses ben Hanokh, both highly respected for their learning. We also studied with the leading Hebrew grammarian of his generation, Judah Hayyudi. There were other teachers for Latin and Greek, Arabic, Aramaic, and Berber. The local language, Ladino, we learned on the streets.

Our father did not neglect to teach his sons business affairs. We both grew up to be practical and self-sufficient, as well as well-educated. In those days, students met at previously set times in the homes of their teachers, sometimes in the synagogue, and sometimes in shops where books are sold. Most wealthy homes, both Islamic and Jewish, have extensive libraries. The teachers lead and direct long discussions of various literary topics, and all the scholars present are expected to participate,to share their insights and opinions. Significant time is set aside for the reading and analysis of all the various meters of both Arabic and Hebrew poetry. Readings are followed by an in-depth discussion about the form, texture, and meaning of the poems.

At an early age, I enjoyed recognition for my understanding of both Arabic and Hebrew poetry. I even received some approbation by Arab scholars who appreciated my writings. As youngsters, Isaac and I decided we had to learn something new every day and share what we had learned. I still feel that if I haven't learned something I didn't know previously, the day has been wasted.

I have made an extensive study of the Qur'an and of the writings of many Muslim theologians. Of course, I studied Torah and both editions of the Talmud extensively. Neither have I neglected the writings of Christian scholars and the New Testament.

Leaders of the large Jewish community of Cordoba often spoke of the accomplishments of the physician Hasdai ibn Shaprut. As a youth, I often daydreamed about matching, or even surpassing, the accomplishments of this hero of all the Jews of Andalusia. Perhaps I have,but that is for others to judge.

Two

AFTER THREE YEARS of strife, during the month of Sivan 4674 (1013), the Berbers took final control of Cordoba. In doing so, they ousted the Arab Umayyads, resulting in the breakup of the Umayyad Empire. That empire was divided into many city-states now known as a *taifa*. During those three years of conflict, the Jews, along with all the other citizens of Cordoba, were under continuous stress and physical danger.

I stoodwith my father in his study.

"Papa, the situation here is too unsettled. We have no idea what these Berbers will decide about how they will rule what they have conquered. I have joined forces with a small group of my friends from the yeshiva, along with some distant relatives of the Umayyads. We have all agreed to leave Cordoba together."

"Sh'muel, your mother and I wish you would stay with us, but you leaving could be the means by which the family is saved. Jewish people, as you well know, have had to move away from many places in this world in order to survive. If you can reach safety and become established, you will provide a safe haven for us if the family has to leave Cordoba. Although you are only twenty years old, you are a man capable of making your own decisions. I hope I have prepared you to live an independent life. Have you discussed this decision with your brother?"

"Yes, Papa. Isaac agrees with you that it would be wise for me to establish myself elsewhere so the family will have a safe place to go. He says he will stay with you here in hopes of retaining our home and business. My friends and I will try to reach Malaga."

"Yes, I hear that the caliph of Malaga has reached agreement with the Berbers. Apparently, they have accepted his tributes and agreed to leave him, his holdings, and his people alone."

"We have the same information."

"It is a dangerous journey. Berber raiders, members of small tribal groups still without taifa to call their own, are creating havoc in the countryside. The regular highways are especially dangerous. It is well-known that these bands continue to rob, rape, pillage, and murder as they please."

* * *

In Archidona, we were told that the roads were safe from Antequera to Malaga, and after spending a night in an inn, two to three in beds infested with biting insects, weate breakfast. Thefood was even more disgusting than the meal the previous night. Fortunately, the owners of the innwere Muslim and obeyed the dietary laws so the food was halal, kosher enough for me and my Jewish companions. The meat must have been from an old male goat. We were confident he did not die of old age and reasonably certain hewas properly slaughtered.

On the road between Baena and Archidona, we were forced three more times to hide from small bands of roving Berbers. In each instance, Donkey heard them before the other donkeys, me, or any of my companions. Each time, we managed to avoid detection. I fully intended to keep that wonderful donkey for many years, and I did.

After twenty days of walking after leaving Cordoba, mostly sleeping in the open and avoiding marauding Berbers, we arrived in Malaga.I found a small house to rent and opened a small shop to sell spices. The gold coins from my cloak provided the capital needed. The business acumen I learned from my father proved valuable.

Over the next several years, my business expanded enough for me to purchase the building that housed the shop. The business provided me an adequate, albeit far from extravagant, lifestyle.

The Jewish community of Malaga was small, no more than forty families. The heads of households were either craftsmen or merchants. All but one of the companions that made the journey from Cordoba with me eventually settled elsewhere, so there were few young scholars with whom I could interact. I did manage to find a measure of intellectual stimulation in the home of Rabbi Judah, the leader of the small Malagan Jewish community. But there was no extensive circle of intellectuals to provide the back-and-forth discourse I was accustomed to in Cordoba. I felt isolated and depressed, except when I was able to interact with my Muslim friend and companion during our exodus from Cordoba.

I believe that friend, Ali ibn Ahmad ibn Hazm, will become one of the most renowned Muslim intellectuals of our generation. He is the son of a high-ranking member of the deposed government of Cordoba. Although he and I were both born and raised in Cordoba, we did not meet until our journey to Malaga. After the takeover by the Berbers, Ali's father was ousted by the new Berber rulers, then imprisoned. He was forced to forfeit a significant portion of his property to obtain his freedom. Despite those family setbacks, my friend continued his studies and acquired a deep understanding of Arabic literature, philology, and the theory of logic. After our journey to Malaga and the long talks we had along the way, he applied his considerable talents to learning Hebrew and studying the Torah and Talmud. He composes beautiful poetry, but his overriding passion is the study of theology.

After our shared dangers on the road from Cordoba, there was the connection of common experience between us. Ali was, and still is, a controversial, sometimes prickly man who especiallyenjoyedarguing. He wouldargue with anyone, especially anyone who heldreligious viewsdiffering from his own, not excluding other Muslim theologians. He also enjoyeddebating literary subjects. We werenot so different. He and I spent many hours engaged in good-spirited argument.

Most of all, Ali enjoyed arranging public debates. He loved to demonstrate his knowledge and debating skills to an audience. Once we were both well settled in Malaga, he challenged me to a series of debates about the veracity of certain sections of the Torah. We held those debates, and my friend published a book detailing them, giving both his arguments and my responses. In that book, he voiced the opinion that I am the most accomplished debater he has ever known. We maintain a respectful, albeit sometimes testy, friendship.

Within the small Jewish community of Malaga, and increasingly within the entire population of the city, my reputation as a scholar increased. There was considerable attention to my ability to write grammatically correct Arabic in the flowery style much appreciated by the Andalusians. It wasn'tlong until those skills were put to use. I was kept busy composing letters. I became a scribe but did not charge friends a fee.

I gave up my youthful dreams of living up to the standards set by Hasdai ibn Shaprut. When I was about to be thirty years of age,my spirits were at a new low. I was unmarried and exceedingly frustrated by the lack of an intellectually challenging life.

The house next to mine was owned by the finance vizier of Granada, a man by the name of Abu l-Abbas. The house and nearby estates of this worthy man were maintained and managed by his steward. One day, the steward came to me.

"I understand that you are an educated man, ibn Nagrela. Would you be willing to correspond, in my name, with the owner of the many properties I manage for thevizier?"

"Of course."

During the following weeks, I answered the vizier's questions about his affairs in Malaga, providing updates on his properties, all from the information supplied by his steward. Abu l-Abbas was impressed by the level of skill and learning apparent in my correspondence with him. One day, he was in Malaga. He asked the steward about the scribe responsible for the correspondence, then insisted the steward bring me to him. I went, and we spoke of many different subjects for over an hour.

"Ishma'il ibn Nagrela, I can see you are a well-educated and intelligent man. I am greatly in need of an assistant with your qualifications. I can offer you access to men of equal intellect, good wages, and a position that will make your life considerably more comfortable than your present existence as a scribe selling spices. What do you say?"

"How soon do you need me in Granada?"

"You will have to return with me. My steward will sell your house and business for you; he is very trustworthy."

I could feel my heart skip beats. I did not answer immediately. Was this really an opportunity or only false hope?

"When do you return?"

"Tomorrow."

"I will be ready in the morning."

"Good."

When I arrived in Granada, the Jewish community made up at least 40 percent of the taifa's inhabitants. It has grown in numbers under my nurturing. After my arrival, life still did not progress smoothly. However, I did become more successful. Sometime before the finance vizier's death,the caliph learned of me, my reputation for honesty, and the work I was doing for the vizier of finance. He appointed me Ha Nagid. This position and title made me responsible for the good behavior of the Jewish community, as well as its tax collector.

Tax collectors are never popular. My appointment inevitably resulted in my acquisition of powerful enemies. The way the system works throughout Andalusia is that the rulers tell those responsible for collecting taxes how much the government expects from their assigned district. The so-called "tax farmers" collect as much as they think they can and keep the difference between the collected taxes and the sum required by their caliph. I wasquite successful in this endeavor, thus I managed to alienate several wealthy and influential heads of old Jewish families.

Rabbi Judah of Malaga had a daughter named Rebecca. She was young, beautiful, and of marriageable age.I wanted to help the rabbi improve his situation, so I secured a tax territory for him and convinced him to move his family to Granada. I made no secret of my interest in Rebecca, but she was already spoken for, promised to a second cousin, one of the rabbi's disciples.

The fact that I brought in an outsider to assume the lucrative tax farmer duties rankled and further alienated those same, already out of sorts, old Jewish establishment families. The situation was made worse because Rabbi Judah was a more recent arrival than I and was dedicated to his work. Those Jewish leaderswere feeling slighted, so they went to the Muslim officials with whom they had long-standing relationships. They managed to convince them that I was collecting significantly more than I should in taxes, keeping enough to become overly wealthy.

One morning I awoke to loud pounding on the door of my house. I opened the door to find six armed soldiers.

"Ishma'il Nagrela?" the largest of them asked.

"Yes."

"You are under arrest for crimes against Granada. Come with us."

I was marched off immediately and put into prison.

When my friends in the Jewish community, along with Finance Vizier l-Abbas and his friends, heard what happened, they reacted immediately. It still took four days before they managed to obtain my release.

My enemies had moved faster. After I was freed, I discovered the same malcontents whoarranged my imprisonment hired a group of thugs who attacked and killed Rabbi Judah and his disciple, the fiancé of Rebecca, while they were out collecting taxes. I was released too late to save Rabbi Judah.

I met with the rabbi's family and suggested I should marry Rebecca and assume the responsibility, and honor, of caring for the family. Despite having to pay huge bribes to help secure my release, I still had considerable financial resources. Rabbi Judah's family agreed to the arrangement but insisted my marriage be delayed for a full year of mourning.

Eventually the *ketubah*was signed, and Rebecca and Iwere married.

One morning, I went to the palace to give the caliph a report. My chief, the son of my mentor, was ill. When I finished,the caliph instructed me to go to the courtyard and wait until he summoned me. For two hours I waited, supplied with food and drink but apprehensive about what was happening. Then I was escorted back into his presence.

"I am well aware that the recently departed Abut l-Abbas was your mentor, Nagrela. He spoke highly of your skills and intelligence. As you know, I followed l-Abbas's recommendation and appointed his son vizier of finance after the old man's passing. The young man is intelligent enough, but his father was negligent in teaching him all he needs to know to be effective.

"This morning when my finance vizier was summoned, you appeared in his stead and explained he was unavailable due to a sudden and severe illness."

He paused, lookingat my face. I did my best to hold the same expression. He smiled and nodded.

"You did an outstanding job of presenting the information I required and answered all my questions regarding the financial status of the kingdom with concise and accurate data."

I kept my face impassive.

"I appreciate your loyalty to your mentor and to his son, but I have learned thatthe son is most dedicated to the pleasures of life. This morning, I am told, his illness was due to him being still under the influence of too much wine and food taken last evening."

He searched my face for my response. Again, I did my best to betray no emotion.

"This is not the first time this has happened. Each time you have filled in for him while presenting the information you have compiled as if he had done the work. I am well aware that my vizier of finance suffers from lack of understanding of the finance ministry and its duties.

"I have had you investigated thoroughly. I learned that you have been the person responsible for the excellent management of our Finance Ministry for some time. I have this day given the son of Abu l-Abbas a large estate near Jaen, to which he is ordered to repair. I have appointed you, Ishma'il ibn Nagrela, vizier of finance. You will return here tomorrow morning to be invested with your office and recognized by the court."

A legend is often repeated in the Jewish community of Granada that I was responsible for the growth in influence and the wise advice of Vizier l-Abbas. According to that legend, my benefactor, the vizier, on his deathbed, admitted to our caliph, Habbus, that the writings and wise counsel he provided for him were all my work, thus securing me the position of finance vizier. This legend is pure fabrication, but it seems to have developed a life independent of reality. It will, no doubt, persist.

Three

IT WAS ONLY a short time after I was appointed vizier of finance that I experienced a significant crisis. Our caliph, Habbus, was infirm with age. For reasons he failed to share with anyone, he had not indicated who his successor would be. This made the Zanhadja nobles very nervous. The heads of the various families and their sons were given governorships of provinces and other honors and responsibilities, but all was at the pleasure of Habbus.

He always made it a point to treat the Zanhadja elite as equals. He avoided summoning any of these worthies to the palace to conduct business. When he wanted their input or opinion, he went to them, demonstrating that he considered them his equals. These men did not want a new caliph who would abandon these practices—or take away their privilege or estates. Prince Yaddair ben Hubasa, Habbus's nephew, courted the chiefs by promising they would retain their privileges. Yaddair seemed determined to usurp the place of Habbus's two sons. A dire family plot was brewing.

Yaddair was one of those people who perused many books but with little real understanding beyond the title and author. He associated with learned men, but his goal was to glean as much as possible from them while expending as little effort as possible. He was clever and well-spoken, and managed to flatter most men. He wanted and needed to give the impression of a zealous Muslim, but I doubt he was or is.

However, Habbus seemed to value his cleverness and employed Yaddair to negotiate with emissaries of other governments, and sometimes gavehim full authority to handle various tasks for the caliphate.

While still alive my mentor, Abu 1-Abbas,proposed to Habbus that the caliph designate Yaddair as his successor. He believed Yaddair to be the most qualified and deserving. However, there was no consensus amongst the Zanhadja tribe.

Various factions lined up as supporters of Yaddair or Badis, while yet another cadre of chiefs supported Boluggin, the younger son. I believedand hopethat Habbus wouldanoint Badis.Amongst his many other achievements and skills, Badis possessedthe one essential personality trait to rule: ruthlessness. He waswell enoughversed in governmental matters. However, a majority of the Berber chiefs seemednot to want Badis as the caliph.

Yaddair thought I caused Abu's son to be removed as financial vizier. More importantly, Yaddair often stated in public that a Jew should not hold such a high position.

That same cabal of chiefs aligned against Badis had close ties to those same wealthy Jews who caused my imprisonment and murdered my father-in-law. All of them resented me because I wielded more power than they could ever aspire to.

I worked diligently to find ways to convince Boluggin that being caliph was a demanding position that required hard work, and carried great responsibility. It was my impression that Boluggin was averse to both. I also needed to gain the support of the majority of the Jews of Granada. I had to convince them that the succession of Badis was in their best interest. At the same time, I needed to do everything possible to convince Badis of my loyalty to him, and to Habbus, and of the value I could be to both of them.

The succession was not the only crisis looming. General Khairhan,the Slav, took over the neighboring taifa of Almeria several years before. He died, and the Slav eunuch General Zuhair succeeded him, becoming even more powerful than Khairhan. Zuhair even controlled Cordoba for a time. Almeria was much more important to Granadaas a friend than as an enemy,so when the caliph of Seville attacked Zuhair, Habbus went to Zuhair's aid. Together they invaded Seville's territory and won a battle over the Sevillian army.

After I was appointed to my position of authority the chiefvizier of Almeria, Abu ben Abbas began to undermine our alliance with Zuhair.Abu ben Abbas was a formidable enemy. He was a young Arab, very wealthy, a true scholar of Arabic literature and an excellent orator. The rumor was that he had five hundred women in his harem, each more beautiful than the previous. My spies reported that Abu ben Abbas was also miserly, egotistical, and conceited. He boasted of his genealogy and traced his lineage to those first Muslims in Medina, who welcomed the Prophet when he fled from Mecca. Ben Abbaswas an unhappy man whom fate forced to serve Zuhair, once a mercenary eunuch slave. This was a demeaning situation for ben Abbas, and abhorrent to him. He believed he was much more qualified to be caliph than was the former mercenary, Zuhair.

I obtained a copy of the following open letter, signed by Abu ben Abbas. Itwas being distributed throughout the territories of Granada.

> *The blessed Qur'an instructs that a non-believer should not hold any office that provides a measure of authority over any Muslim. In keeping with the holy word of Allah, all Jews in the service of Muslim kings must be dismissed. To disobey is to flaunt the law as set down in the Qur'an.*

> *My king, the blessed by Allah Zuhair, has instructed me to demand specifically that the Jew Ishma'il ibn Nagrela be removed from the high office he holds in Granada. The position must be held by a true believer.*

That wasn'tall. One of my spies gave me a copy of the following letter, also signed by ben Abbas:

> *To the most honorable caliph of Malaga, ibn Ali Musa:*

Caliph Habbus of Granada and his Zanhadja have ignored the teachings of the Qur'an by ignoring my advice to rid themselves of the Jews in their government, particularly their vizier of finance, the self-righteous ibn Nagrela. They have placed their own self-interest above the law dictated by the Prophet.

My caliph, Zuhair, respectfully petitions you to join him in renouncing the Zanhadja for retaining the Jews in their administration. If you do this thing, I believe I will be able to convince King Zuhair to form a mutual defense pact with you and Muhammad ben Abdallah, the ruler of Carmona. The alliance of Almeria, Malaga, and Carmona will surround Granada with enemies and force them to adhere to the teachings of the Qur'an. The alliance will also provide other benefits to our respective kingdoms.

During those troubling times I attended several meetings with Prince Boluggin. I was very aware that many of the Zanhadja tribal chiefs preferred to have Boluggin, rather than Badis, as the caliph, because of Badis'sruthlessness. I repeated my previous arguments to Boluggin, in even greater detail describing the responsibilities of the caliph and the restrictions that would be placed upon him, both by the position and by people's expectations. I pleaded with him to consider what he knew about the personality and character of his older brother.

"What do you think Badis will do if you accept the handshake of fealty and allegiance when it is offered by those tribal chiefs most likely to offer support?"

"Yes, Vizier, I agree. My brother will not give up the throne without a fight."

"You surely understand, Majesty, that a civil war between brothers is a terrible price to pay for power. I have nightmares, inspired by my conversations with the one God, whom Jews do not name but the Muslims know as Allah, about the horrors that would come to Granada from a civil war."

That same afternoon, some of those chiefs met with Boluggin. I did not know what Boluggin's response to them was, but I believed he was still not convinced by my arguments and that made my position and standing tenuous, at best.

I spoke again to Prince Badis, as I did on several other occasions during the caliph's final illness. I pledged my support, along with that of the great majority of the Jewish community from whom I hadobtained agreement.

* * *

Three days after my last conversations with the Princes Badis and Boluggin, I was called to Caliph Haddus'sbedside.

"I am aware of my nephew Yaddair's efforts to have you removed as vizier, ibn Nagrela. Which of my sons do you consider to be the best to rule the kingdom after my death?"

"May I be frank, Majesty?"

"I insist that you be so,Nagrela."

"I consider Prince Badis to be better prepared and better suited by temperament and personality to be a strong ruler. I believe he is most likely to follow the example set by you. Although there is strong support for Yaddair, I fail to understand why you might even consider choosing a nephew over one of your own sons, since both are qualified."

"Thank you, Nagrela. As always, you speak the truth as you perceive it. Now I want you to take up pen and paper and write what I dictate.

"Nephew Yaddair, it is my wish and command that you forgo any and all attempts to usurp the throne of Granada. You are instructed to provide your loyalty, support, and counsel to the new caliph. My sons will decide between them who this will be."

I finished the document, and Habbus held out his hand for it. He read it, nodded his head, and held out his hand for the pen. After signing, he called for a messenger.

"Take this and deliver it directly into Prince Yaddair's hands. Report to me his reaction when he reads it."

That same evening, my servant knocked on the doorjamb of my study, where I sat with my son Joseph, already nine years old. Joseph was reciting a passage from the Torahfrom memory.

"There is a messenger from the palace at the front gate, sir," the servant reported.

"Well, Joseph, I expect this is the news I have been waiting for. At least it is a messenger, not soldiers to take me away. All right, bring this messenger to us," I told the servant.

When the messenger entered the study, I looked at him and lifted my chin. The messenger looked at my son and raised his eyebrows.

"This is my son. He does not speak of anything said in this room. Please tell me your message."

"Prince Boluggin refused to shake the hands of those that came to him offering fealty. Prince Badis promised to make Boluggin commander of all the mercenaries, including the Negro infantry from Nubia. He also promised him the choice of several large estates. Prince Boluggin accepted all of these honors and pledged his loyalty to Badis."

"Who sent you with this message?" I asked.

"Prince Badis sent me. He also told me you are invited to attend the ceremony that will crown him caliph."

"When is the ceremony to take place?" I asked.

"The ceremony is scheduled to begin at ten hours after dawn tomorrow morning."

"Thank you. What is your name?"

"I am Ali ibn Quafir."

I reached into my cloak, withdrew a pouch of gold coins, and extended it to him.

"Thank you, Ali ibn Quafir. The news you bring is very welcome. Please tell our new caliph that I will be honored and very pleased to attend."

After the messenger left, I allowed myself a smile of satisfaction.

"Well, the first obstacle had been overcome, Joseph. But Badis has an unstable and volatile personality. He could prove to be less easy to influence than his father. We are entering some interesting and dangerous times. That's enough for this evening, Joseph. I know you listen very intently to what is said in this room. Do you remember?"

"Yes, Papa, I remember everything."

* * *

Several evenings later, Joseph was again in my study. I followed his recitation, reading the copy of the poem I had assigned him to memorize, and smiled.

"Yes, good, Joseph."

I gave him the gold coin I was holding between thumb and first finger, his regular reward for a task done perfectly.

"Sit, Joseph. Tonight, I want to talk about what has happened in the short time since Badis became caliph. Within days after he was crowned as caliph, Badis appointed two brothers as new viziers, Ali and Abdallah ibn al-Karawi. The brothers were classmates of Badis at the school for chiefs' sons. They remainclose friends and spend much time in diversion with the caliph. Their father's family was originally Christian. The grandfather converted to Islam, and the whole family subsequently converted. The family has supplied aides to various Zanhadja chiefs since the grandfather's conversion."

I searched Joseph's face, looking for any sign of boredom or disinterest. There was none.

"The two new viziers have the ear of Badis. I have to make certain I know what advice they give so I can adapt mine to theirs," I continued.

* * *

Badis increased the number of functionaries of his court,and even includeda few native Andalusians, those descendants of the original people who inhabited Andalusia. The native Andalusians seemed always willing to adopt the trappings of any religion they needed to survive. They accepted the different paganisms and gods of the Romans, then the Visigoth beliefs, then Christianity.

When the Muslims invaded, many of them found Islam, although today there are still a few who observe the pagan practices of their ancestors. A few Andalusians even converted to Judaism, but most converted to Islam. It made life significantly easier for them. So now Idealtwith Andalusians, Arabs, Berbers, and Slavs, all of whom envied and hated each other for generations and now struggledfor influence in the court. Of course, most of them hate Jews, especially Jews who occupy higher positions of power than they enjoy.

To further complicate matters, the vizier of Almeria renewed his efforts to oust me. He did his best with Caliph Habbus. After Habbus died, he sent a strong letter to Badis reiterating his charge that giving a Jew high office is forbidden in the Qur'an. He suggested that I was the only obstacle to peace between Almeria and Granada. Without comment, Caliph Badis handed me that letter and waited for my response. I read it quickly, then read it again with considerable thought and concentration before looking up.

I decided to ignore the first part of the letter and focused my attention on ibn Abbas's reference to a recent pact between his caliph, Zuhair, and the prince of Carmona.

"My caliph, you know Carmona's territory abuts our western border. The rulers of Carmona are Zenaga, and closely related to other Zenaga tribes. TheZenagaoften attempt to unite to destroy the Zanhadja. I also know you understand the importance of maintaining a good relationship with Almeria to protect the rear of the kingdom from attack. This will be essential if you are to deal with the generations-long conflict with the caliphate of Seville to the east."

Badis only nodded, his face betraying nothing of his thoughts.

"I suggest you send a respected Arab theologian, such as my friend Abu l'Hassan, as your emissary, to hold meetings with ibn

Abbas. He might be more inclined to listen to an Arab emissary with strong theological credentials. The charge for Abu l'Hassan should be to remind ibn Abbas, and especially Caliph Zuhair, how quickly and forcibly Granada came to the aid of Almeria in their recent conflict with Seville. Surely they can comprehend how mutually beneficial it will be to renew our alliance."

Badis accepted my advice. He sent my friend, the noted scholar, who was also a Sharia judge, to conduct talks with the leaders of Almeria. Badis further instructed l'Hassan to inform the leaders of Almeria thathe considered the Jew too valuable to be dismissed.

Abu l'Hassan returned dejected. He reported that ibn Abbas told him under no circumstances would he advise Zuhair to accept Badis'sarguments. He hinted that with his strong army of Slavs, Arabs, Negroes, and Christian mercenaries, along with his ability to hire additional Catalan troops, Zuhair would not have much difficulty annexing Granada into his caliphate.

After receiving this report, my advice to Badis was to start an immediate buildup of our own army.

"However, we should wait until Zuhair makes the first move. The longer we delay, the more time we will have to gain strength."

Badis followed my advice, and I embarked on an exhaustive study of treatises on military strategies, techniques, armaments, and descriptions of how historically decisive battles had been won.I dispatched agents from throughout the Diasporato purchase books on these subjects and rush them to me by messengers on fast horses. Almost all of these books were written in Latin or Greek. As I devoured the books, I made copious notes to myself in the margins.

When Joseph was born, I was already forty-two years old; I was then fifty-one. At that advanced age, I hired experts to come to the house to teach me the use of the sword, spear, bow and arrow, shield, sling, and all the other weapons in common use. I purchased three well-bred stallions and took the time, at least three times a week, to practice horseback riding along with my physical training for battle.

After two months of daily effort and application I was thin, fit, and muscular. I seemed to be able to hold my own with the various swordsmen I brought to my courtyard for practice and exercise. I have no way of knowing if, or how much, they allowed me to feel their equal. I supposed I would only discover the truth when I faced the real thing.I hoped I was not deluded into thinking my skills were adequate to keep me alive.

Four

IT WAS EARLY spring. The wind rushed through Granada off the snow and ice of the Sierra. Passover was only six days away, and I was in a reflective mood. I asked my wife to tell Joseph to join me in my study.

I heard the rustle as he pushed aside the substantial rug covering the doorway, protecting access to the room as well as affording privacy. The rug was, and still is, dark blue with yellow and red Arabic calligraphy and geometric designs woven artfully through it. Joseph rapped timidly on the thick oak doorjamb. I was bent over my desk rewriting the last stanza of a poem in Arabic, so I did not respond.

Joseph knocked again, harder. I lifted my left hand and extended my index finger. He knew not to expect me to allow him to interrupt me until I finished what I was working on. A full minute passed before I finished and looked up from the paper. I laid down my pen. I reached over and slid one of three stacks of books cluttering the top of my desk to the side and took the top book off the pile, placing it over the poem I had been working on. It wasn't finished, still needed editing, and I was not ready to share it with anyone, not even my beloved son.

"Yes, Joseph, my son, come in," I told him.

"My mother told me you wished to see me, Papa."

The huge table that servedas my desk dominatedthe study. When Joseph was six years old, he was curious about how big the desk was. I instructed him to lay on the floor beside the desk to measure its length against his. I positioned him with his head at one end of the desk and put a book on the floor to mark where his feet reached. Then I told him to put his head next to the book and we would measure again.

"The desk is as long as two Josephs. So, Joseph, I think I will measure and cut a stick to your length; then we can measure everything in Josephs instead of meters. What do you think of that idea?"

"But, Papa, everybody knows what a meter is. They won't know what a Joseph is."

"Ah, that is a good point. Maybe we'd best just continue to measure in meters; but I think you are now almost a meter tall."

I wasfond of the desk. It was a gift from Caliph Badis, made especially for me. On each corner wasa ponderous leg cut from the same cedar tree as the planks forming the top of the desk. The legs werehand-carved to resemble the leg of an elephant. To me, the table representedstudy, learning, creativity, and power. Power because it came, as all power does, from my caliph.

I pushedmy heavy wood chair back from the table. The chair was extracted from the same giant cedar as the desk, and wasadorned with carvings of leaves, flowers, and trees.

I bentover and pattedthe small stool I had been resting one foot on.It wasupholstered with the remnants of a very old silk rug.

"Sit, Joseph."

"I love your slippers, Papa. Do you mind that I sometimes put them on and shuffle about the house, pretending I am you?"

The slippers weremade of soft lambskin, dyed yellow.

I smile at him.

"No, I don't mind, my son. Just don't think to take them from me. I am almost as fond of you as I am of these slippers."

He frowned, so I reached over and mussed his hair.

"I'm just teasing you, Joseph. I will always love you more than anything else in this world, equal to the love I have for your mother and your siblings."

It wasstill my habit to wear white silk clothing. Since the early spring evening was cold, Ialso was wearing one of my several white silk brocade cloaks. These cloaks werevaluable, but minor compared to the many other gifts I hadreceived from Habbus and now his son Badis. All of my cloaks weretrimmed on the sleeves and collars with gold thread. The thread wasa product of a particular Jewish goldsmith, I don't recall his name, but he wasrenowned for producing the most pliable gold thread in all of Andalusia. My head was covered with a high silk gauze *kalansuwa* rather than my usual turban.

The room waspermeated with the smell of old books, parchment, paper, and ink. Only those specifically invited wereever allowed inside. All the furnishings wouldbe Joseph's when I wasgone:the chair, the table, the stool, the deep-red Armenian carpets on the floor, the purple-and-brown rugs on the walls, and the expensive brocade pillows thrown carelessly on the mattress against the south wall. The shelves, covering three walls, werethe resting place of the keepsakes of many years of serving two kings, but books crowdedalmost all the space on the shelves.

"When I am gone, you must be ready to take my place," I toldJoseph after quizzing him about what he hadlearned that was new to him that day.

He nodded.

"Yes, I know, Papa."

"It is important that you are qualified and able to fill the responsibility of taking my place—the welfare of our family, of your new brother, Judah; your sister, mother, uncle, and all the Jewish people. This is true not only here in Granada, but perhaps in all of Andalusia. The lives and happiness of the Jewish people of Andalusia may depend on you, as it does now on me. Is this clear to you?"

"Yes, Papa, I understand."

"However, you need more than the education I am providing for you. You are a smart and clever boy. You learn everything I ask, but you must learn even more as you mature. It will be necessary for you to be able to influence the actions of many different individuals. The people you must deal with will have many different prejudices, fears, schemes, and shifting loyalties.

"As you know, our masters here in Granada are Berbers, of the tribal confederation known as the Zanhadja. Among the Zanhadja, family tribal loyalty is the most important aspect of their lives. Jews will always be outsiders."

"I know, you have told me these things many times before, Papa."

"And I will continue to repeat these facts of our lives, Joseph. There is another loosely united tribal federation of Berbers indigenous to North Africa known as the Zenaga. The Zanhadja and Zenaga will usually form an alliance when threatened by an outside enemy, but when not threatened from without, they will often go to war against each other. This can and oftentimes does result from a minor incident or perceived slight.

"The third race of Muslims is the Arabs. They originated from the Arabian Peninsula and Middle East."

"I don't know these places, Papa. Where are the Arabian Peninsula, the Middle East, North Africa, and what is *indigenous*?"

"Indigenous means the people who are born and raised in a certain place. You are indigenous to Granada."

"Oh."

"That you don't know geography is my fault. Tomorrow, I will start a search for a teacher of geography for you. You must learn all about the countries where our Jewish people can be found—Israel, Syria, Iraq, Persia, and the rest of the Middle East, North Africa, and Andalusia. You must learn the relationship of these places to the Mediterranean Sea. You must also learn about the Christian kingdoms north and east of us, and of Rome and its history. You must know how far away these places are, or how near, and how long it takes to travel to them, and the routes to arrive there.

"You must learn and understand what motivates many of the prejudices, and therefore the actions, of the people who rule over us. The Arabs are a proud race who consider themselves conquerors, traders, and rulers. They seem to be most comfortable living in large towns and cities. The Berbers seem to prefer smaller settlements and the freedom of the countryside. Many Berbers have fair skin and blonde or red hair with blue or green eyes. Arabs usually have darker skin and black or brown hair and eyes. The majority of both Berbers and Arabs are Muslim, but many of the Berbers have retained practices of their previous religions despite conversion to Islam. The Berber Muslims are mostly Sunni, while Arabs may be either Sunni or Shia, depending on where they came from originally.

"We will spend many evenings together, Joseph. I will speak to you about the history and the people who occupied Andalusia, particularly the Zanhadja families who rule Grenada. After they were converted to Islam, the Zanhadja spread throughout the Sudan, and as far away as the Senegal and Niger rivers. They established themselves in the middle of the Atlas and Rif mountains, and to the Atlantic coast of Morocco. Some Zanhadja settled in Algeria."

Joseph started to fidget.

"Sit still and pay attention, Joseph."

"Yes, Papa, but tell me something new that I don't already know."

"At various times the Fatimid, the Zirid, and the Hammadi Arab dynasties controlled North Africa. This all happened before the Berber tribes were converted to Islam. The Islamic theologian ibn Yasin was the person who united those Arabs who had relocated to North Africa. He then converted the Berber tribes and united them under the Umayyad family. The Umayyads eventually conquered Andalusia.

"After the fall of Cordoba, the Umayyad Empire collapsed. When I was your age, I was confused about this history because the Umayyad tribe is also identified in the Arabic historical literature as the Omayyad or Almoravid tribe.In any case, after the Umayyads were defeated and removed from power, the Cordoban Empire collapsed and the taifa, many individual city-states, came into being. Today, some of these taifa are ruled by the Zanhadja, others are ruled by the Zenaga, and still others by Arabs. Some of the taifa are even ruled by Slavs. Some Berbers still want the Umayyad caliph to return and rule all of Andalusia.

"The Berbers, both Zanhadja and Zenaga, will almost always unite to prevent the Arabs or Slavs from taking over. The Slavs are people from Christian Europe, but many are not Christian. The non-Christians follow a variety of pagan religions. All the Slavs were originally brought to Andalusia as slaves. Young boys with the necessary aptitude were, and still are, trained as mercenaries. They admit allegiance to only their unit, army, and commanders. Some of these men, the very best fighters and leaders, are promoted within their units and have become successful generals. The most successful Slavs are freed and now occupy positions of authority and power. A few have even become caliphs."

"My head is spinning, Papa. There is so much to know!"

"Yes, but what I tell you now is most important. The first thing you must do when you meet someone new is identify their background. This is important because the populations in all of the taifa are very mixed. The Zanhadja rule Granada, but our citizens include Zenaga, Arab, Slav, Negros from Africa, Christians, of course Jews, and traders from the rest of the world. Many, except the Jews and the traders, originated as mercenaries, hired for short or longer terms or brought in for a particular war or battle. You must understand that each individual is different. Each has his own personality, prejudices, beliefs, modes of thinking and reacting. To learn about anyone man, you must question him gently, with humor and obvious, sincere interest, not aggressively. Encourage the person to talk about themselves, and especially about their family. You must listen much more than you talk. Joseph, you cannot learn anything if you are talking or thinking about what you are going to say next."

Joseph nodded that he understood, and I smiled.

"By understanding the background and the culture of the people I need to interact with, to learn and know more about their culture than they know about mine, gives me an advantage. For Jews, it is important to maintain some mystery about the way we think and act. Culture dictates the way people live, what they believe to be of significance, and many times, why they do the things they do.

"Now here is something else you must know: The most important thing you must always remember is that rulers are especially difficult, complicated people."

Five

ONE MORNING I was in the hall going to my study and overheard Joseph talking to my wife in the kitchen as I passed.

"Papa told me about the circumstances of how you and he became married. Do you regret not being married to your cousin? Will he always still be your first love?"

I could hear her clothing rustle as she shrugged.

"I never was allowed a choice or an opinion. The decisions were made by my father, then my uncles."

I did not interrupt them. I knew she was preparing the food and sweets for Joseph's tenth birthday tomorrow.

That evening, Joseph was again in my study. I held a copy of the Arabic poem I gave him yesterday to copy and critique.

"What is the meter, my son?"

"That's too easy, Papa. It is an acrostic, written in the *tawil* meter. The first letter of the first word in each stanza spells your name, NAGRELA."

"And what do you think of it?"

"The rhyming is very clever, Papa, but I did not know all of the words, especially some of the rhyming words."

"Did you look up those words in the dictionary?"

"Of course."

"And do you know what those words mean now?"

"Yes, Papa."

"Good." I handed him the gold coin I fished from my pouch. He clutched it tightly, inching toward the door to add the coin to his growing hoard.

I leaned forward and patted the seat of one of my guest chairs.

"Wait, Joseph . . . sit."

Joseph returned and sat in the chair.

"I want you to remember something very critical. Those who occupy important positions, as I plan you will someday, always have enemies. You must work hard to make certain you have at least twice as many friends as you do enemies. Do you know what is necessary for you to make and keep friends?"

"I'm not certain. I don't have many friends other than Samuel ben Yehuda."

"I know his father, it is a good family. Samuel is a big, strong boy, no?"

"Yes, he has been here in the house; we sometimes study together."

"Anyhow, the first rule for making and keeping friends is to follow the words of Rabbi Akiba: 'Do unto others as you would have them do unto you.' The second rule is to always be humble; do not act as though you are better in any way than those you want as friends. The third rule is to care, really care, about their health and wellbeing, and that of their family members. If they need anything, and you have the ability to take care of that need, you must do so. That includes emotional support as well as material support. The fourth rule is to maintain contact. It is hard work to maintain friendships, but if you have not heard from a friend recently, you must initiate contact; let them know you are thinking of them. Ask if there is anything you can do for them. At the minimum, you must arrange some sort of meeting, or a study session, or invite them to a party. You need to be with them in informal as well as formal settings. Do you understand what I am telling you?"

Joseph nodded.

"Repeat what I just told you."

"Treat others as I would have them treat me. Be humble, care about people, especially my friends, and keep in touch with my friends."

I smiled. The boy wasquite quick and bright for a ten-year-old.

"Good. The fifth rule is to do nothing to create bad feelings. This is especially true of your relationships with the Muslims and Christians. You must have friends amongst those peoples. Adapt yourself to their culture and beliefs. You know that our Berber masters are fond of wine, good, rich foods, and women, as well as young girls and boys. Are you old enough to understand this last bit of what I am telling you, Joseph?"

"Yes, Papa, I know of this from your poetry. But you don't do those things, do you? You just imagine them and write poems?"

"Because it is essential for me to not give cause for Caliph Badis and the Berber chiefs to no longer be my friends, I do participate, but with restraint. I never take wine or food in excess. I sometimes dally with the women and children, but I do not consummate. Do you know what I mean by consummate?"

"No, Papa."

"When you are older, I will explain it. Just always remember that I love your mother and all you children. Enough of this."

I studied his face and waited. He said nothing,pursed his lips, and frowned.

"I want to tell you more of my history. Perhaps this will help you understand all I have had to do to achieve my present position. Speaking of these matters aloud also reminds me of events and helps me maintain constancy and clear thinking.

"After the rejection of the overtures by Almeria to get rid of me, my caliph, Badis, instituted regular meetings with his generals. He also spent considerable time drilling his army. It was good that he was personally involved in preparing our defenses. Then we received intelligence that Zuhair was on his way to Granada with a thousand elite troops.

"However, Joseph, I was puzzled by this. Why only a thousand troops? We had at least four thousand soldiers. Why would Zuhair invade with only a thousand? I could only speculate that Zuhair's ego made him reckless. I suggested that Caliph Badis send out scouting patrols in all directions from Granada. Perhaps Zuhair's plan was to distract us in one direction and attack with force from another. Maybe the whole thing was just an attempt at intimidation, overconfidence, and hubris. In any case, my advice to the caliph was to wait. I suggested he should act surprised when Zuhair appears. Time would reveal his intentions. Was it possible Zuhair was so deluded he thought Badis would become his vassal without a fight?"

* * *

Zuhair and his army arrived late this afternoon. He made camp on a hill just south of the Jewish section of Granada. His arrival at the head of so many soldiers, without prior announcement, was rude and provocative. Caliph Badis rode out to greet him with only his personal guard, myself, and three tribal chiefs. When Badis asked the reason for this breach of manners, Zuhair's explanation was that he had come to pay his respects at the grave of his great ally and friend Caliph Habbus. This was, of course, complete nonsense, since he had never offered condolences to Badis when Habbus died.

We returned to the alcazaba, where Caliph Badis followed my advice to not precipitate a confrontation. This was contrary to the angry response of the majority of his tribal chiefs. With considerable effort, he restrained his outrage and waited to see what Zuhair would do next.

The following day, after presenting Zuhair with many gifts, Badis hosted a dinner with all the ceremony and honor befitting a guest caliph. I was present when Badis and his most trusted chiefs sat with Zuhair to discuss relations between the two states. Zuhair was attended by Ahmad ibn Abbas and two of his generals, but he said nothing. He allowed ibn Abbas to do all the talking for him. I remained in the shadows, silent but observant. Zuhair sat on his cushions, arms folded and a smirk on his face.

"I would be most pleased if you would annul your pact with Carmona," Badis remarked.

"Are you aware of the thousands of experienced soldiers my caliph Zuhair commands?" asked Ahmad ibn Abbas. "My caliph is strong enough to do as he pleases. You, Badis, are already dependent upon Almeria's strength and goodwill for your very survival. You should be thankful for the protection my caliph Zuhair extends."

I could see our chiefs were seething, ready to snatch their swords and begin a slaughter. Warning stares from Badis kept them silent and under control.

"Your Excellency," Badis said, ignoring ibn Abbas, speaking to Zuhair directly. "Only two years ago you pleaded for my help. Now here you are, at my gate as an uninvited but welcomed guest. Your chief vizier presumes to suggest that you are somehow entitled."

Ahmad ibn Abbas was not satisfied with the consternation he had wrought. He persisted. I sat quietly, my face a mask, while ibn Abbas continued to infuriate. He turned his face to our chiefs.

"You must force your caliph to rid himself of the Jew there in the shadows, but part of this meeting, as if he is your equal. If you want peace with Almeria, force Caliph Badis to do this."

Isaw that Badis was seething. He glanced at me, then fought to conceal the malicious smile tugging at the corners of his mouth. The arrogance of Zuhair and his minion had brought several of the chiefs, who previously had only tolerated me, to my side. They were now my friends and supporters. Badis and I saw this happening. Ahmad ibn Abbas and his master seemed to be oblivious. I may have overestimated them.

"I believe this evening has run its course," announced Badis, and got to his feet.

Zuhair and his entourage left the alcazaba and returned to their camp. Badis stalked the room where he had hosted the meeting. He cursed, waving his arms and shouting his anger. His manhood had been denigrated and he was ready to fight. His honor—and that of all his Zanhadja chiefs and their people—demanded they not succumb to this Slav eunuch and his arrogant Arab vizier.

"None of the patrols we sent out found an Almerian army close enough to cause problems," I noted.

"We will drive them out of our country in the morning!" screamed Badis.

"Please, brother," said Prince Boluggin quietly. "Allow me to try one more time to convince the vizier of Almeria not to renounce their pact with Granada."

Badis glanced at me, and I nodded in agreement. There was nothing to lose by allowing it.

That very evening, Boluggin went to the tent of ibn Abbas in this last attempt to prevent war. While Boluggin was gone, I suggested to the caliph and assembled chiefs that Boluggin would be a good choice to command our army. There was unanimous agreement.

He returned within the hour. Badis, his chiefs, and I were still waiting.

"Yes," Boluggin reported, "I am convinced. Ibn Abbas, the troublemaker, with Zuhair's approval, fully intends to either annex or destroy this Zanhadja kingdom."

Boluggin was distraught about the outcome of his peace initiative, but he was honored by Badis's offer to appoint him commander of our forces. He accepted.

I retrieved from my satchel a large map I had commissioned. I spread it out on a low table. Badis and the others crowded around the table, some sitting on cushions, others on their knees, all straining to see what I would suggest.

"With your permission, Excellencies, I have made an exhaustive study of the strategies and tactics of some famous Roman and Greek generals who published books on the subjects. I wish to suggest for your consideration a strategy for battle that is very different from the type of warfare to which you are accustomed. You have traditionally emphasized the use of cavalry. This requires that you meet your enemy on open ground where you can maneuver your horses. The intent of the strategy I suggest to you is to bring Zuhair's cavalry into the range of our archers and crossbowmen. Cavalry battles inevitably end in hand-to-hand combat, and large numbers of both sides are injured or killed. Force of numbers usually prevail, but we would lose many of our brave men.

"I learned that this is the route Zuhair used to come to Granada. It is the same route he is most likely to use on his return. I doubt he will risk the forces he brought with him in an open confrontation. I cannot believe he is stupid enough to do that. To arrive, he skirted the western slopes of the Sierra Nevada, here." I pointed out his route on the map. "He crossed over the Genil River here, using the bridge at the small village of Al Fuente. On their return, Zuhair and his army will have to pass through this narrow gorge before reaching that bridge."

Everyone leaned forward to see where I was pointing.

"I believe our archers and foot soldiers should take advantage of the topography. We hide them in the hills on either side of the gorge, here, and here. We send, this very night, engineers to destroy the bridge prior to Zuhair's arrival. Our forces should wait until the tail of their column is in the gorge. He and his army will be trapped in our ambush. Their only escape will be into the mountains, where their cavalry will be of little use."

It took less than ten minutes of discussion before Badis and his chiefs agreed to my plan. Badis and I looked over Boluggin's shoulder as he wrote out orders to all his commanders, making certain his troops were distributed in the most advantageous sites for the ambush. The first order was to the commander of his engineers, who were immediately dispatched to destroy the bridge. Everything wasnow in the hands of God.

Six

THE DAY OF my first battle was a clear Friday morning. Joseph watched me from his bedroom window as, in full armor, I mounted my stallion. I departed in the first gray light of dawn.

Badis, two of his tribal chiefs, a trumpeter, Boluggin, and myself, protected by twenty of the caliph's personal bodyguards, watched from one of the highest hills as the battle unfolded. The early morning mist was soon burned off by the sun, and I felt the warmth of it on my shoulders. I smiled as Zuhair, at the head of his army, reached the bridge at Al Fuente, only to find it destroyed. Boluggin raised his right arm and the trumpeter blew one long blast. Our soldiers, hidden above the gorge on both sides, rained arrows, crossbow bolts, and stones from slings down onto Zuhair's baggage train bringing up the rear of his army. They had no place to go except forward, further into the gorge. All of his troops were crowded into the gorge. Adonai was paying attention to us this day.

Zuhair had two hundred mercenary Nubian foot soldiers among the thousand troops of his little army. On the day we first went to greet him, I had observed the commander of our Nubian mercenaries talking with a young man from Zuhair's Nubians. I questioned our commander and learned the man he was talking to was a younger brother, a captain in the employ of Zuhair. The Nubian commander and I had a private discussion. He agreed to contact his brother. His charge was to outline a course of action that would be very profitable to his brother and to his brother's men.

As soon as our troops attackedthe baggage train, Zuhair's Nubians scurriedto plunder the supplies.Then they joined their relatives fighting for us. Zuhair didnot rise to his position, lacking courage. He quickly formed his remaining troops into battle array, but his cavalry was trapped in the gorge without room to maneuver. Some of his foot soldiers, with Zuhair goading them on,managedto fight their way out of the gorge, but Boluggin rushed to lead our cavalry and cut them down.

Ahmad ibn Abbas was screaming invectives against me. His voice echoed off the rock walls of the gorge. He blamed me for all of Islam's ills. His high-pitched voice could be heard clearly above the din of battle, melding with the screams of wounded men and animals.

The commander of Zuhair's Slav cavalry was thrown from his horse. Our Nubians took him captive. When Almeria's cavalry saw that their commander was captured, they brokeranks and scattered, our cavalry in pursuit. A smile tuggedat my lips. The remainder of Zuhair's forces had no choice but to run for the foothills.Each man was intent on making his individual way up into the relative safety of the Sierra Nevada.

The strongest men struggled to reach the edge of the snow and make their escape. The men on foot were unable to keep pace with those mounted. Those not cut down by our men turned, raised their arms, and submitted to capture. Those men still mounted braved the steep slopes and deep precipices, their horses stumblingon the rough terrain. Some men were pitched off their mounts. Several horses fell off the edges,some with, some without, their rider. I felt deep sadness about the fate of the horses, but the men had freedom of choice.

I spotted Zuhair, who appeared to be struggling to control his horse as he fled the gorge. The terrified animal pitched thentook the bit in his teeth and joined other horses running out of control along the edge of a cliff. Zuhair's horse stumbled and fell, carrying his burden into the void. I couldn't hear it, but I sawZuhair's head explode on the large boulder that arrested his fall.

No fewer than threehundred Almerians were slain. The rest were taken captive. General Boluggin gave me the honor of putting Ahmad ibn Abbas in chains. We waited as the plunder of the battlefield was gathered and our woundedwere cared for. Zuhair's men with minor wounds were treated after our own men were as comfortable as possible. Those enemieswith severe wounds were humanely dispatched.

As darkness engulfed the battlefield, tents were raised for Badis, his officers, and the tribal chiefs. There was also a separate tent for me. We were served a meal by slaves and retired to sleep the sleep of the just. In my tent,I murmured the Shabbat prayers that usher in that holy day, mindful of the fact there was no minion but secure in the knowledge Adonai was with me. Our soldiers slept on the ground, wrapped in their cloaks, close to their campfires. The guarded captives huddledtogether for warmth.

* * *

The following morning, Shabbat, I felt no remorse or guilt for being away from the synagogue. I was doing the Lord's work. Ahmad ibn Abbas stumbled along in front of my horse, his hands and feet bound in chains. I held the ropearound his neck in my right hand. He cursed me all the way back to Granada. While still holding the rope, I reached inside my cloak and caressed the tiny,rolled-up Torah resting on my chest, in contact with my skin. The writing is miniscule but readable. I had the Torah copy commissioned when I first decided I would participate in war. I vowed to carry this miniaturized Torah with me in every battle I participated in. I planned to fight praying that our Lord would give me the strength and courage of David. It was his will that we defeated the Almerians.

Ahmad ibn Abbas was brought to Granada defeated, disgraced, humiliated. He shuffled, head down, carrying heavy chains, in front of the same man he railed against so publicly for so long. Mounted on my stallion, with Abbas dragging his chains and shuffling his feet in the dirt in front of me, my heart filled my chest. I was as content as any man couldbe, but I was also troubled by the emotions.

Caliph Badis came back from the front of our troops. He turned and matched his stallion's gait to mine, riding at my side.

"I want you to instruct the chief of one of my smaller tribes to imprison this poor excuse for a man in his compound," he toldme.

I recognizedthat this wasan honor shrouded in a threat.

"Tell whomever you select as jailer that Abbas is to be treated as a guest, but he must be constantly watched, not allowed to escape."

If ibn Abbas escaped, the chief must understand that he wouldpay with his life.

Ibn Abbas wasa haughty Arab, overly proud of his education, intellectual achievements, and heritage, andwasa very wealthy man. He knewthat Badis was, as are all rulers, avaricious and always in need of cash. After we were safely home, word reached me that he had offered to pay Badis a huge ransom for his freedom. Badis prevaricated. His excuse was that he needed to consult with his chiefs and with his viziers.

The situationwas difficult for me. I knew Badis would be tempted by the magnitude of the ransom, butif ibn Abbas was released,he would do everything in his power to conspire against me. He had even more reason to hate me, holding me responsible for his defeat.

Ibn Abbas always considered himself destined to be caliph of Almeria. I felt it was necessary to remind Badis, at every opportunity, that ibn Abbas wasan Arab and a sworn enemy of the Zanhadja. He was also vindictive in nature and would, as long as he lived, seek revenge for his defeat and humiliation.

The evening we returned, I was in my home. I paced the house, charged with energy and excitement. I was still too excited to sit still. Rebecca cornered me in the hall. She put her arms around me and held me tightly.

"Did you have to fight, my love?" she asked.

Joseph could notrestrain himself and raninto the hall.

"Did you kill anyone, Papa?" he asked. "Did you receive any wounds?"

My wife took my hand and led me to a chair in the dining room. She pushed me gently into it then sat on my lap, her arms around my neck, her face buried in my chest. She was sobbing with relief. I patted the small of her back. My brother-in-law joined us. He pulled another of the chairs closer to hear my account of the battle.

"No, I did not have to fight," I told them. Joseph seemed disappointed.

* * *

A month passed. Ibn Abbas was still a prisoner. Various caliphates and principalities throughout Andalusia sent emissaries to our court. Some of these emissaries requested that ibn Abbas be set free; others asked for his death. Badis listened with a serious face to all the entreaties, nodded his head, but said nothing.

Rosh Hashanah came, then Yom Kippur, and still Badis made no decision concerning the fate of ibn Abbas. Sukkot arrived, and I was unable to maintain the normal light-hearted banter and good spirits I usually felt for this holiday. I was preoccupied, concerned about Badis's decision about the fate of my enemy.

Every year, on the fifteenth day of Tishrei, we celebrate *Sukkot*. Sukkot is the Hebrew word for a hut. Each family builds a small temporary structure and lives, eats, and sleeps in the sukkot for seven days. The purpose is to commemorate forty years of wandering in the desert and the giving of the Law on Mount Sinai. During this wandering, the Israelites lived in frail huts.

This is a festival, a season of rejoicing. It also celebrates the fall harvest. The sukkot is decorated with fruits and vegetables. We also make a *lulav*, a combination of date palm, willow, and myrtle branches held together by a woven palm branch. The lulav is held in the right hand and the *etrog*, a lemon-like fruit with a strong citrus smell, is held in the left hand. The two are waved simultaneously in six directions—north, south, east, west, up, and down—symbolizing that Adonai is found everywhere. This year, the mood during our feast in the sukkot in my courtyard was somber.

Rebecca always closely supervised the preparation of theSukkot meal for the first night. She prepared the main course herself. It is called *buraniya,* and consists of layers of fat lamb, eggplant, and spiced meatballs made from veal. It is one of my favorite dishes, but Rebecca's version does not compare favorably with my memories of my mother'sburaniya. One of my favorite memories is sitting in our kitchen watching as my mother prepared and cooked this dish. First, she cut up the lamb into chunks and put them in a large pot sitting over the fire after the olive oil she put in the pot first started to smoke. She stirred the meat while adding coriander, cumin, and saffron. After the seasoned lamb was browned, she added a spoonful of soaked *almori.*

Perhaps you are not familiar with almori. It is a mixture of salt, honey, raisins, pine nuts, almonds, hazelnuts, and a small amount of flour. This is all pounded into a paste and formed into a roll that is allowed to harden in the sun. Many of our dishes contain this ingredient. The cook breaks off as much as needed for the dish, soaks it in water, and then adds it to the dish.

After Mother added the almori,sheadded a couple of spoons of spiced vinegar. Perhaps that is the difference. I think Rebeccausedless of the almori and leftout the vinegar, or maybe usedthe wrong vinegar. The mixture is cooked until the meat is about half-done. While Mother prepared all the initial ingredients, our cook mixed the veal, onion, garlic, and parsley, chopped everything together into small pieces, then made meatballs and fried them in olive oil.

Next,Mother dipped slices of eggplant in boiling water, then grilled the slices. She selected a large pan and made alternating layers of eggplant, then lamb, then more eggplant, then the meatballs. Each layer was seasoned with saffron. She covered the dish with chopped almonds andpoured whipped eggs with lavender and cinnamon over the mixture. Finally, she topped everything with egg yolks and put it in the oven until the ingredients blended together and all the wet ingredients were dry. After this, she put the pan on the edge of the embers of the kitchen fire to keep warm until it was time to cut it into slices and serve it. My mouth is full of saliva as I write this.

My worries about ibn Abbas persisted. The beginning of Simchat Torah starts at sundown, the holiday when we complete the annual cycle of Torah readings and begin a new cycle. The next morning, I learned that my caliph was out strolling that previous evening with his brother, General Boluggin, and one of his other viziers, Ali ibn al-Karawi. As they passed the house where ibn Abbas was being held, Badis decided to enter, along with his companions and two bodyguards. Following the customary greetings and offering of food and drink, he instructed their host to bring ibn Abbas before them.

Ibn Abbas, arrogant as always, thought Badis was going to accept his ransom offer. He decided to make his release more certain by doubling the offer. Badis was incensed. He considered Abbas's arrogant demeanor, and the increase of the ransom offer, as denigration of his hospitality and his honor as caliph. He grabbed the spear from one of his bodyguards and stabbed ibn Abbas in the abdomen. Boluggin quickly grabbed the other guard's spear and struck ibn Abbas inthe chest. Ibn al-Karawi joined the slaughter with his knife. The jailer chief covered his eyes to avoid watching the butchery. The three of them stabbed ibn Abbas seventeen times before he finally died.

The same evening ibn Abbas was murdered, but prior to my learning of it, I handed Joseph a poem I'd recently completed with the following instructions:

"I want you to take this to my students, and I want each of them, and you, to make copies of this poem. You will check all copies for errors and make any necessary corrections yourself. I will send copies of the poem to our courts and yeshivas in Jerusalem, Baghdad, Egypt, Tunisia, and elsewhere. The poem is written in Hebrew with an Arabic superscription explaining that the poem is a description of the malicious plans and actions of Zuhair and ibn Abbas. It tells how God was instrumental in rescuing me from their evil intentions and punishing them. The title of the poem is "Shira." It is written in one hundred and forty-nine lines, each stanza ending in words with the sound *ruh*. You see,the poem has the same number of lines as the number of Psalms. This is not a coincidence.There are also numerous references to the Scriptures. I did this to draw parallels between this story and those told in the Torah. The poem will inform all Jews of our victory at Al Fuente and what it means for us as a people. On second thought, make enough copies to distribute throughout the Diaspora. I intend that this poem be used in a celebration to rival that of Purim."

* * *

Only a month after the death of ibn Abbas and the final victory over Almeria, Granada was buzzing with the news of the arrival of Abu l-Futuh Thabit ben Muhammad al-Djurdjani. He entered the city with a dozen well-armed warriors. The writings of this dignitary were well-known, as was his reputation as a mercenary of great skill. Josephcame to me with the news of al-Djurdjani's arrival.

"Ah yes, al-Djurdjani. He is a furious and skillful warrior, Joseph. His writings indicate he is also a formidable scholar, thinker, and writer. I am concerned and somewhat anxious to know why he came to Granada. I know he asked for an audience with Caliph Badis, but Badis, after our victory and all the adulation from his peers, has become even more distracted and difficult than usual. He avoids the day-to-day obligations of his position, forcing me and the other viziers to make decisions he should be making. His chiefs and their men are flush with spoils from the capture and appropriation of several of Almeria's towns and fortresses. Notables, including myself, have been given some of the appropriated estates. Our traders have benefited by gaining direct access to the sea and trade. With all of this distraction, Badis has neglected to pay some of his chiefs the attention and acknowledgement they feel they are owed. He is too preoccupied with hunting, his harem, wine, and other diversions to cultivate his friends. You remember I spoke to you about the importance of cultivating your friends."

"Yes, Papa, I remember that conversation very well."

Seven

MY HOUSE WAS built on a small hill in the northeast corner of the Jewish sectionf of Granada. From my rooftop terrace I hada clear view of the snow-covered Sierra Nevada. Looking up,onecouldsee the alcazaba of Caliph Badis, again being renovated. The fort and palace complex occupiedthe top of a rocky hill that dominatedthe city. The triangular top of the hill was flattened by the labor of men, probably in Roman times, and cameto a point. The tower located closest to that point lookeddown on my house and, in fact, on all of Granada.

My house was also built in many stages. The basic, original structure consistedof both quarried rock and handmade bricks. The ground floor wasreached via a stout, solid cedar gate in a high wall that facedthe street passing in front of the house. There wereno houses across the street from ours, only a low retaining wall with a view of the valley below. Our front gate openedoutward, making it more difficult for anyone to force their way in. Once through the gate there wasa large courtyard dominated by the sound and smell of fresh water. In one corner of the courtyard, water felltwo meters over a rock wall into a pool. That water passedthrough a fountain in the center of the courtyard, sending out a cooling mist. The water from the waterfall also circulatedthrough a series of ponds filled with fish and water flowers.

On the roof of my house wasa small windmill that poweredthe pump lifting the water up into a tank, also on the roof, that fedthe waterfall. There wereseveral stone benches in the courtyard, and many planters filled with exotic plants and fruit trees. Birds sangto us from the trees, and there werealways flowers, or flowering bushes, or flowering trees, depending on the season, to add their sweet aroma.

One enteredthe house proper from the courtyard through an iron gate that protecteda huge oak door. Both couldbe locked to prevent entry into the house. Through the doorway there wasa long, narrow room lined with wooden benches. Those waiting to see me usedthe benches to wait if the weather wasbad, or if they wereuncomfortable about waiting in the courtyard.

This waiting room hadthree other doors in addition to the one leading from the courtyard. The first of these doors openedonto a hallway with an arched ceiling. The first doorway on the right out of that hallway ledto the salon and adjoining dining room. Off the dining room wasthe kitchen, then a storeroom with a door to a small back courtyard. The back courtyard containedthe privy. There wasa stout gate to the narrow alley that passedin back of the house.

The hallway continued, ending at the stairs leading up to four bedrooms, then up another flight to the large bedroom that my wife and I shared. The rooftop terrace wasreached from a separate doorway from the top stair landing.

The first door on the left off the waiting room openedto a short hallway leading to my study. Off the study wasan adjoining room containing a small bed, covered in bright silks, and silk pillows stuffed with cotton. This waswhere I sometimes nappedin the afternoon. The third door openedinto a large room filled with floor cushions and bookshelves along three walls. This wasthe room where I metwith my students. I also usedit for meetings when there weretoo many people to fit into my study.

Shortly after I was appointed finance minister, I started a *yeshiva*. I selectedmy students using three criteria. The first wasan evaluation of their skill as calligraphers. I coulddiscern a great deal about a person's personality, attention to detail, and reliability from their calligraphy.

If the prospective student passedthe calligraphy test, I interviewedhim to evaluate his knowledge of the Torah and Talmud. Finally, I askeda series of questions designed to evaluate honesty and moral character.

My mode of instruction wasto arrange the students in a semi-circle in front of where I sat. I dictatedto them from the Torah, or from one of my books of the Talmud, or from some other work of theology or poetry. I then inspectedwhat they wrote down and madecorrections before initiating a discussion of the possible interpretations and meanings of the text. When not teaching, I put the students to work making copies of important writings, mostly mine. Copies of the Torah and Talmud weredestined for poor communities or scholars throughout the Diaspora. Copies of my and other authors' poetry, in both Hebrew and Arabic,weredistributed to friends, acquaintances, and scholars I believed would be interested.

After the defeat of Zuhair and ibn Abbas, it wasn't long before our own Prince Yaddair initiated another crisis. This was made possible because Badis neglected to do what was necessary to maintain his popularity with several of his chiefs. Muhammad al-Djurdjani also felt slighted by Badis, who never bothered to respond to his multiple requests for an audience. Yaddair, with minimal effort, was able to recruit al-Djurdjani to his cause. He hired him, and all of his retinue, as his personal bodyguards. He then conspired with al-Djurdjani to organize a rebellion involving those chiefs who felt slighted by Badis. His new colleague made all the necessary contacts and organized the treacherous rebellion. Yaddair convinced himself that he kept his own hands clean.

Even though Yaddair's dislike of me is well-known, the schemers invited me to join their cabal. Al-Djurdjani wasa clever man. He involved me believing that by doing so, I could not act against the plotters. He even pressed me to host one of their meetings, where he said they would plan Badis's assassination. I believe they wanted me to host this meeting because they were certain I would learn of their plot in any case and hoped to make me guilty by association.

I found myself in a very sticky, tricky situation. I thought long and hard about how to deal with it. I was not certain of a course of action. There was a real possibility that Prince Boluggin was also party to the scheme. At the least, he no doubt knew of it. Badis was failing to demonstrate true leadership, and that was especially troublesome. I also learned that some of those same stalwarts of the Jewish community responsible for the murder of my father-in-law were involved in the plot, and that fact made my decision final.

The clandestine meeting was to take place that same evening I learned of the involvement of my Jewish enemies. I called all the servants into my study. They crowded in with worried expressions on their faces. I had never had such a meeting with them; Rebecca was always the person to direct their activities.

"I want each and every one of you to leave this house and visit your relatives," I told them."Do not return for two days. I see many of you have questions. Do not bother to ask. Just do as I say. I want all of you to be gone after the noon meal, or earlier. You are dismissed."

I left the study after they cleared it and went to find my brother-in-law, who actedas my steward. I found him in the kitchen with Rebecca.

"Solomon ben Judah, I have something I need you to do, without asking any questions. Today, immediately after the noon meal, I want you to take Rebecca, and my children, to my farm at Guevejarfor a three-day holiday. I cannot explain why, but I need you to do this for me. Will you?"

"Of course, Ha Nagid. I will go now and make everything ready."

"Good. Thank you, Solomon."

Then I found one of the male servants and sent him to the alcazaba with a sealed note asking for a meeting with the caliph on an extremely important subject as soon as possible.

Badis was seated on a nest of cushions when I was ushered into his presence. He held a cup in his right hand and had his left arm around one of his concubines, who was groaning softly as she moved her body along his left side, a hand resting on his privates.

"What is it that is so important, Nagrela?"

"I have information that is very sensitive, Your Excellency. It can be for your ears only."

"You are certain?"

"Yes, Your Excellency."

He pushed the girl, who could not have been more than fourteen years old, away.

"Go, leave me. I will call for you later." He then shouted, "Everyone who can hear my voice, leave these rooms. If I find anyone listening, I will have your ears cut off!"

The smile he directed at me involved only his lips; the rest of his face was serious.

"Thank you, Your Highness. I have gained knowledge about a plot to assassinate you and take over the caliphate. They have made the mistake of involving me, thinking thus to gain my assent and support."

He jumped to his feet. "Who are these people? I will have them arrested and executed immediately!"

"The plot involves Yaddair and is being organized by al-Djurdjani. Some of your tribal chiefs are involved, and even some members of the Jewish community. Unfortunately, I do not know who all of the participants are. I urge patience, Excellency. There will be a meeting at my house this evening and I believe most, if not all, of the plotters will attend. If you are agreeable, I will arrange a place for you to secret yourself so you can identify for yourself who is involved and the truth of what they are planning."

"What do you suggest?"

"If you will come to the back gate of my house shortly after the sun sets, I will let you in and take you to a place where you can see and hear for yourself what is planned."

When the planet Venus was just visible in the darkening sky, I stood in my back courtyard, waiting. After a short time, there were four heavy raps with the pommel of a sword on the heavy oak door. The door rattled and echoed from the blows. I swung it open and Badis, clothed in a heavy cloak, his face covered with the tail end of his turban, entered while sheathing his sword. I closed and locked the gate, then led the way up the stairs to Joseph's bedroom, located directly over my meeting room. I had previously drilled a hole in the floor so Badis could listen to what transpired during the meeting and see who the plotters were.

Less than an hour later, I ushered the last of the conspirators into the meeting room. I knew Badis was sitting on cushions near the hole in the floor. He told me later that it was not necessary for him to lie on the floor with an ear to the hole to clearly understand the conversation being held in the room below.

"I was tempted, on several occasions, to look through the hole to see who was talking. Their treachery will be rewarded. I feared the movement might be noticed and I would be discovered, but they were all too focused on their evil intent."

Yaddair was not present, but al-Djurdjani was clearly speaking for him. As the men arrived, I acknowledged each of them by name for Badis's benefit. I did not speak during the meeting. The plan to assassinate Badis was discussed, and assignments as to who was to do what were made. Al-Djurdjani detailed the sequence of events that would make Boluggin king. Then he talked about making Yaddair the king after Boluggin was induced to abdicate or, if necessary, assassinated. Perhaps they were still unsure of me, so they avoided any discussion of the time and place for the plot to unfold.

The meeting ended, and the more than twodozen men left the house in groups of three or four. When the last of the traitors left, I showed Badis the way out to the back courtyard and opened the gate. Neither of us spoke, but before disappearing into the narrow alley, Badis put his left hand on my right shoulder, gave it a squeeze, and nodded his thanks.

Badis now knew all of the conspirators. The day after the meeting he summoned one of them, the head of one of the Zanhadja tribes, ostensibly to offer him a new position of responsibility in the government. I was ordered to be present.

"I know all about the meeting you attended last night. I want a written list of everyone involved in this plot. If you do not reveal the names, and when and where the assassination attempt is to be made, your whole family will be killed while you watch. After they are dead, you will be slowly, painstakingly tortured until death releases you from your agony. I estimate the process will take several days. You are fortunate to be the first I ask this of. I know the other conspirators. I am certain one of them will give me the information I seek."

The man gave it up immediately.

"I was on my way to tell you of this plot when I was summoned, Excellency. The plan is to surround you and your bodyguards at the horse races scheduled for this weekend at the nearby village of Zubia. The traitors know that you are looking forward to attending the races since several of your horses will compete."

Badis motioned to one of his bodyguards.

"Take this man away and lock him up until I decide the truth of what he says—and his fate."

He looked at me.

"Well, ibn Nagrela, since you are a student of military strategy and tactics, what do you suggest?"

"I have given the matter some thought, Excellency," I answered. "My suggestion would be for you to attend the races accompanied by me, no more than four bodyguards, and two of the tribal chiefs, one of whom is on your list of conspirators. You should secret at least fifty of your best Zanhadja warriors, all from your own family, to mingle with the large crowd. The weather will be cool, and all of your men should wear long cloaks to conceal their light armor and swords."

* * *

At the races, I soon spotted al-Djurdjani and his men, along with eight of the coconspirators, maneuvering individually through the crowd trying to get close to Badis. Badis had informed his men of the identitiesof the conspirators. As they moved toward the caliph, each was cutoff, separated, and held at knife or sword point by Badis's men. After they were disarmed, the conspirators were quietly led away.

When al-Djurdjani was accosted he managed to draw his sword, but he was surrounded by five skilled warriors. He attacked the man in front of him, who warded off the blow while another of Badis's kinsman standing to his right sliced at al-Djurdjani's sword arm. The arm was cut to the bone.Al-Djurdjani's swordfell to the ground.

Badis pushed his way to where al-Djurdjani was being held.

"So, this is the one who wants to assassinate me," he declared. "One of you tear a piece of his clothing and bandage that wound tightly. I do not want him to die before I am done with him. Now let us return to the alcazaba as quickly as possible."

Al-Djurdjani was led away with a rope around his neck and his hands tied behind his back; a rough, tight,bloody bandage bound his wound.

Yaddair and most of the other conspirators were waiting at the palace, poised to take control. They received word of the events at the races before we were able to return. They fled Granada, eventually reaching Seville. Among those whofled were those same affluent Jews who had caused me so much grief. I was not unhappy to see them gone. I made it easy for their families to join them in exile.

"Ibn Nagrela, once again you have proven your loyalty. I am giving you all the houses and property of those Jews who supported this rebellion and who escaped to exile."

"Thank you, Excellency. Am I free to dispose of this wealth as I see fit?"

"Of course, it is yours."

I decided to allow the families all the wealth they could carry as they departed and payed them a fair, albeit discounted, price for their properties. The Talmud teaches that sins of the father should not be paid for by the innocent son.

I was also present when Prince Boluggin came to Badis.

"I am sorry, brother. I knew of this plot but failed to warn you. I beg you to forgive me. I will never do anything of this nature again."

"I am not terribly impressed by your expressed remorse, Boluggin. But I must respect the honor of our father. You will retire to your estates and remain there unless you are summoned to my presence. Do you understand me?"

"You are banishing me?"

"I could have you executed for treason. Be thankful. Now go, I am tired of looking at your worthless face."

Eight

DESPITE THE SETBACK, Yaddair was not deterred. The throne of Granada continued to beckon him; he could not ignore it. He still had strong supporters in Granada who preferred him to the caliph they had. Badis relied on me more and more to oversee the day-to-day administration of the caliphate. Unfortunately, he was also reverting to behavior that hadalienated many of his Zanhadja by neglecting to court, praise, thank, and reward them.

I learned that Yaddair sent emissaries to visit Granada with instructions to evaluate the political situation. I also learned that from time to time, he received communications from secret admirers—fortunately, not secret from me—who were still living in Granada. It was clear to me that he still wanted to take Granada and make it his.

While Yaddair continued to plot, I was busy developing my growing network of spies. I now had a list of the names of at least two hundred Zanhadja warriors who supported Yaddair. I went to the alcazaba to communicate this information to Badis.

"Who are these traitors, Nagrela? I command you to give me your list. I will execute all of them immediately."

"That could prove to be dangerous, Excellency. Many of these men are well-connected and well-respected. Their executions would likely force their friends, colleagues, and certainly their family members into Yaddair's camp."

I handed him the list.

"My advice would be that you make your knowledge of these men known by giving some of them large gifts for no apparent reason. This will make those not given gifts wonder if they have been exposed. I am mulling over other strategies to turn the traitors against each other."

"Nagrela, you are one devious bastard. I like you and the way you think. You have earned yourself even more respect from me."

The Arab caliph of Seville, Granada's longtime enemy, supported Yaddair's scheming. He was concerned about the growing strength of Badis's caliphate. After the defeat of Zuhair, and the takeover of much of Almeria's territories, Granada was the most powerful state in Eastern Andalusia, thus a growing threat to Seville.

After Joseph and I finished my review of his educational assignments yesterday evening, he had a question for me;

"Papa, why does Seville hate us so much?"

"It's all politics and long-held grudges, Joseph. As you know, Granada is a Berber kingdom, and Seville is Arab. Seville came to be as a result of the struggles between the Umayyad and Hammudite dynasties. The Berbers support the Hammudite dynasty, while the Arabs have always supported the Umayyads. The first three Hammudite rulers took the title of caliph and ruled all of Andalusia after deposing the original Umayyad caliphate. Since that time, the war between the Arab supporters of the Umayyads and the Berber supporters of the Hammudites has never been completely settled. Seville emerged as the Arab-supported Umayyad stronghold with a puppet they installed as the Umayyad caliph. The kingdom is actually ruled by the crafty and power-hungry Abu l-Kasim ibn Abbad. That despot's goal is to rule all of Andalusia."

Late that same morning, a messenger arrived with coded dispatch from one of my Jewish spies living in Carmona. The message was written in Hebrew, disguised as a chatty letter, but I am the one who devised the cipher. Abu l-Kasim had sent his army to invade the borders of Carmona five weeks ago; the message took more than a week to reach me. Instead of moving his army the short one-day march east and slightly north, directly to Carmona, l-Kasim's general circled first south and then east, subduing several small towns and cities along the way before taking the Carmona-ruled city of Osuna. The army then moved directly north to take Ecija. The object of this strategy was obviously to protect their rear when laying siege to Carmona.

The ruler of Carmona was Prince Muhammad ben Abdallah, a Zenaga Berber. Historically, he had done his best to maintain good relations with Seville, his close eastern neighbor. The caliph of Seville gave the responsibility of his army to his son Ismail, an experienced and successful general. Following the subjugation of Ecija, Ismail turned back east and laid siege to Carmona. My spy said that it wasn't until Ismail started to approach Carmona that ben Abdallah sent emissaries to both Badis and the Hammudite king of Malaga, Idris ben Ali.

I went immediately to our alcazaba to find out if Badis had received ben Abdallah's emissary yet.

Carmona is well protected by its alcazaba that occupies the top of the largest hill in the region. That fortress is built on the ruins of the original Roman and Visigoth fortresses,as are most in Andalusia. The caliphs of Granada and Malaga understoodthe obvious threat to their own kingdoms if Carmona fellto Seville.

When I arrived, our alcazaba was in turmoil. Soldiers, functionaries, and servants were scurrying in every direction, their heads down, worried expressions on all faces.

"Ah, Nagrela, here you are. I assume you know what is going on."

"Yes, Excellency. I received a coded message from one of my spies in Carmona this morning. I am told that Ismail has taken Osuna, Ecija, and several small towns along the way. He now lays siege to Carmona."

"Yes, this is the same information I have. We will, of course, respond. The orders have been given to mobilize. I am in communication with Caliph Ali of Malaga. He is ill, but he is sending an army under the command of his vizier, ibn Bakana. I will head our army, but I insist that you join me, Nagrela. We will have need of your knowledge and sage advice."

I nodded my agreement and said, "I never doubted that you would see and understand that responding in this way to the caliph of Carmona is in your own best interest. It is a necessary and smart diplomatic move."

We marched northwest on the road to Cabra, a town located on the western edge of Granada's territory. There we joined forces with ibn Bakana. Our combined armies trekked west over forty kilometers before fording the Genil River. After crossing the Genil, we moved further west to the plains just east of the small town of Los Arenales.

Badis, the other high officials, the generals, and I all had our own tents and servants. Badis's pavilion was of heavy silk in blues, reds, yellows, and greens, strips all sewn together to make a large enough shelter in which to hold court. The tents of the other leaders were only marginally smaller and slightly less ornate. Badis, the other officials, and the generals all had cotton- and down-stuffed mattresses to sleep on. My tent was just large enough to house the heavy carpet that served as my bed, some cushions, my traveling desk, and the books I must have. There was room for one or two visitors to crowd in if necessary. My tent was made of heavy, close-woven, blue silk. The tents of the lesser officers and administrators were slightly smaller than mine, single-person canvas tents.

Our servants set up the tents of their masters at each camp. They cared for the horses, and cooked and served their master's food. The soldiers were divided into platoons of ten to twelve men. They drew their rations from the supply wagons, foraging for fresh food along the way. The soldiers made their own cooking fires and slept on the ground, rolled up in their cloaks. To show solidarity with the soldiers, I did not use a mattress. I slept on a carpet on the ground, but inside my tent. I made certain my servants made my sacrifice well-known throughout the camp.

As we moved west, we made no effort to obscure the fact we were coming to the aid of Carmona. As intended, Ismail's spies warned him of the size of our approaching army. Not wanting to be attacked from the rear, he abandoned the siege of Carmona and marched his army to meet us. When we had confirmation that Ismail was moving to intercept our forces, I sought out Badis and ibn Bakana.

"Excellencies, I have in my service a young Jewish man who was raised in Carmona. This young man is willing to make his way into the city where his family still lives. He can take a message to ben Abdallah from you and instruct his forces to attack Ismail from the rear as soon as our armies are engaged."

"That is an excellent idea, Nagrela. Go to my groom and tell him to give you a fast horse to send this young man on his way."

Three days later, the armies faced each other on open ground just east of a small village. As the armies prepared for battle, ben Abdallah and his army of Carmona appeared on top of a hill to the rear of Ismail's forces. Ismail, being prudent, ordered his army to retreat to the southwest rather than engage our forces on two fronts.

As Ismail retreated, the three leaders of our combined forces held a meeting to celebrate the bloodless victory.

"I will keep my army here until tomorrow morning to begin our return to Granada," Badis announced.

"I will do likewise," said ibn Bakana. "I am anxious to return to Malaga and learn of the health of my caliph."

Ben Abdallah only tarried for an hour before beginning his return to Carmona.

The next morning, we bid farewell to ibn Bakana and started east for Cabra. To reach Cabra, we had to recross the Genil River. Badis followed his usual practice of sending scouts out ahead of his army. I was riding next to Badis when we saw a man approaching, whipping his horse for more speed.

"That's one of my scouts," exclaimed Badis.

The rider pulled his lathered, panting horse to a sliding stop in front of us.

"Excellency, Ismail force-marched his army to the east, circled around us, and reached the ford across the Genil. He is there waiting our arrival. His troops are ready and anxious to do battle!"

Nine

"NAGRELA, WRITE OUT a request to our allies to come to us as quickly as possible," Badis instructed, then he turned to one of his generals."Choosefour of our best horseman, two to go by different routes to ibn Bakana, and two to go to ben Abdallah. Each rider will ride one horse while leading another and switch horses every time the animal he is on tires. I will sign each message and affix my seal."

"Of course, Excellency. I will prepare a message immediately. Why do you want two messengers for each of our allies?" I asked.

"I want each man to take a different route in case some accident, mishap, or capture by our enemies prevents one of them from reaching Bakana or Abdallah."

Each messenger carried the following sealed messages addressed to our departed allies:

Esteemed Sir,

We are stopped in sight of the ford of the Genil River. Ismail has surprised us by circling around. He and his army are now ensconced between us and an open plain, the only ford of the river for some distance at his back. Caliph Badis requests that you immediately join us and reunite our forces. Only this action will enable us to deal with this threat to the security of all three of our caliphates.

The messengers who arrive with this plea will lead you by the shortest route possible so we can join forces in this endeavor. May Allah grant you speed.

The messages were signed and sealed, and two riders and four horses galloped to the east, to Carmona, and the others rode south to find ibn Bakana.

While waiting for our allies to rejoin us, I studied the terrain and sketched a map of the area. I considered all the possible variables that could affect the outcome of the coming battle. With the Genil protecting his rear and an open plain between us, I realized that Ismail was in a much better position to maneuver his forces and win the day.

Shortly after dark, ibn Bakana and ben Abdallah, with their armies, arrived, faster than I had anticipated. I was summoned to Badis's pavilion.

"Nagrela, I want you to stay for our meeting. The meeting will begin shortly. Ibn Bakana and ben Abdallah will bring all their regimental commanders, and ours will be present as well."

After everyone assembled, Badis turned to me.

"Have you a plan, Nagrela?" Badis asked and smiled. "I suspect you do."

"I have something in mind, yes, Your Excellencies."

"Ibn Nagrela is a wise and learned man. He has made an exhaustive study of military tactics and strategy. It was his plan that was responsible for our recent defeat of Zuhair at Al Fuente. I ask only that you be willing to listen to his ideas. If you don't like his plan, I am open to consider other options. Will you all agree to listen to what he says?"

He waited for each man present to voice or nod his assent.

"I suggest we offer our best fighter as our champion, to challenge their champion to single combat," I began. "Tonight, under cover of darkness, we position the cavalry of ibn Bakana to attack the right flank of their army."

I spread out my sketched map on top of a low table, positioned under a hanging lamp in the center of the pavilion.

"We position ibn Bakana's cavalry here, out of sight, behind this hill. While the enemy troops are focused on the outcome of the fight between the champions, ibn Bakana's forces attack. After the right flank is fully engaged, the cavalry of ben Abdallah should attack the left flank. Ismail will have to shift troops in response to the second cavalry attack. As soon as he does so, our foot soldiers will attack the middle of his defenses. Our archers, sling-throwers, and crossbow archers should be positioned in ranks behind our infantry. The infantry will advance until the archers are in range of the enemy. The archers and crossbow soldiers fire, in volleys. Each rank reloads while the next rank advances and fires, until the slingers are close enough to cause damage.

"The commanders of these units must maintain discipline and keep their ranks close. We hammer the enemy until they start to spread out or scatter. Badis's cavalry should be held in reserve to attack the weakest point when it is exposed. Small units of Badis's Nubian infantrywill also be held in reserve to be quickly dispatched to block any enemy cavalry attacks. The Nubians, with their long spears, have proven to be very successful in the face of charging cavalry.

"It is imperative that our infantry continues to press the attack forward until they reach the river. The objective is to split Ismail's forces. By concentrating overwhelming numbers in the center, our archers, slingers, and crossbow soldiers will make maximum impact. Our three leaders have personal guards numbering approximately fifty men each. I suggest that these men, all mounted and itching to participate in the battle, be held in reserve until the enemy shows its first signs of breaking ranks; then you release your men to go in and clean up."

Badis cleared his throat.

"Ibn Bakana, what do you think?"

"Yes, it could work."

"Ben Abdallah?"

"I agree, it is a good plan."

Badis looked at the generals crowded around the table on which my sketch of the battleground was spread out. He raised his eyebrows at each in turn. Each nodded his agreement.

"It is settled then."

He turned to the opening of the pavilion and shouted, "SHARIF!"

A fully armed man filled the opening, his feet spread while standing at attention. He was at least two meters tall. His huge shoulders, arms, and chest tapered to a narrow waist, but then his body flared out again with bulging thighs and calves.

"Sharif, you command my Zanhadja bodyguard. Who is the best fighter amongst you?"

The man smiled.

"I have never been defeated, Sire."

"I know that, but can you defeat any other man in my army?"

"Yes, Sire."

"I thought so. I need a champion. Are you that man? Are you willing to fight to the death against the champion of these forces blocking our return home?"

"I am honored to do so, Sire."

"Good. You may ask for anything you wish tonight, and it will be granted. In the morning, you will represent the honor of Granada and of our allies."

The man nodded, bowed, and backed out of the pavilion.

I spent the night worrying. Would Ismail agree to a battle of champions? If he did, would our troops follow the plan and react with the necessary speed and commitment? At midnight I left my tent to make certain ibn Bakana's cavalry were well hidden behind the hill I had identified.

The sun broke through wispy clouds hugging the horizon behind us. The two armies were arrayed, ready to do battle, in the plain, the river Genil rushing past behind Ismail's forces. Somewhat less than half a kilometer separated the two armies. Sharif marched out a hundred yards in front of our troops, stopped, and shouted:

"I AM SHARIF, CHAMPION OF BADIS, CALIPH OF GRANADA! I CHALLENGE YOUR CHAMPION, IF ANYONE IS FOOLISH ENOUGH TO ACCEPT, TO MORTAL COMBAT. ARE ANY OF YOU RABBITS BRAVE ENOUGH, MAN ENOUGH, TO ACCEPT?"

I sat on my stallion, watching. At least a dozen men crowded around Ismail, clamoring for the honor of killing the loudmouth. He sat on his warhorse, pondering the meaning of the challenge, frowning. Finally, he pointed at one of the men begging to be honored as his champion. I could see that the man chosen was Sharif's equal in size and, no doubt, fighting skill.

The two came together in front of the massed troops. They fought on foot with sword and shield, evenly matched, for over thirty minutes. While they were thus engaged, and the enemy soldiers were focused on the spectacle, ibn Bakana waved his hand at a runner who disappeared down the back of the hill we were watching from and raced, out of sight of the enemy, to give the order for the cavalry attack on the right flank of Ismail's position.

The two champions, both exhausted, bent at the waist, sucking in deep breaths of air filled with the dust from their exertions. They paused for less than a minute, then reengaged. The cheering from both sides reached a crescendo. Ibn Bakana's cavalry circled the hill and charged into Ismail's right flank. Ismail reacted, deploying his infantry to intercept, but his troops were slow and somewhat disorganized.

As soon as our cavalry made contact, ben Abdallah's cavalry attacked the left flank. This time, Ismail's remaining infantry responded a bit faster. As soon as both flanks were engaged, our center moved forward. The champions broke off and rushed back to their units, both leaving blood on the ground.

Badis, his two colleagues, and I, all of us mounted, watched the unfolding battle from the top of our hill. The personal guards of the vizier and the two caliphs were arrayed behind each of them.

Waves of noise rolled up toward us. Signal calls from bugles and drums competed with the clash of swords and spears clanging against shields. The sounds of weapons breaking and horses neighing and screaming with pain merged with the shouts of men and their battle cries, screams of the wounded, and moans of the dying. The whoosh from volleys of arrows, bolts, and missiles flying through the air punctuated the pandemonium.

I clutched the small Torah under my cloak. I silently murmured continuous prayers to God. Then I noticed that the Berber mercenaries who had been recruited and employed by Ismail's father seemed to be reluctant to enter the fray.

"Look there, Excellency," I pointed. "That unit on the slope of that small hill over there are spectators. I think their standard identifies them as Berber mercenaries."

"Yes, you are right."

Badis turned in his saddle.

"Sharif!"

In a moment, Sharif was at his side.

"You see that group of men just watching the battle from the side of that hill?" He pointed.

"Yes, Sire."

"I believe they are mercenaries, but they are Berbers, do you agree?"

"Yes, Sire, I know that banner. Those men are from Ecija."

"Make your way to them. Offer them what you believe they will accept to join us in this battle against the Arabs."

"Of course, Sire."

No more than ten minutes passed. I saw Sharif leading the turncoats into the fray.

As our infantry steadily advanced, it was easier for our archers, crossbow, and sling soldiers to pick individual targets rather than just sending volleys into the air. The massed group in the center of our forces moved resolutely toward the river, toward Ismail and his bodyguards, who were fighting furiously. Badis could restrain himself no longer. I dismounted and watched as Badis and his two allies rushed into the fray, leading their mounted bodyguards, everyone but me eager to join in the slaughter.

Ismail was on the ground, dead. What remained of his army fled to save themselves.

Badis spurred his horse over to where Ismail's body lay oozing blood into the dirt. He dismounted. I remounted and rode to him. As I approached, Badis severed Ismail's head from the dead body.

"Bring me the highest-ranking officer we have captured!" he shouted.

The order was repeated several times as soldiers milled around looking for a captured officer. Badis stood, holding Ismail's severed head by the hair;the blood dripping into the dust at his feet made small circles with raised edges.

"Well?" he shouted, clearly impatient.

An Arab officer, a rope around his neck, his arms tightly bound behind his back, was shoved to his knees in front of Badis.

"You see this?" Badis asked. He tilted the man's head up by placing the tip of his sword under the shaking officer's chin. Then he shoved the severed head into the man's face, the dead nose pushing against the living one.

"You are a lucky man. You will live this day. I will supply you with a donkey. You will deliver your commander's head to his father, with my compliments."

"He will have me tortured to death, Sire. Please do not require this of me."

"You coward! Would you rather be tortured by me, here and now? Act like a man, a soldier. Do as you are ordered."

"Yes, Sire. I will do as you command."

"Good. Give this man food and drink. Give him one of the captured horses. I will save him from the disgrace of riding a donkey."

Our soldiers took the rest of the day to remove all valuables from the dead and wounded. Those badly wounded and not likely to survive were dispatched. The others, along with those captured without injury, would become slaves or be ransomed if we found their families to have the financial resources.

It took all of the following day to fairly divide the spoils Ismail's troops had garnered from Ecija and Osuna, and from the many small towns and villages they had conquered during their depravations. Three even piles of valuables were stacked, and shares were awarded by our three leaders to the commanders of each of their regular and mercenary contingents. Those commanders were left to decide how to distribute the share to their men. The commanders, of course, retained a significant portion for their own use.

While the division of spoils was taking place, I retired to my tent and started writing down a hymn of praise to God. I named the work "Prayer Before a Battle." I vowed to recite this poem to myself before every battle in which I wasinvolved, from that time forward. I also vowed to keep my miniature Torah safe and secure, over my heart.

Ten

AFTER RETURNING TO Granada following the successful campaign against Seville, I received a messenger from the alcazaba who brought me this letter:

> My servant, Ibn Nagrela,
>
> I require your presence in the throne room four hours after the sun rises tomorrow morning. At that time, you will accept the positions of chief vizier to the caliph and general-in-chief of his armies.
>
> Be prompt and dress accordingly.
>
> Badis, Caliph

A few days later, I started composing a long poem about the Battle of the Genil and the victory over Seville. I finished the poem and gave it the name "Tehilla." The poem, as does "Shira," consists of 149 lines, the same as the Psalms. This I did on purpose. In both poems, I provide many references to biblical events. These biblical references are analogies, praising Adonai for the victories over my enemies, Granada's enemies.

The Arab ruler of Seville, ibnAbbad, had a long-term goal to usurp the Berber kingdoms, especially that of Badis. He wanted to unite all of the Arab and Slav rulers of the various taifa and provinces of Andalusia. He, of course, envisioned himself as the supreme caliph. This ambition was further fueled by a new and overwhelming desire for revenge for the death of his son, Ismail.

It had been three weeks since I completed "Tehilla"and put Joseph and my students to work making copies of it. This morning, one of my spies reported that Prince Yaddair hadprovided ibn Abbad with an opportunity to exact a measure of revenge for Ismail as well as to movehis political goals forward. The caliph of Seville decided to encourage and provide support for Yaddair's efforts to recruit and mobilize a force of elite Slav mercenaries. I neededto recruit more spies working in Seville. It wasessential to keepa close watch on Yaddair's efforts.

Summer, fall, and winter came and went. I received word after midnight that Yaddairhad finished recruiting his mercenary army. He led his rabble through, and around, several taifa bordering Seville, then invaded Granada's territories from the north. The same spy told me that Yaddair and his forces took the city of Arjona. To exact a measure revenge for ibn Abbad, and to gain the continued support of that still grieving monarch, Yaddair ordered the execution of the entire garrison. He also allowed his troops to strip the city and its citizens of all their valuables before moving south.

A week later, I learned that Yaddair had bypassed Jaen, deeming that city and its fortress too strong to overcome quickly. He moved steadily south, forcing several smaller towns and fortresses to surrender.

As if these developments were not enough, I received word that my brother Isaac, who now livedin Loja, wasseriously ill. I immediately asked for a meeting with Badis.

"Excellency, I am in a terrible state with worry. My brother is seriously ill and I do not know if he is receiving adequate care. I must travel to Loja and make certain he is receiving the best care available."

"You would leave me here to cope with my nephew's depravations on my own? How can you even consider that, Vizier?"

"Sire, I am unable to concentrate my attention on the affairs of your caliphate while not knowing if my brother is adequately cared for."

"No, Vizier. You are the general-in-chief of my armies. You must take the field and stop Yaddair's invasion."

"Please, Excellency, you have several generals capable of halting the advance of Yaddair and his mercenaries. As soon as I see to my brother, I will return, take command, and deal with Yaddair once and for all time."

"Leave me a list with the names of the generals you believe are capable of stopping Yaddair's forces until you can return and deal with him, and which one to put in overall command. I will send for you after I have thought about this for a few days. I will tell you then if you can go to your brother's bedside or not."

"Thank you, Excellency. I am happy you will consider doing this for me."

A week later, I was back.

"All right, Vizier, I have given the Zanhadja tribal chief and general ibn Ziri the task of intercepting Yaddair's mercenaries and forcing him to take refuge in whichever nearby alcazaba is available to him. Ibn Ziri will lay siege to wherever Yaddair takes refuge and await your arrival to finish the job. You may hurry to your brother, and then hurry to your duty."

During that very difficult week, while Badis prevaricated, I could not avoid worrying about Isaac. I started a poem entitled "Does Isaac Live?" I also convinced the leading physician of Granada, Abu Mudin, to accompany me if Badis allowed me to go to my brother's sickbed. As soon as I left the caliph, I collected the physician and we proceeded to my house, where everything was ready and waiting for an immediate departure.

We were twenty kilometers from Granada on the road to Loja when we were met by a man riding a horse flecked with saliva and sweat. I recognizedhim as Isaac's steward.

"Ha Nagid, I am very sorry to report that Rabbi Isaac died peacefully in his sleep last night."

I was distraught.

"Abu Mudin, there is nothing for you to do now. Please return to Granada, inform my family of my brother's death, and expedite arrangements to make certain my family arrives in Loja in time for my brother's funeral. The distance is less than sixty kilometers, but they will have to travel hard to arrive in time. I must continue on to organize Isaac's funeral and provide care for his wife and children."

Two days after the funeral, we were standing in the barren Jewish cemetery of Loja. Twenty family and friends, all dressed in white mourning clothes. We stood stark against an overcast sky. Despite the season, there was nothing growing, nothing green to break the mood of that dreary place. Everything was depressing: the brown dirt covering the ground; the gray pebbles resting on the many gray gravestones, signaling visits by mourners;my brother's silhouetted mourners; and most of all, the mound marking the newly filled grave. We were gathered once again in a circle around Isaac's grave, as we hadbeen every day since the funeral, to pray.

When I was finally done praying and weeping, I gathered my family and Isaac's. We left the cemetery and returned to Granada, where I sequestered myself in my study. The only time I came out for the next five days was to lead the prayers for the dead during *Shiva*. The Jewish community of Granada demonstrated their support and love for me by crowding my meeting room with many more than the ten men necessary for a minion for the Shiva ceremony.

My caliph, uncharacteristically, seemed to understand my attachment to my brother and my grief. He made no demands of me until the official mourning period was completed.

Before I returned to my responsibilities and duties, I gave my son Joseph four new poems for him and my students to make copies of. The first wasnamed "A Curtain of Stones." In it, I spokeof Isaac's unexpected death, my own anguish, and the realization of my own mortality. The second poem, entitled "I Carried Him to His Grave,"spoketo Isaac's role as a mentor and teacher to me and many others. I described Isaac's magnanimous nature and how he provided aid to all who were in need. I also described carrying my brother to his grave and how I rent my cloak as dictated in Samuel 13:31,where it says those mourning should tear their garments over their heart. The third poem, "A Day Ago I Buried You,"spokeof my pain that my brother could no longer communicate with me, and the fourth, "Within the Earth They Have Locked You Up,"wasanother expression of my deep grief over the loss of my brother, mentor, and friend. I do not believe that another day of my life will pass without me thinking about my brother and saying a prayer for him.

My time of mourning was soon ended by Yaddair's evil deeds. Badis summoned me and declared that I had done my duty to my brother and his family.

"It is now time for you to resume your responsibilities and duties to the caliphate. Enough with your mourning and depression. You need to focus your thinking, studying, and actions to confront the threat from the north."

The barrier of the Sierra de Alta Coloma, north of Granada, separated Yaddair and his activities from us. While I was distracted, neither Badis nor ibn Ziri were able to organize an adequate response to Yaddair's invasion. Our army was unable to confront Yaddair's in a decisive battle or annihilate it or even force him to retreat into a fortress.I worked long hours to reorganize the army, making certain it was fully supplied and properly equipped. In ten days, I was ready to deal with Yaddair.

It was the month of Elul 4802 (August 1041) as I led a sizable army out of Granada.

The previous day, I had met with Badis to tell him all was ready.

"Ibn Nagrela, I know you understand that it is not appropriate for me to be the direct cause of the death of my first cousin. I am staying home," he smiled without humor.

I believed the excuse was understandable, given Badis's character, but some degree of laziness was probably also involved in his decision.

During the next several days, my army marched through the foothills, splashed through creeks, then forged a river. The men, with our long supply train following, climbed up twisting roads into and through the heavily forested and rocky mountain passes of the

Sierra de Alta Coloma. As the army came down from the last pass, my scouts reported sighting a contingent of Yaddair's forces in the valley below. I paused and made camp in a small valley with good forage and water. I sentout six scouts, all mounted on fast horses.

"I must have reliable information about the strength of Yaddair's forces before I attack," I told them.

The scouts returned in less than two hours. They said that Yaddair's army was inferior to oursin every way. One of myscouts was even able to penetrate their camp and talk to some of the mercenaries. They were happy to gain the spoils after overcoming poorly defended towns and villages, but were not overly pleased to be facing a real army, especially one led by me.

I called for the commanders of my cavalry units, my mounted archers, the mounted crossbowmen, and the mounted slingers to report to my tent for orders.

"I want each of you to lead your units out of this camp, with as little noise as possible, at midnight. At first light you are to attack Yaddair's camp. As soon as you make your attack, I will bring along the remainder of our forces to clean up; the supply train will follow. Is everyone clear on what I expect?"

Silent nods of assent.

The attack, with our overwhelming numbers, took place while Yaddair's men were still wiping sleep from their eyes. My men overran the enemy camp. Many of the mercenaries were killed in the first mounted charge. After their first run through the camp, the cavalry, mounted archers, crossbowmen, and slingers whirled and charged back. Those men able to catch a horse, fled. Yaddair and a number of his close supportersmade good their escape and took refuge at Fuensanta de Martos, the closest fortress to the battle.

Fuensanta de Martos is perched atop a steep, rocky promontory known as the Rock of the Garlic. It dominates the large valley, spread out as far as a man can ride a horse across, or the length of, in half an hour at a full gallop. A mountain ridge east of the fortress rises some considerable distance above the fort. From that ridge's summit, the eastern approach to the fortifications is down a steep, rocky slope.

It is too difficult and dangerous to mount a serious attack from that direction.

The fortress itself has the classical three levels of defense. The first level of defense, an outside high wall with battlements built, as usual, on the remains of a Roman fortress that was later rebuilt and used by the Visigoths. The wall protects the northern, eastern, and southern approaches. The second line of defense, the alcazaba itself, is built up to the very edge of a steep rock precipice. It protects the western approach and has battlements from which the defenders can fight off attack. In the center of the alcazaba stands the tower. From the tower, any attack directed at the fortress can be seen and forces deployed to counter it.

The only regular access to the fortress is via a huge solid oak outer gate in the south wall. That gate opens into an enclosed space with a second, even stronger gate and high walls on all sides fronting the alcazaba. From those walls, defenders can pour rocks, hot oil, arrows, crossbow bolts, or javelins down on any invaders who manage to breach the first gate.

Although Fuensanta de Martos is formidable,I decided it could be taken. I surrounded the fortress and prevented people or supplies from entering or leaving. Once the siege was established, I directed my troops to conduct a variety of maneuvers all designed to make the defenders believe they had temporary numerical advantage. The maneuvers were successful. I was able to entice Yaddair to send out contingents of cavalry to attack. These sallies resulted in furious fighting, but Yaddair's forces were always driven back into the fort with significant losses. While these diversions were taking place, my engineers constructed artillery machines.

I brought with me the four books of *Epitoma Rei Militaris* written by Flavius Vegetius Renatus. I met with my engineers and shared the drawings and descriptions of the machines with them.

The immediate vicinity of the fortress was covered with low bushes, scrub oak, grasses, and small clusters dwarf pine, but the steep, rocky slopes of the mountain range east of the fortress provided stands of yellow pine and oak of sufficient size to construct *mangani magribi*, the siege weapons that Renatus calledtrebuchet. I held numerous conferences with my engineers, and while my cavalry and archers distracted Yaddair and his defenders, the engineers constructed three *Spendore*-type ballistaesling machines. These machines require men to pull on ropes to cock them and sling boulders with great force. We also built two light *Alakatrom Farangi*-type trebuchet. These trebuchet have baskets that can be loaded with larger boulders. The boulders would be used to batter down the walls.

"We can also use the baskets to lob sealed jugs with Greek fire of three different types," I explained.

Greek fire is a mixture of naphtha, turpentine, and oil. When mixed with saltpeter, the mixture is explosive. We were able to throw large clay pots full of the stuff, with a lighted fuse attached, over the wall using the machines. Smaller jarswere used as grenades by the slingers.

In Arabic, the word *naft* refers to petroleum; the Hebrew word is *neft*. It can be crude oil or tar diluted with oil. Even the pitch from certain trees can provide the neft. I didn't have much petroleum in my supplies, but I did have ample stores of turpentine and olive oil. The pine trees on the mountain provided us with pitch. I also ordered the artillery officers to add some quicklime to the mixture. This combination ignites when it contacts water, so if the defenders tried to douse the fires with water, the fires wouldflare, almost explode.

The machines were placed in locations easily accessible to cavalry coming out of the fortress. This was done to tempt Yaddair to send his men out in an effort to destroy the machines. I positioned infantry, crossbowmen, and archers so they were not visible from the alcazaba. As soon as the enemy horsemen were within range, my men attacked, driving them back to the fortress. This tactic was effective, and I was able to reposition my men each time so the next time the enemy sallied forth, they couldn't predict from where the counterattack would come. I ordered the artillery commanders to concentrate their attack on the southeast portion of the wall.

The bombardment continued for eleven days, constant during the day and throughout the night. On thetwelfth day, I instructed the artillery to concentrate all of their heavy projectiles at the base of one particular section of the wall that had visibly weakened. After four hours there was a breach in the wall. I ordered the machines moved closer and continued to attack the breach until it was large enough to gain entry. Before the first waverushed through the breach, I orderedmy archers to target any exposed enemy personnel. Two units of infantry were deployed to protect the archers. Then the infantry, armed with spears, javelins, longswords, daggers, and shields, entered to do their close work. They were followed through the breach by two cavalry units and mounted archers, followed by three ranks of crossbowmen. The first rank fired a volley, then paused to reload while the next rank moved forward and fired, repeated by the third rank. By that time, the first rank had reloaded. The onslaught was continuous.

Yaddair's mercenaries knew they would be shown no mercy after what they did to the towns they conquered, so they fought on. Our veteran Nubian infantry were well-armed and well-protected with new and improved armor. I was able to supply them with chainmail coats, iron helmets with nose protection, and chainmail hoods under the helmetsto protect the neck and the throat. Once inside, they were able to use their spears and shields in the limited space within the fortress against Yaddair's ineffective cavalry counterattacks.

After they unhorsedthe cavalry, the following ranks of infantry were able to throw their javelins and use their swords and shields to great effect. Hand-to-hand fighting wasall confusion. The shouting of the soldiers as they attackedwas muffled by the screams of the wounded. The sounds of battle mixedwith the smell of fleshburning from Greek fire grenades; all this was overwhelmed by the penetrating, acrid smell of blood and evacuated bowels of men and horses.

Our artillery focused on the inner wall, and after it crumbled, my men gained control of the fortress. Our physicians treated only our wounded. Their wounded were of little concern, since they were to be executed, as were any unhurt who were captured. I was determined to never face these particular men again. Dead enemies do not have to be fought in the next battle.

Two of Yaddair's most trusted generals were captured and brought to me. One of them died of his wounds as he was thrown to the ground at my feet. The other survived.

"Behead this one in the morning."

"Please, Excellency! I have a family, a wife, children. Mercy! Is not your Jehovah a God of mercy?"

"I will show you the same mercy you showed for the innocent people you slaughtered in the towns you conquered."

I ordered that every possible hiding place be searched to find Prince Yaddair. Somehow, during the confusion of the battle, he managed to escape with a half-dozen supporters. Yaddair managed to make the considerable distance to Cordoba, where he thought he would receive asylum.

* * *

After my return to Granada, I initiated negotiations with the caliph of Cordoba. Two of that ruler's viziers, both reasonable men, represented me. They managed to convince the caliph that Yaddair was not only a threat to Granada, but also to the stability of all of Andalusia. Yaddair was imprisoned in the alcazaba of Baena. However, he still had many wealthy followers, as well as his own financial resources. Within two months he managed to escape from Baena, probably by bribing his jailors. The next intelligence I receivedwas that Yaddair was in Carmona as a guest of honor.The sands of loyalty were always shifting.

Joseph and I were, again, in my study.

"But I thought Muhammad ben Abdallah of Carmona was our friend and ally. Why doesn't he turn Yaddair over to you?"

"Ah, Joseph, your political education and insight are still lacking," I explained. "The growing strength and power of both Seville to the west and Granada to the east are perceived as a threat by Muhammad ben Abdallah. He suspects, and rightly so, with respect to our caliph, that Granada lusts after his western provinces and perhaps all of

Carmona. Nothing the caliph of Seville says or does gives him any reason to believe Seville is any less interested in the annexation of Carmona."

I knew we had not suffered the last of Yaddair's schemes. Before long, my spies reportedthat he had organized another army. He was still intent on gaining the throne of Granada.

Eleven

A YEAR PASSED and another crisis was looming, this time unrelated to Yaddair. After Zuhair and his vizier were no longer ruling Almeria, the important families of that taifa invited the caliph of Valencia, Abdurrahman ben Abdurrahman, to take possession of Almeria and provide governance. Abdurrahman accepted. He traveledto Almeria with one of his sons, Ubaidallah. At the time, Ubaidallah was only five years old. The caliph stayed only long enough to establish a working government then returned to Valencia, leaving Ubaidallah to rule with the boy's uncle, Abdurrahman's brother-in-law, Abu l-Ahmas Ma'n, as regent.

After I finished checking the work Joseph completed, I brought him uptodate on the events involving Almeria.

"Abu l-Ahmas Ma'n is not content to rule Almeria until the young Ubaidallah is old enough to take over. He aspires to rule all of the taifa of Almeria and its neighboring provinces, but as caliph, not regent. I recently learned that he approached the governors of three Valencian provinces he knows are not particularly happy with the rule of Abdurrahman. Each of the governors he approached want to be caliphs, desirous of more power and control. The conspirators cooperated, synchronized their plans, and simultaneously orchestrated revolts in four different locations. Do you know where Lorca is, Joseph?"

"Yes, Papa, it's about a hundred and fifty kilometers north and east of Almeria."

"What about Jodar?"

"That's about two hundred kilometers north and west of Almeria."

"And Xativa?"

"About four hundred kilometers northeast of Almeria."

"That's very good, Joseph. Do you enjoy the study of geography?"

"Yes, Papa. I like to look at the maps and learn where places are in relation to other places."

"Good.Well, within the taifa of Almeria, Ma'n staged a bloodless coup, an easy task, since he was already in control."

"Did he kill the little boy, Ubaidallah?"

"No, Ahmas Ma'n sent the boy back to his father in Valencia. It seems Ahmas Ma'n does have some scruples. He was reluctant to execute his sister's son, or perhaps he was more concerned about retribution if he did so."

"So how did the caliph of Valencia react to this?"

"No surprise to me,Abdurrahman ben Abdurrahman reacted quickly and decisively. He mobilized and marched his army to Xativa. Do you know Xativa's location relative to Valencia?"

"Yes, of course, Papa. It is located only sixty-five kilometers south of Valencia."

"Yes, and he quickly subdued the revolt there. Now he has hired experienced Catalan mercenaries to join him in campaigns against Lorca and Almeria. He also petitioned the caliph of Denia, on the coast and only a hundred kilometers southeast of Valencia, to join with him to defeat the revolutionaries."

"Why would Denia agree to that?"

"Good question, Joseph. It is important for Denia to maintain some balance between Valencia and Almeria. Almeria is located an easy five days' ride to its southwest. Denia's goal is to maintain its position as an independent caliphate between the two larger taifa. Deciding the best course of action was difficult, but the caliph of Denia finally decided his best option was to join Abdurrahman ben Abdurrahman. His decision was, according to my spies, bolstered by considerable remuneration. If Abdurrahmanis victorious, Denia may be able to maintain its independence."

"So Ahmas Ma'n is in trouble now?"

"Yes, the Denia-Valencia alliance is a major threat to Ahmas Ma'n. He has asked Badis for help. He swore to be a 'forever faithful ally' if Badis comes to his aid."

"What will you advise our caliph to do?" asked Joseph.

"I advised Badis to delay his response for four days so I can fully investigate the situation and consider all possible ramifications of Granada choosing a side in this conflict. I have spent the last four days interviewing emissaries, spies, and viziers of other taifa. I also took great care to determine how Badis would analyze the situation and toward which side he would lean. I, of course, recommended the approach he already favored. I recommended that Granada join Ahmas Ma'n, since Valencia is our common and historic enemy. He understands the rationale for fighting against the regime of Abdurrahman ben Abdurrahman, even on the side of a traitor."

"And what did our caliph decide?"

"Badis agreed. He ordered me to mobilize the army and insisted, since I am general-in-chief, that I be in command of all strategy and tactics despite his, Badis's, presence. There is a long, difficult journey to complete before Granada can play an active role in the war. The strategy I have laid out with Ahmas Ma'n is for Granada to retake the city of Lorca while Ahmas Ma'n and his rebel allies fight against those forces of Abdurrahmantrying to retake Almeria and Jodar."

"So, you will soon leave us to fight another war, Papa?"

"Yes. As you know, Lorca is about two hundred thirty kilometers east-northeast of Granada. The most direct and fastest access for our army is to penetrate and cross the north end of the Sierra Nevada. That road is impassible for wagons, so baggage and supplies will have to be carried by a huge number of mules. The route is too steep and rough for the men to traverse while wearing their armor and carrying their weapons, so they will march in their bleached linen tunics embroidered with the colors and insignia of their unit.

"As you know, the men wear loose linen trousers and most wear leather boots, although some of the infantry, especially the Nubians, prefer sandals. Each man carries a closely woven, woolen cloak that is water-resistant but not waterproof. At night in the cold mountains, the passes of the Sierra Nevada will still be covered with snow in midsummer. The soldiers will roll up in their cloaks, huddled as close to a fire as possible. I will share in my men's discomfort, although my officers and I do have tents. Badis, of course, has his large pavilion and sufficient servants to ensurehis comfort at night. While on the march, all the officers will be well-mounted but still exposed to the elements."

"Going through the mountains, it will be difficult to keep your army close together, won't it, Papa?"

"Yes. The army and our supply train of mules will stretch out over five kilometers through the mountains. A good day's march in the mountains will be twenty-five to thirty kilometers. On more level ground, we will be able to cover about fifty kilometers and keep closer order.Badis and I will be at the head of the column, each of us mounted on spirited stallions. You have seen my saddle, Joseph."

"Yes, Papa, it is richly decorated with gold and silver. But isn't the caliph's saddle even more ornate?"

"Of course, it has to be.I hope you have also observed the saddles we use are all of the same basic design, with only medium-high pommels and seat backs. The heavy cavalry of the Christians of Northern Spain, France, and Germany use saddles with high pommels and high seat backs. They ride with their stirrups long so their legs are straight. Because much of the fighting in Andalusia happens in mountains or hill country, our saddles have lower pommels and seat backs. Our men usually have the iron stirrups set short enough to ride with their knees bent. This is a much more secure manner of riding and fighting in rough terrain, and I think it is also more comfortable. All our saddles have both breast and rump straps to make them more secure on the horse. Saddle blankets are sheep skin with the wool clipped and are either cut or folded to afford the horse as much protection and comfort from the saddle as needed. All of our cavalry and mounted archers are equipped with chain mail armor. That armor will be carried, along with most of their weapons, by the mule train.

"As Badis and I ride sidebyside out of Granada, we will pass by this house. Perhaps your mother and you will stand on our rooftop terrace to watch us leave."

"How do the soldiers keep track of where the others in their unit are during battle?"

"Another good question, Joseph. The horses of the commanders are adorned with plumes, dyed the color of their unit. Single plumes for each unit are attached to the headpiece of the bridle, or the cheek strap, or hangfrom breast or rump straps. Each color and placement isdifferent enough to make identification easy during the confusion of battle. My horse and that of Badis have plumes on all parts of our equipment. Our standard-bearers, who ride directly behind us, carry poles with our individual flags and the banners of all the units. I make certain that scouts are deployed, in all directions, at least an hour before the army departs each day. We will not be surprised by our enemies."

The evening before we left Granada, I showed Joseph my armor and that of my horse.

"You see, Joseph, my armor includes this."

I held up a long chainmail coat, the links attached to soft leather and to each other.

"This is called the *zardfaa*;it reaches to my knees and elbows. You see, it is burnished to shine brightly in the sun. I also have these."

I took up the chainmail hood that protectedmy throat and neck and a solid iron helmet.

"The helmet is held on with these straps that go under my chin. It is held off my head by this leather harness inside. You see, there is also aroyal-blue plume on top of my helmet."

He took the helmet from me and inspected the leather harness, then put the helmet on his head. It was much too large.

"There are also these. They are called vambraces, for my forearms. They are also made of chainmail,but instead of attaching the chain mailto soft leather, it is attached to thick oxhide. I also wear these, called greaves, to protect my knees and ankles. These are also backed with the thick, heavy, oxhide leather. I also have stiff gauntlets of the same basic manufacture as the vambraces and greaves to protect my hands and wrists."

I allowed Joseph to try on my armor, but everything was, of course, too big and heavy. He staggered under the weight, walking with his feet widespread, as we made our way to the courtyard. There I helped Joseph out of each item and piled all the armor onto a canvass tarp on the tiles of our courtyard. Joseph could only lift one corner and was unable to slide the loaded tarp along the smooth tiles.

"What about your horses, Papa? Are they not protected?"

"Yes, each horse has its own set of armor, custom fitted. Their armor consists of three separate parts of chainmail, each again sewed to soft leather and the chain links attached to each other."

I held up each part of the horse's armor.

"This first part covers the head of the horse, except for his eyes, nose, and ears. This second portion protects the neck and hangs down to the breast. The third section is like a large blanket draped over the horse's back, with an opening for the saddle. This section reaches to the horse's knees and is split in front to allow movement. See? Some of the horses, including my three, are trained to rear and strike soldiers on the ground, or other horses. Their hooves are shod with heavy iron. Some cavalrymen want less weight on the horse. They prefer an apron-like protector, also of chainmail, but this protection only covers the horse's chest and front legs."

"What weapons do you carry, Papa?"

"My two-and-a-half-foot curved sword. I carry it in a scabbard that hangs from a silver-encrusted, and highly decorated,baldric. I wear it over my left shoulder, like this."

I hefted my long lance.

"This is called a *kontos*. As you see, it isslightly more thantwice the length of my body. I carry it on my back, held on by this strap. My shield travels attached to the left side of my saddle. You see, it is in the shape of a teardrop. It is about half my height and about an arm's length across at the widest part. I also carry this, it is called *bardoukon*, a spiked mace. It is held in a case attached to the right-hand side of my saddle, its handle within easy reach. While on the road, I only carry my sword and the dagger that is always in my belt. All of my armor, and the rest of my weapons, along with the armor and spare weapons of my soldiers,will be carried by the mule train."

The following morning, as the sun peeked over the eastern horizon, we rode past my house. Rebecca and Joseph were on the rooftop terrace, her hand resting on his right shoulder. I waved at them and saw her squeeze his shoulder hard enough for him to flinch.

As we moved into the first mountain pass, I looked back. Dust hovered over the troops as they trudged along. The hovering dust mixed with the smell of horses, mules, manure, and sweat. As we entered the pass, I heard our brave men counting cadence, some units singing, and the sounds of tramping, hard-soled boots, sandals, and iron-shod hooves. It was colorful, noisy, thrilling, and ominous. I grasped the miniature Torah inside my cloak and recited my prayer before battle. I hoped Joseph had been reassured by his mother's touch. I wished for the same.

We marched for three hard days in the Sierra Nevada, then came down to the city of Guadix. Our route was filled with steep ascents and descents. The trails were rocky, thick with brush, thistles, and scrub oak. We lost a total of three horses and six mules during the tiresome, dangerous passage. Several animals stumbled, twisting their legs, and were too lame to be of further use, so we abandoned them to fend for themselves. Two horses and one mulefell off the steep edge of a cliff and were dashed against rocks as they fell. The cavalry officer riding the first horse to go over the cliffmanaged to kick loose and jump off, but he broke his leg when he landed. The other horse, a pack animal, lost its balance when the load it was carrying shifted. The mule was shoved to the side by another mule trying to squeeze past on a very narrow portion of the trail. The shoved mule lost itsbalance and went over the side.

Although the route was difficult, we made it through with almost all of our troops, animals, and supplies in good condition. In Guadix we rested for a day and resupplied with fresh food. The following day we crossed the valley, skirting the Sierra de Baza. That road took over hills that were sometimes rocky and steep, but lacked the yawning precipices we experienced in the Sierra.

We rested again for a day in the town of Baza, then entered the long valley between the Sierra de las Estancias and Sierra de Maria. That valley broadenedout before climbing into mountains again to arrive at the ancient city of Valez Rubio. From there, we united with the forces of Ahmas Ma'n. Our combined forces were able to descend to the hill country, circle around, and approach Lorca from the southeast.

While we were traveling, Abdurrahman learned about our progress. Spies wereeverywhere. His army waslinked up with the army of Denia, soAbdurrahmanwas able toconcentrate his resources. Aftersubduingthe revolutionary forces in Murcia, hemoved his army to the stronghold of Lorca.

During these events, I was able to send emissaries to the king of Denia. These faithful men, all with relatives and connections in Denia, pointed out that it was quite obvious that Abdurrahman'slong-term goal wasto rule all of the taifa of both Valencia and Almeria. The caliph understood that it was not in Denia's best interest for Abdurrahman to be that strong. The caliph of Deniawas only fighting to keep an independent Almeria. He knewthat if Almeria and Valencia were combined, they would be strong enough to threaten the wellbeing of an independent Denia.

So,the caliph of Deniawent to Abdurrahman and demanded immediate payment of the fee that Abdurrahman had agreed to when Denia joined him. As the caliph of Deniano doubt anticipated,Abdurrahman was strapped for cash after paying his Catalan mercenaries. He was unable to meet the demand for payment, so the caliph of Denia took his army and went home.

Word of our imminent arrival reached Lorca by way of several spies I sent into that place. They carried inflated reports of our size and strength. Abdurrahman's Catalan mercenaries decided the odds of defeating us, thereby collecting booty and reward, were not in their favor. They also went home.

Abdurrahmanwas out of options. His army consisted of many conscripts whohad been fighting all summer. Fall was looming, and his conscripts were anxious to return to their homes for the harvest season. He abandoned Lorca and returned to Valencia. Two days after Abdurrahman left, we entered Lorca in triumph. We secured a strong ally for the future, Almeria's caliph, the usurper Abu l-Ahmas Ma'n. We also gained another dedicated enemy.The caliph of Valencia wouldnot soon forget who responded to support his turncoat brother-in-law.

Twelve

AFTER HIS ESCAPE, Prince Yaddair made his way to Carmona seeking aid for yet another attempt to claim the crown of Granada. The caliph of Carmona, that same Muhammad ben Abdallah we had saved and who had given an oath to always remain a friend and ally of Granada, listened to him. It was a propitious time for Yaddair. Carmona was feeling pressure from both Seville, its near neighbor to the west, and from our expanding Granada to the southeast. Ben Abdallah was very cognizant of this dual threat. He received reliable information indicating individuals in both Seville and Granada were proposing plans to annex portions, or all, of his kingdom. Yaddair promised ben Abdallah that when he was made caliph of Granada, he would never consider taking any of Carmona's territory. He promised that ben Abdallah would be his permanent ally. To sweeten the deal, he promised to cede two adjacent provinces of Granada to Carmona. The caliphs of Andalusia were well-known for making promises, then forgetting them when the situation warranted.

Ben Abdallah agreed to this pact and that spring, Yaddair initiated isolated raids into several of Granada's provinces closest to Carmona. He was testing to see our reaction. Badis was incensed. He immediately ordered me to mobilize the army. He sent me, in command of a large force, to find Yaddair, defeat his forces, and punish Carmona for ben Abdallah's duplicity and complicity.

"This ben Abdallah speaks from both sides of his mouth!" Badis shouted at me. "His plotting and collaboration with Yaddair are the acts of a traitor, a most treacherous traitor. This is unacceptable behavior from an ingrate ally. I came when he was desperate, without asking for anything in return. I fought battles and lost Granadian lives to save him from Seville. He must be punished, Nagrela, along with that upstart nephew who will not stop trying to take my caliphate from me. Do you hear me, General?"

"Yes, Sire. I will do my best to bring them both to heel."

"Not do your best, Nagrela. I am counting on you to bring me their heads."

Before I was put in official command of Granada's armies, the annual summer wars of the various Berber, Arab, and Slav rulers were not much more than forays into enemy territories for looting and exacting tribute. The main purpose of these "wars" was to achieve honor and respect for their martial prowess, to satisfy their inclination for thievery, and less than incidentally, to pay their soldiers and mercenaries. All of the individual soldiers and officers in these armies had a vested interest to do everything possible to avoid being killed or wounded while collecting as many portable valuables as possible. Pitched battles requiring strategy and tactics were not something their commanders spent much time or intellectual energy on. The major consideration was to avoid confrontations in force. The swift horses of the Berbers and Arabs enabled them to strike quickly while fighting for honor and reward. This mode of conflict especially appealed to both the Berber and Arab cultures and personalities; it was their nature.

I instituted strategies and tactics proven successful by the Romans and Greeks, before the birth of Christ, to force our enemies to engage. My purpose was to defeat, decimate, and annihilate any army aligned against me. This strategy empowered me to force the capitulation of towns, cities, and lands, thus increasing the holdings and influence of Granada.

Fortified towns surrendered to avoid the horrors of a long siege, starvation, or death from projectiles hurled over the walls.

The alcazaba are always built on the highest ground available. This means limited access to water, so thirst is a major weapon to force capitulation. Large jugs of Greek fire hurled over the walls start fires. This forces the defenders to use scarce water supplies to fight the fires.

I initiated the war against Carmona by attacking outlying towns and small cities, capturing them quickly using overwhelming numbers. While on the move, my army foraged for food, animals, and valuables. I forced any people we encountered to swear loyalty to Granada and pay taxes to Caliph Badis. If they refused payment, they were driven from their farms and holdings, and all their valuables were seized. When a fortified city or town decided to resist, I brought up my engineers, with their mobile siege machines, and attacked the fortification at its weakest point. After the fortress was taken, I allowed my regular troops to join my mercenaries in raping, murdering, and pillaging. This was calculated. It was done as an example to other fortified populations that might consider resistance. These extreme measures ensured that other cities would be less likely to resist, thus reducing the risk to my men. I let it be known that if the people did not resist, and avowed their loyalty to Granada and Badis, they would be spared the savagery of my soldiers. Although some tribute was required. I must be able to pay my troops. I was never able to reconcile this brutality with the teachings of the Torah. It gave me pause.

So much booty was accumulated during the initial stages of the campaign against Yaddair that I was forced to appropriate every mule, horse, and wagon we could find for transporting the loot. I assigned space on pack mules or in the wagons to specific groups of soldiers from each unit. This enabled them to transport their confiscated treasure. The number of animals and wagons in my baggage train became larger, and longer, than my army. When we were on the march, the baggage train sometimes took many hours to catch up when we made camp for the night.

Midsummer, I forced Yaddair to take refuge in a rather small and poorly constructed alcazaba. I ordered the attack, and in only two days the fortress was in my possession. This time, Yaddair did not escape. Badis's order was to rid Granada of the menace once and for all. I separated Yaddair's head from his body with one swift swing of my sword and sent the head back to Granada.

* * *

After I returned home, Joseph and I resumed our regular evening meetings to review the progress of his studies.

"Joseph, I must tell you that despite our Lord's injunction against killing, I found the execution of Yaddair, the man who caused so much trouble for our caliph and for myself, quite satisfying. It was not nearly as troubling to my soul as I anticipated it would be. The slaughter of some innocents does trouble me, but while I am forced to do this,it clearly enables me to save many of our soldiers from death or wounding."

"So, Papa, with Yaddair dead, you don't need to go to war again?"

"Unfortunately, Joseph, the killing of Yaddair does not settle things between Badis and ben Abdallah. However, recently ben Abdallah became ill and died. His son Ishak assumed leadership, thus continuing the ruling dynasty. Among the cities of Carmona that I captured and added to Granada is the city of Ecija. It is the second-most important city in the territory formerly ruled by Carmona, and only a day's ride from here. After I executed Yaddair, I stationed a garrison in Ecija before returning home with the army."

A few weeks later, I was again closeted with Joseph. He was making remarkable progress in his learning. I was and am proud of his accomplishments. He wasa good listener, rememberedeverything said, almost word for word, and never repeatedanything he heardin my study. He understoodthat I frequently think out loud and my thoughts werenot to be repeated.

"So, Joseph, the citizens of Ecija, and the other cities and towns that resisted me, didn't forget the brutality of my army. They never do; but they are all still loyal to the dynasty of Carmona. Ishakmoved to relieve the occupation of Ecija. As soon as Ishak and his troops left Carmona, the citizens of Ecija made it impossible for our garrison to move about the town, except in large numbers. The commander of the garrison realized that with the threat of Ishak's army, and the mood and actions of the citizens of Ecija, it would be impossible to defend the city. He abandoned the city and returned to Granada with his soldiers. Ishak entered Ecija as a returning hero.

"When Badis learned of the loss of Ecija, he was furious. Because Ecija is so close to Seville, Badis and I agreed it should be under our control, to prevent any encroachment by Seville. Our intention was for Ecija to be a constant threat to Seville, that ancient enemy of the Zanhadja."

* * *

The following fall and winter, I mobilized another large force. In late spring my army again surrounded Ecija. Again, I created situations to entice the defenders out of their fortress by placing what seemed to be easy targets of foot soldiers and archers, but those troops were bait for the trap. I situated much larger forces hidden from sight. Once the enemy cavalry sallied from the fortress and was within range, I unleashed hidden units of archers, crossbowmen, and slingers. I was amazed that although I had employed this tactic many times, it was still so effective.

I also incorporated another tactic I learned from my military reading. While still in Granada, I formed a separate and elite unit of men who showed aptitude in the use of slings attached to short poles. I pay them to train year-round. These pole-slingers are capable of flinging rocks and small boulders longer distances with great accuracy. They are also able to fling small jugs filled with Greek fire. This grenade is particularly scary to opposing troops.

"We have created a small army of Davids," I bragged to my commanders.

After suffering losses from several of my ambushes, Ishak decided that his honor required him to engage. The two armies met on the same battlefield where we had defeated Prince Ismail of Seville. However, this time my army guarded the ford across the Genil.

I instructed my engineers to build two long trenches with mounded barricades behind the excavations. They were positioned to funnel any attacking force toward the ford, which I left open, defended only by my cavalry and mounted archers. I positioned my archers, crossbowmen, slingers, and the highly trained and elite pole slingshot unit so they could fire salvos from the tops of the mounds of soil and rocks excavated from the trenches. Ishak's soldiers had to somehow get over the trenches and force their way up the mounds to get to the men firing at them. After firing, each rank was ordered to retreat behind the mounds to reload while the next rank moved to the top and fired.

My cavalry was spread out in front of the ford. Ishak's cavalry had to attack through the flanking gauntlet to reach us. He sent his foot soldiers in first, and we decimated them. His cavalry fared little better. They were all but completely routed before I finally ordered our cavalry to attack. His archers and crossbowmen were never seriously engaged and fled for their lives when our cavalry charged.

* * *

"I tell you, Joseph, my head was ready to burst with excitement and energy; I was possessed. After I ordered our cavalry to charge, I joined them while praying aloud to the Lord to make my arm strong and help me smite my enemies. Despite my misgivings about killing, I was flushed. My conscious mind, and my conscience, were lost in the exhilaration of battle. The blood of those soldiers I slew mixed with the dust and dirt beneath my stallion's hooves."

My son gazed at me, his forehead furrowed, slowly shaking his head, his eyes wondering who I had become.

Thirteen

WHILE THE CAVALRY was mopping up, our other soldiers were occupied stripping the dead and wounded of their weapons and valuables. Ishak fled to Carmona with very little left of his army. Ecija was once again part of Granada. All the rich farmlands and fields of the province were ours as well.

The day after my return, I was summoned to an audience with Badis.

"Nagrela, I am very pleased with what you have accomplished. I have given you title to these two large estates in the conquered territory as your reward."

He held out a handful of documents.

"Thank you, Excellency. It is my duty to serve you; I expect no reward."

"Nonsense. Would you have my people think I am ungrateful and miserly? You must learn how to accept gifts graciously. It is one of your only failings that you do not. Take these."

"Yes, Sire. I will do my best to correct this deficiency." I smiled. He returned my smile, but only with his lips. This wasnot uncommon for him, and I no longer fretted over it.

I then owned seven properties consisting of fruit and olive orchards, vineyards, and irrigated farmland, most of them in the richly soiled river valleys called Vegas, in Ladino. Two weeks after receiving the most recent additions to my properties, I called Joseph to my study. It was still early in the day, and he was surprised to be taken from his studies.

"Pay close attention, Joseph, because one day, perhaps soon, if I continue to fight battles, I could be seriously wounded or even killed. If that happens, you will be responsible for the family's estates."

He nodded but did not say anything.

"Three men are waiting in our courtyard. Two of the men were stewards of the two new estates in the province of Ecija that our caliph gave me. The previous owners of these estates have absconded to Seville. I ordered each of the stewards of the properties to bring all of their records for the past five years. I want you to help me inspect the expenses and income of these new properties, along with the records of harvest, the size, and the loyalty of the labor force. I want you to learn all aspects of the operations."

"Of course, Papa. Whatever you wish."

"One of the properties consists of fertile bottomlands on either size of the Genil River, ten kilometers north of Ecija. There are over four hundred hectares of tilled land irrigated by a small dam and canals that divert water from the Genil. The land produces good quality sugar, as well as wheat and sunflower seeds, amongst several other crops. The other property is located in hill country that was, in ancient days, covered with wild olive trees. It is planted with three different varieties of domesticated olives and four different varieties of wine grapes.

"The third man who will join us is a very experienced agriculturalist by the name of David ben Abraham, a Jewish citizen of Ecija. After we inspect the production and financial records of the properties, and take the measure of the two stewards, we will decide, with ben Abraham's input, if the two will continue to manage the day-to-day operations of these properties. If not, we will first look to the workers on the farms for replacements. If any of the laborers are Jewish and are reasonably educated, they will have preference. Ben Abraham will be able to recommend other Jewish farm workers if we need to look further.

"As our overall manager for these properties, ben Abraham will receive an annual stipend plus ten percent of all net profits. The onsite stewards will receive a house, food for their families, a modest annual stipend, and five percent of all profits. All workers will share in the profits as well, one or two percent, depending on the profitability of the holding on which they labor. Do you understand the difference between gross and net profit, Joseph?"

"Not really, Papa. Isn't profit how much is left after all expenses are paid? I didn't know there were different kinds."

"If we press our own olives, the value of the oil is more than if we sell the olives to someone else who will press them for the oil. However, if we don't have a press, the cost of constructing one might be more than what we could receive for the oil. Plus, we have to hire someone who knows how to operate the press. The same is true for grapes. We can sell the grapes to a vintner to make wine, but if we want to make our own wine, we will bring in more money. However, making good wine is a skill and an art. We would need people who are very good at this to make good, valuable wine. What we must do is calculate the cost of building an olive oil press and purchasing containers to store the oil, and the cost of establishing a winery and paying someone to oversee the making of the wine. Then we have to estimate how long it will take for us to cover the cost of these improvements and show a profit."

"This is all complicated, Papa."

"Yes, it is. However, you and I cannot afford the time to learn all that is necessary to operate any of our agricultural properties profitably. What do you know about when and how to irrigate a bean field, for example? We could learn how to do it, and when, but it would take too much time away from more important things."

"Yes, I understand. I don't know anything about irrigating fields."

"Exactly. So, our strategy is to hire people with the necessary skills and knowledge, and remunerate them with an additional incentive for them to control expenses and maximize profit. I also have a policy of rewarding effective and honest stewards by deeding a portion of the property to them after seven years of service. You know that our

Lord commands that we allow our fields to go fallow; that is, not to plant anything on them, every seven years?"

"Yes, Papa, I remember that."

"On all our properties, I insist that we rotate crops so only a portion of the fields are allowed to go fallow each year, on a seven-year cycle. So, we obey that law and have a harvest every year."

"But only from a portion of the lands."

"Exactly. But we avoid having zero income every seventh year. In any case, when they are partial owners of the property, my stewards are even more motivated to make a profit. However, any kind of agriculture is a risky venture. Drought, too much rain at the wrong time, hail, fires started by lightning or other causes, disease of the crops or animals—many things, including the value of our products at the time we sell, are only controllable by Adonai. This can mean one or several years in a row of loss. Luck, and our Lord, as well as good workers and managers, determine the success of our agricultural endeavors.

"I have been fortunate in finding good stewards for the other five farms we own. All of those stewards are Jews whose families have been involved in agriculture in Andalusia for generations. Because they are honest Jews, I can trust them, and they know they can trust me. So, Joseph, are you ready to help me make a decision about the men who are waiting for us?"

"Yes, Papa."

"I don't want you to say anything while they are with us. I want you to watch and listen carefully. All right, son, please go to the courtyard and escort the men here."

Joseph stood and watched, listening carefully as I greeted each of the three men as they came into my study. I embraced David ben Abraham and we spoke in Hebrew, exchanging greetings and news of our families. I introduced ben Abraham to Joseph, and my son showed proper deference. My chest swelled with fatherly pride when ben Abraham embraced Joseph and murmured the prayer for a long and healthy life for him. Then I turned to the other two men.

I extended my right hand to each of them as a mark of respect and courtesy, not something commonly done for employees.

"Do either of you speak Hebrew?"

Both shook their heads no. I switched to Arabic.

"I apologize for being discourteous by excluding you from the conversation with David ben Abraham."

Ben Abraham smiled and nodded his head, immediately understanding what I was doing and why I was doing it.

"Please sit, all of you."

I indicated the three chairs I had placed in front of my desk and waited until they were seated to take my own seat, the desk separating us. Joseph stood leaning against the wall.

"So, first I want to learn something about each of your families and how they are now faring under the new regime."

I turned slightly to face the steward of the Vega property and locked eyes with him.

"I am thirty-five years old and have been married for ten years, Lord Vizier. I have only one wife, but we have been blessed with two sons and a daughter. My father and mother and my maternal grandfather all reside under my roof. We are all doing well, sir."

"Good. I trust the God we share will continue to bless your home. I am very pleased to hear that you accept the responsibility for the care of your elderly. I assume you will continue to do so when your wife's parents need it as well."

"Of course, Excellency. Her parents are still young, and her father continues to support his family."

I turned to the steward who managed the olive groves and vineyards.

"I am only twenty-four years old, Excellency. I wed only two years ago and now have an infant son. We believe our lives will improve under your stewardship."

Next, I questioned each of the men about their level of education and asked questions designed to evaluate their understanding of literature and mathematics. Then I enquired about the specific agricultural practices they utilized for the properties they managed.

After that, I asked them to tell me specifically about the books they had most recently read.

The younger man responded first, mentioning a book dealing with management of olive groves and another book of Arabic poetry.

"Ah, so you read poetry. Do you have a favorite author?"

"Yes, Excellency, I especially like the poetry of Abu Ahmad Abd al'aziz ibn Khira al-Munfatil."

I was surprised.

"Can you recite the opening lines of one of his poems that you favor?"

He did so, much to my satisfaction, then I recited the next two lines of that poem. I could see he was impressed. I turned to the other manager and questioned him along the same lines.

Satisfied, I started a detailed examination of the records from each of the properties. I called Joseph to look over my shoulder as I added columns of figures in my head, asked Joseph for his totals, and nodded when his and my totals agreed and matched the entries in the journals. I corrected the few journal totals that did not.

While completing the inspection of the records, a task that occupied close to three hours, I noticed the two stewards started fidgeting in their chairs after the second hour. Ben Abraham sat quietly, his hands folded on his lap.

"I find the records of both properties incomplete for my purposes, especially for the Vega farm. I will write down the changes I require. Ben Abraham will oversee the recordkeeping. There is nothing seriously wrong, but I will organize the bookkeeping to make certain there is a more detailed accounting of expenses, and in the future, I want all sums to balance. I understand that the recordkeeping for the Vega property is significantly more complex, since many different crops are raised, and the crops are harvested at different times. I also understand that prices for crops will vary widely depending upon the current availability, and many other factors."

The meeting lasted into the late afternoon. The only break came when Rebecca brought food into the study at noon. We continued working while we ate. Joseph continued his task of silent observation and learning, but I noticed that he managed to enthusiastically partake of the cold lamb roast and three kinds of cheese,two hard, one soft. There was also fresh-baked bread with a hard, brown crust that showered crumbs when bit into and a softly textured pure white inside.We washed everything down with freshly squeezed orange juice.

"All right, thank you, gentlemen. You may be excused. Please return to the courtyard. I have some thinking and deciding to do, but I will call you back when I have come to some conclusions."

The three men left and I turned to Joseph.

"Sit, son. Do you understand what I was looking for in the close examination of the recordkeeping?"

"Not exactly, Papa."

"I was looking for inconsistencies, and especially for unexplained expenses that would indicate the previous owner was being taken advantage of. I didn't find anything of that nature.

"So, Joseph, what do you think, should I keep these men on?"

"David ben Abraham is very nice, and I think he is very knowledgeable and intelligent, Papa. The man in charge of the Vega farm seemed confused about what you expect of him but ben Abraham will, I'm certain, be able to explain everything in terms he can understand and will monitor what he does closely. I saw ben Abraham nodding his agreement when the man spoke about the actual farming. I think the olives and grapes are being well cared for, and that man seemed to understand what you expect of him. Both seemed very surprised, and pleased, to learn that if they were retained, they would share in any profits. I don't believe the previous owner did anything like that."

"So, you think we should keep both of them in place and monitor the results?"

"I wouldn't want to cause financial or other problems for their families. What will you do, Papa?"

"I am very pleased to hear you are thinking of the welfare of the families of these men, Joseph. I am proud that you think in terms of the impact of our actions on not only the men, but also their families.

If you agree, we will give them each a year to demonstrate their worth, but under David ben Abraham's close supervision."

That fall and winter, I frequently brought my son into my study while conducting the state's business. I repeated my strict instructions to only watch and listen each time he was present.

"You are to be like a fly on the wall. I am relying on you to be especially mindful of the reactions and facial expressions of everyone in the room when someone else is speaking. This is especially important when I have more than one visitor. I want you to learn to interpret their reactions to what is said by their expression and body language. You should be able to guess if they agree or disagree with what is being said by changes in their face, especially the eyes and mouth. Some will fidget or shift body position when uncomfortable. When you notice anything unusual, we will talk about what you think their body and facial expressions meant after they leave. This is a most important skill, Joseph. It is essential that you be able to detect when you think someone is lying, or holding back some of the truth, or being evasive. When I think someone has done this, and you don't catch it, we will speak of it, and I will describe what made me think so."

From that timeon, I included Joseph in meetings with ambassadors and emissaries from other governments. We arranged cushions against the wall on the right-hand side of my desk so he could observe the faces of the men I met with. I also included him when I gave instructions to the ambassadors and emissaries being sent to other kingdoms. I always wantedthese men to achieve specific goals. Iprovidedsuggestions on how to accomplish my aims, and I wantedJoseph's take on how well they listenedand if he believedthey woulddo as instructed. When I metwith my spies, or men who wereplotting some action in another government, I excludedJoseph from those meetings, but I often sharedthe substance of the meeting or report with him afterward.

"You do understand, Joseph, that along with being general-in-chief of the armies and chief vizier to our caliph, I have retained the office of vizier for finance?"

"Yes, Papa, but I do not understand why you must take responsibility for all three positions. Isn't one of them enough to keep you well occupied?"

"Although it seems to be the least significant, the office of the vizier for finance is the most important, my son. Everything we do as a government depends upon having the financial resources available to do it. At the same time, we must keep Badis happy by providing him with the means to do whatever he wants to do. We must always be mindful of the historic tensions between the tribes of our Berber masters. Even the lowest Berber tribesman will feel himself superior to us. Other dignitaries of the court, and even the common citizens of Arab descent, all believe in their superiority. But if we control the finances, we control the government, and they can all believe what they want.

"However, we must also be ever mindful of disputes that could impact our position. As soon as I hear of any situation that could result in confrontation, and I usually hear of such things early, I bring all those involved together. I listen attentively, and with understanding, to all sides of the dispute. By giving people the opportunity to air their grievances, and listening carefully without comment or judgment, I am usually able to suggest a compromise that all can live with. These are skills you must master."

Fourteen

I'D BEEN FORCED to deal with more than the usual number of disputes between tribal chiefs and the other viziers. The caliph's vizier for internal affairs was involved in a plot to bring back Prince Boluggin. Badis was aware of the plot and instructed me to deal with it. All of this intrigue and palace politics seemed to stress me more than it used to. The result was that I was uncommonly curt with Rebecca. Joseph witnessed me barking at her for no justifiable reason, and he came to my study to voice his concern.

"Joseph, I am extremely agitated and upset about the situation at the alcazaba. There is a plot to bring Prince Boluggin back and assassinate Badis. The caliph learned about it and put me in charge of doing something to make it go away. He doesn't want to bring his brother to trial for treason, but wants the schemers gone. I am considering several options to deal with the situation, but all are complicated and any one of them could backfire. That is why I was curt with your mother. I will apologize to her, but talking aloud about what I am considering doing will help me reach a decision. I appreciate that you are a good listener, and I know nothing I say to you will leave this room.

"Thank you, Papa. But it upsets me when you are unkind to my mother."

"I'm sorry, Joseph. I promise I will make amends to her. This has been a particularly difficult time for me."

I told him about the various options I was considering. We both sat silently for maybe fifteen minutes, then suddenly, a course of action popped into my head.

"All right then, what do you think of this?I will just visit the vizier of internal affairs and describe all the evidence we have of his plotting. I will tell him that our caliph is aware of the evidence. I will suggest he take advantage of my good nature and depart Granada, with his entire household, within twenty-four hours. If not, he will be arrested and tried. Prince Boluggin's role will be revealed during the proceedings and he will, no doubt, share the vizier's fate, certain to be a public beheading."

Joseph nodded.

"Yes, I understand that Caliph Badis wants to avoid putting his brother on trial."

I nodded, pleased that my son understood the dilemma, then I changed the subject to something else that had been troubling me.

"You understand, Joseph, that I am obligated to mingle and interact with all of the chiefs of the tribes of the Zanhadja, as well as Badis's several sons from different mothers, including those of his concubines. There are also a number of nephews, and a host of other Berber dignitaries with ancillary powers. Although it is onerous to me, I am forced to join with these people when they drink to excess, gorge on rich foods, and comport with the young girls and boys who serve at their parties.

"The Berber leaders of the Zanhadja are warriors. They are amazingly unsophisticated, and are Muslim only for convenience. They pay lip service to the laws of Islam, ignoring those that encroach on their carnal pleasures. They are, for the most part, not interested in literature, or science, or any intellectual pursuits. Because they are mostly uneducated, they are uncomfortable around intellectuals, writers, and poets. They feel, but would never admit to being, envious of learning, and are especially hostile to Arabs of learning. I must be able to convince these men that although I am well-educated and can hold my own in any kind of intellectual debate, I am only their servant. I cannot do, or neglect to do, anything that might cause Badis to think less of me, or for his nobles to gain the impression that I feel myself superior to them in any way. This requires that I constantly act against my nature, even more so against our religious principles. I am particularly resentful of having to deceive your mother. I suspect she knows what transpires at the Berber orgies."

I paused, silent. Joseph did not interrupt my thoughts.

"I will give you an example. Last night, a well-known and learned Arab writer attended the party, and I wasinvited to participate,Badis's invitation. Badis is clever enough to know that men of this ilk want to convince him that they have exceptional talents and learning, and that they are willing to provide those exceptional skills for the good of the kingdom if offered employment. You must remember to never underestimate Badis. He is relatively uneducated but extremely intelligent and intuitive. He is also extremely clever, especially when he feels threatened in any way. He expects me to provide entertainment for his friends by demonstrating the limitations of the interlopers' learning and abilities.

"The one last night, as have all such men previous and future, displayed his extensive knowledge of Arabic literature by replying to the unsmiling questions of Badis and the other nobles at the gathering. He used quotations from the Qur'an and famous Arabic poetry. Of course, the Berber courtiers understood practically nothing of what the man was expounding, but waited with anticipation for Badis to introduce me as his Jew chief advisor.

"When he finally did so, this particular scholar, as have all others, immediately turned the conversation to religion. They all seem to want to initiate a debate, secure in the idea, fed to them with their mother's milk, that Islam is superior to any other faith. Badis and his minions leaned back in their cushions to enjoy the show. They expected me to not only respond, but to soundly defeat the man. I did so on this occasion, but I know that eventually I will meet my match. When that happens, I expect Badis and the others will turn against me."

"Why do you subject yourself to these situations, Papa?"

"I must, Joseph. When you are older, I hope you will understand, and agree, that by occupying this position of great responsibility and power, I—and I hope and pray that you—do everything possible to protect our people. Nobody in all of Granada, save the caliph, dares to raise a hand against any Jew for fear of my retribution."

"I'm so very sorry you have all these worries, Papa. Maybe if you think back to a happier time, you will find something to calm you."

"What happier time are you thinking of, Joseph?"

"Do you remember the party you hosted in our home the night of the Mahradjan, the longest day of the year? Your guests started to arrive as the sun turned the sky pomegranate and orange. After walking up the hill to our house, most of them paused at our gate, then crossed the road to stand at the low stonewall, tarrying to enjoy the view of the Sierra. That evening the vega was painted with the greens, blues, and purples of the vineyards. The verdant, ordered rows of the growing crops contrasted with the black-green of the olive groves extending up the foothills. The peaks of the Sierra formed a backdrop capped by the ever-present snow.

"I watched as some of the guests looked up to their left at the steep hill topped by the alcazaba and its tower, with the top of the king's palace just visible above where the walls come to a point at the tip of the long mesa. They could see the king's terraced and manicured gardens interspersed with the forest of trees and shrubs covering the steep slope up to the alcazaba."

I laughed. Joseph looked puzzled.

"What?"

"You deny that you have any poetic ability or inclination, my son, but your description of the scene is poetic."

Joseph shook his head and continued.

"I watched them from our rooftop terrace, hidden from their view. Although I knew that all of them received a personal note from you inviting them to the party, they seemed apprehensive. They were reluctant, perhaps shy, to knock at the gate to be admitted. Then you called to me to run fast, to let the guests into the courtyard and lead them to the salon.

"That night, the tile floor of the salon was completely covered with thick, red Armenian carpets. You waited until all were in the house before you came out of your study. I thought you were a most imposing figure in your elegant cloak, standing half a head taller than the next tallest man in the room. You greeted each man by name and embraced him. Most of the men clasped your right hand in both of their hands and bowed. After greeting everyone, you faced east and cleared your throat. Everyone turned to face the east and recited the evening prayer with you.

"I counted nineteen guests, including some young men from your yeshiva. I also noticed two of the rabbis from the yeshiva and several elders of the community, their hair as gray as yours. Your guests sat on cushions at low tables covered with soft leather squares draping over all four sides. You spoke briefly to three of the younger guests, and they went to one of the three tall serving tables, picked up jugs, and poured wine into glasses. They then passed around the room, serving all the guests. As the wine was distributed, our servants arrived with large bowls of fresh and dried fruits, and sweet cakes stuffed with almond and pistachio nutsand with slivers of cinnamon and sugar running through them. I am very fond of those particular sweet cakes. There were other pastries stuffed with fruit."

I chuckled.

"Why do you laugh?"

"You do have a good memory for sweets, as well as an appetite. You must learn to control your urges to overindulge, otherwise you will become fat."

Joseph nodded and continued.

"The guests conversed quietly, in small groups. Occasionally, a person would leave one group and migrate to another. One of the students from the yeshiva stood and recited one of your Hebrew poems, much to everyone's delight. Shortly after that, a servant escorted a man, almost as tall as you, into the salon. You stood and embraced him, then bade him sit at your table. You offered him food and fruit juice, but no wine. You did not introduce the man by name.

"'This gentleman is from Cordoba, a friend of long standing,' you announced.

"The man then stood and recited a long poem in Arabic. Everyone voiced their appreciation and admiration. I also thought the poem wonderful. Then the stranger gathered his large cloak around himself and said goodbye to all in the room. As he went out, he patted me on the head. After he was gone, you told us that the stranger was the famous Arabic poet Abu Ahmad al'aziz ibn Khira al-Munfatil, the same poet you quoted to the young steward of the olive and wine grape orchards. I had no idea the poet was your good friend."

I smiled at him and nodded my head to encourage him to continue.

"Shortly after the poet left, a group of musicians, all wearing identical scarlet-and-yellow tunics, arrived. They made themselves comfortable, rearranging some cushions, then started playing, first slowly and quietly, then progressing into more animated melodies. One of them sang poems set to music. I remember that one of the musicians used what he told me afterward was the feather from an eagle to coax music from a strangely shaped harp of only five strings. Some musicians strummed guitars and sang; others played flutes of various sizes and tones.

"After the musicians departed, some of the guests went to stroll in the courtyard. A few continued their quiet conversation inside. Some of those who went outside walked around the fountain inspecting the plants, while a few sat on the stone benches. All seemed to be taking in the calm night air and tranquility. You joined those in the courtyard. One of the men noticed that your eyes sometimes closed in long blinks. The man circled around, murmuring to each group. One at a time, the men came to take your hand again and to thank you for the evening.

"The next morning, at breakfast, you told me that most of the men were Jewish government officials. You had personally appointed those in the highest positions. Others were given their positions because of your recommendation. Some were appointed by the directors of various agencies who wanted to gain your goodwill by giving positions to your Jewish friends."

"Thank you, Joseph. Yes, I remember that evening and the pleasure I derived from it. Thank you for reminding me, providing such an accurate and detailed description of what you observed, and making me realize that life is still good."

During that period and to this day, many Jews came to Granada because of me. They came to take advantage of the opportunities, safety, and lack of persecution. Other Berber rulers were aware of the loyal service I provided for Caliph Badis and they gave positions to Jews, especially as managers of their finances and estates. Many Jews, because of the security I provided, and my influence throughout Andalusia, became wealthy, acquiring land and estates. Jewish families immigrated to Granada from someArab-ruled Andalusian states, as well as from other places in North Africa and the Mediterranean, including the Middle East.

The Jews in Andalusia and beyond, once my accomplishments were known, referred to me only by the title Ha Nagid. In addition to being chief vizier to Caliph Badis, I wasthe chief rabbi of the Jewish community of Granada, a position I have the utmost respect for. I didn'ttolerate quarrels or disputes within the Jewish community because such disputes wouldundermine both my position and the goodwill the Berbers hadfor the Jews. Every important lawsuit in the Jewish community wasbrought to me. Many legal questions weredirected, by correspondence, to me from communities beyond Granada. I always respondedas promptly as possible to these enquiries. I often tasked Joseph to make copies of my responses.

I always foundtime to teach, not only my chosen scholars. I gaveinstruction on Torah at the Talmudic Academy of Granada. I supportedneedy scholars with regular stipends, gavegenerously to the programs of my yeshiva, and payedmy students and other scribes to make copies of the Torah and Talmud. The copied volumes I gaveto poor students and scholars, and also distributedthem to yeshivas in Morocco, Tunisia, and throughout the Middle East.

I alsomaintainedan active correspondence with Talmudic scholars throughout Andalusia, North Africa, and the Middle East. These men wereclearly my equals, some my superior, in learning and academic accomplishment. These scholars sharedwith me their various interpretations of sacred law, the books they wroteand those authored by others, as well as news of what they werecurrently studying and preparing to write about in the future.

When I wasout on military campaigns, I stillmanagedto maintain my correspondence, as well as writescholarly opinions and poems. When I returned, I orderedcopies made of everything written while gone. I distributedcopies, using convenient traders on their way to the destinations where the people with whom I wantedto communicate resided. I also usedspecial messengers to send writings to favored scholars throughout the Diaspora.

I communicatedregularly with the *gaon*, the leader of the Talmudic academy in Tunisia, Rabbi Hai. I heldhim in high esteem and respect. I also correspondedwith Rabbi Hezekiah, the recognizedhead rabbi, known as the exilarch. Rabbi Hezekiah wasthe leader of the yeshiva of Pumbedita, the Babylonian community responsible for the Babylonian Talmud.

Concurrent with the increasing importance and stability of the various Jewish communities in Andalusia was the significant growth of our economy. Sugar, cotton, and grain werecash crops grown on irrigated vegas and exported. Exports of olive oil and wine producedwealth. Gold, silver, copper, iron, and marble wereextracted from the hills and mountains, especially in the provinces of Elvira, just northwest of Granada. The mined gold and silver werealso used by goldsmiths and silversmiths, particularly those in Granada. Iron and copper providedraw materials for tools, weapons, and other trade goods.

Jews participatedin these industries as both artisans and merchants. They helpedto market all the products of Andalusia. Some wereespecially skillful and successful as traders, even into the surrounding Christian kingdoms. Wherever they traded, they wererespected for their honesty and integrity. As Ha Nagid, I didall I couldto foster this positive reputation of the Jews. I encouragedthem to honor all deals made, no matter the consequences or cost, and to make real the perception of integrity. I consider this to be the true strength of my people. The disdain, displeasure, and disappointment I displayedfor those who didnot adhere to these high principles wasusually enough to make compliance certain.

By some estimates, the Jews of Granada accountedfor at least 40 percent of the total population. Besides artisans, merchants, royal officials, and tax collectors, Jews werealso physicians who tookcare of all citizens. We also hadseveral scholars and teachers, along with scientists who discoveredand disseminatedtheir new knowledge. All the people of Andalusia benefiteddirectly or indirectly from the activities of members of our Jewish community.

I was a student of the renowned Rabbi Hanokh when I was a youth in Cordoba. I write extensively on the subject of Halakha, Jewish law. I spend many hours studying, and thinking about, the ideas and arguments presented in both the Babylonian and Jerusalem Talmuds. As a youth, after my exodus from Cordoba, I wrote commentary regarding some rarely discussed and relatively unstudied chapters in the Gemara. That work was designed to counter the ideas of the Babylonian academics while enhancing the reputation of Andalusian scholars, especially the work of my teacher, Rabbi Hanokh.

While I was in the field during our last campaign, I began an extensive Talmudic review using the style of the Talmudists. I entitled this work *Hilkh 'ta g'bharadta.*My purpose wasto write a more complete, more precise, and better-organized argument than any existing works of that nature. I organized the work by citing a specific law, as discussed in the Babylonian Gemara. Then I juxtaposedthe Jerusalem Talmud's interpretation of that law. Then I citedthe relevant writings of the various leaders of the scattered yeshivas and scholarly academies throughout theDiaspora. Finally, I addedmy own interpretation and thoughts. I speak of this only because I believe we can achieve a measure of immortality by doing good scholarly work and writing the truth, as we interpret it. In this manner, the generations that follow can learn from our writings and judge for themselves the value of what we teach.

Fifteen

WITH THE PASSAGE of time,Joseph celebrated his thirteenth birthday. That Shabat hehad his bar mitzvah;he wasnow officially a man. I wasvery proud of him. He did all the prayers and readings perfectly, and gave a scholarly interpretation of the Torah portion he was responsible for.

The state of Granada was growing; the people prospered. The realm spread south to the sea and to the east all the way to Baza. To the north our lands extendednorth of Jaen, to the borders of the Christian territories, then west to Ecija. All of the people who inhabited the cities, villages, mountains, hills, valleys, and lands within our borders payedtribute to Caliph Badis and answered to his administrator, me.

The Jewish communities prospered, spread, and expanded throughout Andalusia, especially in the cities and towns. There were also many Jewish agriculturalists. They brought their skills, ethics, morals, devotion, and love of the land with them from wherever they had lived previously. Jaen's Jewish community was second in size only to that of Granada. Jews engaged in all types of agriculture and trade in Jaen, but controlled the tanning and leather-producing industries that community is famous for.

The leather products wereconsidered to be of the highest quality throughout Andalusia and beyond. Recently, during services in the synagogue, I overheard that two families from Jaen are moving to

Palestine to start a leather products importation business. Due to my influence and protection, Jews are also free to migrate to places of opportunity throughout Andalusia and beyond.

Joseph and I were again in my study. I quickly scanned the most recent copy he had made of one of my long poems.

"This is a good job, Joseph. Your calligraphy has improved significantly in the last two months. Are you beginning to understand more of the references to Torah passages?"

"I think so, Papa, but I'm certain I don't find or understand all of them."

"Well, let's do this. If you think a phrase may be a reference to Torah or Talmud passages, but aren't certain, you must ask me. If it is, we will find the passage, discuss it, and see if we can arrive at an interpretation we are both satisfied with."

"Thank you, Papa. May I ask you about something else?"

"Of course, anything."

"I know you have had problems with the Hammudite tribe of Malaga, but I don't know the history."

I squinted my eyes and could feel the furrows deepening on my forehead. The smile I produced was more of a grimace, involving only the lower third of my face.

"That is a long and complicated history, Joseph, but it will be good for you to learn it. Perhaps you will obtain a better idea of the kind of people I must deal with almost daily.

"About fifty years ago, Ali—a former general in the army of Caliph Suleiman, who was, incidentally, just a puppet caliph—was given Malaga as a reward for his service to the caliphate. Ali was a member of the Berber Hammudite tribe of North Africa. The Hammudites are related to the Umayyads who, you should remember, originally established the caliphate. Because of that relationship, Ali believed he had the right to claim the caliphate of Cordoba, so he did.

"He was a cruel and unpredictable ruler. He managed to alienate almost everyone living in Cordoba. He was assassinated only three years into his rule. His brother Kasim succeeded him as caliph, but the caliph of Cordoba, prior to Ali's arrival, had a son, Yahya. This

Yahya, of course, enjoyed a more legitimate claim to the crown than Kasim did. The inevitable result was a civil war. Remember, in those days,the caliph of Cordoba ruled all of Andalusia."

"That all happened when you were still young, didn't it, Papa?"

"Yes. I was in my early twenties when it happened. Those were very troubling times."

For a long moment I was lost to Joseph, remembering. He did not interrupt my thoughts. Then I shook my head and returned to the history lesson.

"Anyhow, Kasim lost the civil war and fled to Seville, but the governor of Seville turned him and all of his followers out. Seville was rewarded for turning Kasim away by obtaining nearly total independence from Cordoba. Yahya's forces fought a few more major battles, but mostly just skirmishes with the very depleted army led by Kasim. Those were difficult times. There were two forces, mostly consisting of small bands of robbers and thieves, running amok throughout the countryside. Kasim was eventually captured. Yahya imprisoned him and kept him in prison. After thirteen years he learned that Kasim was planning an escape, so he had him strangled.

"The civil war and the level of independence granted to Seville caused many other cities to strive for equal or even complete independence from the Cordoban caliphate. Eventually, those desires resulted in the taifa, the multiple city-states we now have. Yahya tried to retain and maintain the caliphate in its entirety, but these efforts required constant warfare. In 1035 he made a pact with the Zenata tribe that controlled the province of Carmona. He brought them back into Cordoba's sphere of influence as an almost equal ally. Next, Yahya invaded Seville, but the Carmona Zenata betrayed him. He died in battle while fighting the army of Seville.

"My old enemy, Ismail ben Abbad, was in command of that victorious Sevillian army. The treacherous Slav, ibn Bakunna, the same evil man who conspired with Zuhair and ibn Abbas of Almeria to destroy the Zanhadja and me, installed Yahya's brother Idris as caliph.But Idris lacked any real power; he was just another puppet of ibn Bakunna.

"Idris died not long after he became caliph. Ibn Bakunna tried to engineer the crowning of Idris's young son, who was also named Yahya. This was all done so he, ibn Bakunna, could continue to rule through a puppet caliph."

"Papa, my head is spinning. I don't think I will ever be able to keep all of these alignments and betrayals straight in my mind."

"You must try, Joseph. It is important that you learn from history and understand how things happen at the level of rulers. Another Slav vizier of Malaga, by the name of Naja, supported a cousin of the young Yahya ascaliph. This cousin was Hasan. He and Naja moved too quickly for ibn Bakunna. They sent a large fleet into Malaga's bay. Ibn Bakunna panicked and fled to hide in one of the ancient hill towns northeast of Malaga. Hassan sent a messenger to him promising sanctuary, and ibn Bakunna, feeling much relieved, returned to Malaga. He was immediately arrested and brought to his knees to beg for his life at Hassan's feet. Hassan looked on as ibn Bakunna was slowly strangled to death.

"Hassan knew that the unpredictable loyalties of the Berber tribes might result in them uniting under young Yahya, so he ordered the boy murdered. However, one of Hassan's wives was the older sister of that same Yahya. This wife decided her husband was acting with considered malice and treacherousness against her family, so she poisoned him."

"That whole family sounds crazy, Papa."

"I think so too, Joseph, but wait, the story is not over. After Hassan was murdered by his wife, Naja continued scheming to regain power, but he was running out of male Hammudites. Hassan's young son and Hassan's younger brother were still in Malaga. Naja made a bold move. He killed Hassan's son and threw his brother, a studious and anything but ambitious young man, into prison. Subsequently, he convinced the various Berber clans in the province of Malaga to swear allegiance to him as the new caliph. They agreed to this, but not with enthusiasm.

"Naja still had one more Hammudite to deal with, the ruler of the small taifa of Algeciras. So, he mobilized an army to attack

Algeciras and eliminate that potential threat. He encircled the alcazaba at Algeciras, but the various Berber chiefs with him began to disappear,along with their men. Because of his murderous behavior and obvious lack of respect for them, they no longer believed Naja was the best possible choice for caliph.

"After losing a significant portion of his army, Naja reassessed the situation and decided to return to Malaga. The road he chose went through a narrow gorge. The Berbers still with him, and some of those who had previously deserted, organized an ambush. Naja's carcass, as far as we know, is still rotting in that canyon.

"The Berber chiefs of Malaga freed Hassan's brother, and he was crowned ruler, renamed Idris II. This poor fellow was a good man, very pious and reverent. He instituted policies to help the poor and unfortunate, supported artists, musicians, and poets, but he lacked the fortitude and ruthlessness necessary to rule Berbers. He also failed to recognize and counter the ambitions of our Badis.

"Badis began by demanding Idris II concede a specific tract of land. This demand was based on a trumped-up claim that it had always been part of Granada. Idris II conceded. So, Badis invented other stories to claim one small village, then another, then towns and fortresses as he expanded Granada to the south. Eventually, Badis took control of Casabermeja, only twenty-four kilometers from Malaga itself.

"Idris II's chief vizier had a large extended family who owned property in and around Casabermeja. This man made a crucial mistake. He encouraged his brethren to obstruct the decrees of the governor Badis appointed to administer the newly annexed territories. The most devastating thing he did was to advise his relatives to remit their taxes directly to Idris II instead of to Granada. Badis demanded the vizier be brought to Granada to answer for his sins. Idris II, afraid to confront Badis, dispatched the poor fellow into Badis's clutches.

"The vizier arrived at our court with his hands bound at his back. I had to avert my eyes and focus on our master's smiling face as he watched the poor soul be strangled. After the fellow slumped to the floor dead, Badis turned his gaze on me. With my heart pounding in my ears like the surf in a storm, I managed to force a smile and nodded my head to show my agreement with his action. May God have mercy on me for this, and for the many other sins I have committed to appease Badis and to maintain my authority."

Joseph came to me, hugged me, then tried to climb onto my lap. It was a childish attempt to comfort me. I pushed him off and patted his shoulder.

"You are too old for me to hold you in my lap, Joseph. You are now a man and must grow up fast and learn even faster. Do you want to know what happened next?"

He took two steps back and again sat on his footstool. His face was red with embarrassment.

"Yes, Papa."

"Well, the Berber chiefs of Malaga could no longer stand such a weak ruler. They sent him into exile with his books and replaced him with a distant cousin, named Mohammed. Mohammed is now the ruler of Malaga, and he is mean-spirited, ambitious, cruel, and foolhardy, a perfect Berber ruler. I doubt he will last long."

"Thank you, Papa, for telling me all of this. I believe I have gained a different perspective and a better appreciation for the problems you face maintaining your position so you can protect our people. I now begin to realize the difficulties you have reconciling your actions that are contrary to the teachings of morality and fairness of our religion."

Sixteen

MOHAMMED IBN ABBAD, caliph of Seville, finally died. He wasno longer able to create difficulties for me or Granada. His son, Mu'tadid, was only twenty-six years old when ibn Abbad died. Badis and I, along with all the Zanhadja chiefs, considered Mu'tadid too young and inexperienced to be a serious threat. The Sevillian army wasa collection of mercenaries, and I hadmanaged to defeat them in every encounter. Seville had recently begunto pay tribute to an adjoining Christian state, and all the Berbers consideredthis a significant sign of Mu'tadid's weakness. These factors indicated to the Zanhadja, as well as to several smaller taifa states with leaders craving expansion, that Seville was no longer a force to be reckoned with.

Then the situation changed. Mu'tadid emerged as a viable threat. During the first two years of his rule, he worked diligently to acquire allies and rebuild his army into a cohesive force. Whenever smaller taifa states launched an attack to acquire Sevillian resources, his reaction was immediate, aggressive, and brutal. Most dangerously, he showed signs of mental instability. He collected the heads of his enemies.He ordered that all the heads of leaders killed in battle be brought to him. He also insisted that any captured leaders be brought before him. He beheaded the captured leaders with his own sword, then added those heads to his collection. My spies reportedthat Mu'tadidkeptthe pickled heads of his enemies in containers in his bedroom. He reportedly tookthe heads out of their containers by the hair, then linedthe heads up on the floor facing him and shoutedat them, recounting all the transgressions of their previous incarnations.

His cruelty and madness didn't end with severed heads. Anyone who did something to displease him, or even if he suspected the person was considering a course of action that might displease him, was strung up in the courtyard of his palace to slowly strangle.

So, Seville was again ruled by a strong and ruthless Arab. Once again Seville took its place, with Granada, as one of the big two Islamic powers. The Christian states to the north remained a threat to encroach on Islamic territories. The conglomeration of smaller independent taifa ringing the borders of the big two were constantly mounting raids to obtain loot and to grab land. Various Berber, Arab, or Slav tribes ruled each of the small state taifa surrounding both Seville and Granada, and there was a constant shifting, loss, or gain of power and reforming of allegiances among the taifa.

Joseph and I were in my study. I spoke to him about the situation in Seville and the small taifa. He listened, nodded his head in understanding, didn't interrupt, and stored away everything.

"Joseph, I also need to tell you a little about the Slavs, another interesting story. Most of the people we identify as Slavs originally arrived in Andalusia as child slaves. They were children captured in raids or wars from Christian Europe or kingdoms to the east and brought to Andalusia to be sold. Some of these waifs were even sold to traders by their parents. I am sorry, and ashamed to admit, that many of the slave traders have been and still are Jews. They justify their participation by saying, 'Trade is trade.'They salve their conscience by saying, 'Aman must provide for his family the best way he can.'

"These men are well-versed in the Torah passages that describe the acceptable manner in which slaves are to be treated. Thus, they justify acquiring, keeping, and trading slaves."

"That certainly is not in keeping with what the Talmud teaches, is it, Papa?"

"No, I agree with you on that point, Joseph, and have written extensively about it. But profit seems to supplant all arguments. The truth is that the practice continues, and will do so, as long as there is profit to be made, I'm afraid.

"No matter how they are acquired, most of the female children brought to Andalusia as slaves are trained as servants. Male children, those deemed to have potential, are trained as mercenaries. Their brothersinarms become their only family. The Slav mercenaries are trained with severe discipline, and they become fiercely loyal to theirs brothers-in-arms who have experienced the same initiations. The cream inevitably rises to the top, and those individuals with greater intellect and bravery, or with innate wisdom, or special skills, become courtiers, generals, provincial rulers, and even some rulers of states. Most of these overachievers convert to Islam and practice the religion as a convenience, but they also maintain strong connection and loyalty to their origins.

"With the passage of time, the number, influence, and power of the Slavs has grown. They became as ruthless as the Berbers and Arabs by whom they were schooled. Today, Slav caliphs rule a significant part of EasternAndalusia."

"How does this impact Granada?" asked Joseph.

"So far, the Muslim taifa, including those controlled by Slavs, seem to be most interested in raiding, plundering, and looting each other. This behavior is necessary for them to keep their standing armies and mercenaries happy and paid. They do not seem particularly anxious to wage prolonged wars or pitched battles, or even to expend their resources to limit the slow advance of the Christian states. I predict this weakness regarding the Christian states will be problematic in the future."

"How so?"

"The Christian rulers, especially the long line of popes and their anointed kings, have all been dedicated to the expulsion or conversion of all non-Christians from their territories. They consider Andalusia to be part of what they call Spain. If they are successful in retaking lands they consider to be theirs, it will go badly for the Muslims and the Jews."

"What can be done to prevent that from happening?"

"The best thing would be to unite all of Andalusia in a strong caliphate, but that seems unlikely to happen, especially since Granada and Seville cannot coexist, at least not for now. I am always working to find ways to unite the Muslim taifa to prevent a Christian takeover. So far, these efforts have not borne results. Let's leave that subject, however. I want to continue to tell you about the dangers caused by the caliph of Seville.

"As Mu'tadid gained strength, he realized that a successful strategy against Granada relied on gaining the support of four key small taifa: Carmona, Ronda, Moron, and Arcos. All of these states are ruled by Berbers, natural enemies of the Arabs, but all four rulers are Zenata, and they have long-held grievance against the Zanhadja as well. Because of these consuming hatreds, they can and do align themselves with either Granada or Seville with enthusiasm whenever it suits their purpose."

I smiled as Joseph shook his head, clearly bemused by the perfidy of the Berbers.

"The Birzali tribe of Zenata rules Carmona. They are known to be ambitious, full of natural energy, and more intellectual than is common amongst the Berbers, but they are not overly thoughtful. Carmona changes sides often, depending on the direction of the wind. Moron was founded and is still ruled by the Dammon tribe. Their leader is Muhammad ben Nun. The Dammon tribe strives to achieve the same intellectual level as the Birzali, but lacksthe energy of the rulers of Carmona. Moron is important because it occupies a territory critical to the ability of Seville to maintain its outlying provinces to the west."

"Yes, I know how physically close Carmona is to Seville. That is always a problem, right, Papa?"

"Yes, my son, but we'll deal with that. Most important for us is that Ronda is situated geographically between Moron and Malaga and is governed from an alcazaba built on a natural fortress almost immune to seizure. It is the strongest of the four small taifa and is ruled by the Yenfreni tribe. Ronda has a long history of aligning itself with Seville and is an ideal location from which to launch raids in any direction while maintaining a secure retreat. It is positioned to attack the rear of any Granadian army invading Seville, or vice versa. We must keep a close watch on Ronda and make certain it doesn't go over to Seville.

"Arcos is located about eighty-five kilometers directly west of Ronda. It is the least significant of the four taifa, but is somewhat protected by the Sierra de Grazalema. It is ruled by the Krizun tribe. It is also critical to any meaningful strategy involving us and Seville."

Joseph sighed, a prolonged and hopeless sigh. I ignored his mood and continued.

"Mu'tadid's plotting and growing strength in Seville is becoming more problematic for us. My concern about that growing threat causes me to spend significant time and energy planning counter moves and trying to anticipate how the almost inevitable attack from Seville will materialize."

Only a week after that conversation with my son, a tragedy struck my family. Both Joseph and my daughter contracted smallpox. Only five days later, my dearly loved daughter died. I mourned her passing while doing my best to encourage Joseph to struggle and fight off this horrible disease. Four different physicians visited our home daily. After they finished their various treatments, I questioned each of them. It wasnot uncommon for one or two to disagree about what constitutedan effective treatment or prognosis, but the diagnosis wasunanimous. When the physicians disagreed, I gatheredthem all together in my study and questionedthe basis of their opinions. I soughtmore than anecdotal evidence for the proper course of action. I also prayedwith them for Adonai's guidance and intervention.

A full month passed and Joseph was recovering, but ever so slowly. I rewarded all four physicians equally and handsomely. I am far from certain who was the most instrumental in my son's recovery. Shortly after Joseph had regained his health, but not yet his strength, I sat on the edge of his bed.

"We must give thanks to Adonai, Joseph. The treatment was successful because heinspired the physicians, or listened to their prayers and mine. Or perhaps you recovered despite the treatments because our Lord willed it. Regardless, we must thank him."

A few weeks later, I took Joseph with me on an excursion to demonstrate to the people that my son has recovered and I wasno longer distracted or obsessed withhis illness. First, we went to the synagogue and prayed for over an hour. Then came his reward. We went to the market.

Joseph had gone to the market many times with his mother when he was a young child. Later, he accompanied various servants on errands. When healthy, he went with his friends from the yeshiva. Butthat day was special for him, I believe. It was his first visit to the market with me.

During the long weeks he was kept in bed, I sometimes despaired that he would ever get up. I held his arm as we strolled through the tunnel formed by three-story houses leaning into the street on both sides. Ahead, the tunnel opened to Market Square, shielded from the sun and occasional rain by overlapping canvas awnings. The sound of vendors shouting as they touted their wares rolled up the narrow street to engulf us, like waves from the Mediterranean breaking over the feet of waders walking into the sea. The day was wonderful, full of sunshine. The temperaturewas pleasant; warm in the sun, cool in the shade. The sky was devoid of clouds, an effervescent blue.

As we entered the square, we were constantly stopped by lines of people who wanted a word with me, or to thank me for a favor I did for them, or to ask for a favor, or to just touch my hand and receive a blessing. We were pressed by the crowd of people, inundated by the sounds of many voices speaking many languages: Arabic, Berber, Hebrew, Ladino, and sprinkles of various Slav tongues.

A bewildering array of objects, people, colors, and sounds assailed us, all accompanied by mingled smells, not unpleasant but impossible to ignore. We strolled past vendors with baskets and mounds of seasonal vegetables,and butcher stalls with hanging carcasses of lamb, veal, beef, goat, chickens, game birds, ducks, venison, and rabbits. There were seafood stalls displaying tuna, shad, and sardines, along with other fish I did not recognize.

There were many stalls selling both fresh and dried fruits, and spice stalls too numerous to count. There exist, I believe, thousands of aromatic herbs and spices. Many of them were unfamiliar to me, but I didrecognize the aroma of cumin, aniseed, mint, cinnamon, pepper, nutmeg, coriander, parsley, mustard, and the golden, pungent but delicate saffron. All of these, especially the saffron, are standard for any Andalusian kitchen. Some recipes, Rebecca has explained to me, call for nearly three grams of saffron, that most expensive of spices, tiny threads plucked by hand from the blossoms of a fall-flowering crocus.

Our wandering through the narrow pathways enclosed by stalls took us past the bakers to the drink vendors. I gave one of the vendors a coin for two cups of steaming-hot, sweet tea, perfumed with fresh mint. Joseph and I sat at a rickety table outside the stall and sipped our tea while a line formed to pay me homage.

After finishing our tea, we walked past the prepared food stalls. Here we were assaulted by the powerful fragrance of spiced meatballs of many different flavors:*mirgas*, a spiced sausage; fried fish; *churros*, a type of fried fritter dipped in boiling honey; and *almojabana,* a sweet cake made with cheese.

We finally arrived at the destination I knewJoseph was hoping for—stall after stall of sweet treats made with sugar, honey, almonds, walnuts, hazelnuts, eggs, candied fruits, cinnamon, and other spices. The possibilities were without number, and I was pleased that Joseph had an appetite. I allowed him to choose four sweets.

"You can eat three of those, but you have to give me one," I told him.

After considering the choices for a long moment, he extended one of the sweets to me. As I chewed, the flavors exploded on my tongue. Slivers of almonds crunched under my teeth, the sweet taste of honeyfollowing. The next chew encountered the resistance of a piece of candied cherry. It broke apart, inundating the other flavors with its unique,sugary essence.

Next, we came to the stalls selling vinegar, too many different flavors and types to name. The Andalusian kitchen uses vinegar in most recipes, especially vegetable dishes. Next werethe olive oil stalls, with different varieties of olives and different stages of pressing. Again, too many differences to account for.

The day turned hot. The sun traversed the sky from high in the east to midway to the west. I saw Josephwas tiring.

"Papa, I am thirsty."

"Of course, Joseph, as am I. Let us find another drink vendor and sample something cool."

Ihada word with one of the men who hadbeen following us. He had been trying, not very successfully, to engage me in a conversation, sohe was pleased to be of help. We followed him to the stall of an Arab selling jugs of fresh spring water kept cool sitting in snow from the Sierra. The vendor explained that the icy snow was delivered to him early each morning. He kept his drinks always in the shade, in a box insulated with straw. His water was infused with either rose or orange blossoms. He poured each of us a glass after asking what flavor we wanted. Joseph tookthe orangeblossom, and I chose the roseblossom, but I let him taste mine. Then I noticed another jug of flavoring.

"What is in that jug, sir?" I asked.

"That is *rubb*," he answered. "It is a syrup I make from the Corinto grape and sugar. It is also used to flavor the water. Do you want to taste it?"

Joseph looked at me; I nodded.

"Yes, please," Joseph said.

The vendor poured a generous amount of the thick syrup into a glass, added cold water, stirred it with a silver spoon, and handed it to my son.

"It tastes of fresh, sweet grapes! The flavor is soothing and long-lasting," heexclaimed, and smacked his lips.

The vendor and I laughed as he polished off the refreshing drink.

After we returned home, Joseph went immediately to the kitchen and began describing all we had seen and done to his mother. I stood in the doorway observing their interaction. She was busy making a pumpkin sweet she knows I am extremely fond of. I watched her and Joseph as she measured flour, water, a dash of vinegar, salt, and butter, then kneaded it, gradually adding cold water until she decided it was the consistency she wanted. She rolled out the dough, then spread butter over the top, folded it, and rolled it out again, spreading more butter. She repeated the process six times.

Finally, she divided the dough into several equal amountsand used her hands to form each into a ball, thenrolled each out into a thin round. She covered one of the rounds with grated candied pumpkin, then put the second rolled-out round on top of the first. She painted the edges with a beaten egg, then pinchedthe dough to connect the two layers. The completed pastryfit exactly in Joseph's hand.

Rebecca put a metal tray of the completed pastries into the oven. They baked while Joseph continued his recounting of the day. Just before the treatwas done, Rebecca removed the tray from the oven, dabbed each crust with another beaten egg, and sprinkled the top with a mixture of cinnamon and sugar. She put the tray back in the oven, checkedit frequently, then removed it. I saw the crusts were all golden.

"Do not look at these and me with those sad eyes, Joseph. Your father and I spoiled you when you were ill, but now you are cured. A small taste of this will be for a treat, but only after you eat your entire dinner tonight, including all your vegetables."

Seventeen

JOSEPH AND I were together again in my study.

"I have mentioned the importance of agriculture to life in Andalusia, Joseph, but perhaps now is a good time to describe the extent and variety of that industry.

"When the Romans came to this country, they named it Hispania. They recognized the fertility of the soil, the moderate weather, and long growing season, so they stayed, making slaves of most of the indigenous people. When the Visigoths arrived from the north, they recognized the same attributes and also stayed.

"The Arabs, Berbers, and Jews added new expertise. They worked to improve the irrigation systems developed by the Romans and Visigoths, and imported new crops from North Africa and beyond. They discovered that sugar cane, brought from the Nile Valley, thrived in the lower Guadalquivir Valley, especially in the environs of Malaga. The lemon trees brought into the region by the Romans were improved, and new varieties of both bitter and sweet oranges were added. Several varieties of olive trees were planted in vast orchards; many of these were brought from Israel. Grape vineyards, growing several wine varieties, eating varieties, and the wonderful seedless and sweet Corinto, found new soils and new climates.

"Vast irrigated fields of wheat, rye, and barley were developed, as were orchards of date palms, almonds, coconut palms, bananas, and hazelnuts. Pine nuts, harvested from the forests, added to the cornucopia. Fruit orchards provided cherries, apples, and pears, and from the Ebro and Jalon river valleys, figs.

"Irrigation also enabled several varieties of beans, endives, spinach, chard, radishes, leeks, carrots, celery, onions, eggplant, and artichokes to thrive. There were melons, too many different kinds of melon to list, and squash, many kinds, each with its own texture and flavor that was enhanced by knowledgeable chefs."

"How did we learn to dry fruit to preserve it, Papa?"

"I don't know when that first happened, my son. I suspect that very long ago, some fruit dried out in the sun and a very observant person discovered it could be kept for a very long time in that condition, which made it perfect for exportation or for use in recipes throughout the year. We are lucky that there always seems to be a fresh fruit in season and available to us here in Granada.

"Oh yes, I forgot the silk industry. Mulberry trees were grown to harbor silkworms for silk production. We also have an abundance of wheat and other agricultural products made possible by the fertility of the soil, irrigation, and our sunny, warm weather. Silk, linen, and other textiles, along with the work of our gold and silversmiths, also constitute our exports to the world. We've talked about all of these previously."

"Yes, I know."

"Well, exportation and trade accounts for some of the wealth of our citizens. Any civilization can only endure if its economy is strong. That is why I take an active interest in making certain all aspects of Granada's economy grow stronger with time. I am doing my best to suggest programs and initiatives to Badis that will continue economic growth, but there is unspoken resistance to my ideas. The caliph takes them under advisement. I know he discusses the ideas with some of his other viziers and tribal chiefs, but it is uncommon for him to do anything without my approval. I am doing my best to discover the reasons for the opposition to some of my projects, and from whom it originates.

"Well, Joseph, let's turn again to our problem with Seville and Ronda. The Romans occupied the place now known as Ronda over

1,490 years ago. The Roman commander, his name was Scipio, ordered a fortress built from the partially standing ruins of an original fortification scraped together by the indigenous peoples of the area. The original builders used boulders and stones from the edge of the huge cliff. The Roman engineers hauled additional boulders and stones to the site, where they raised a formidable cliff-side alcazaba controlling all of the surrounding countryside.

"After they were secure and well-established, the Romans expanded and improved the existing irrigation system in the valley below the fortress, developing a robust agricultural economy in the region. With time, and no invasions to disturb the peace, the need for the alcazaba evaporated and it crumbled from neglect.

"After the Visigoths took over, the battlements were repaired and renovated, adding more modern design styles. But with no outside invasions during the following several hundred years, again the walls crumbled."

"How did its name come about, Papa?"

"Abd al-Aziz was the son of General Musa Ibn-Nusayr, the commander of the original invading Muslim army. He occupied the town in 4562 (713). Abd al-Aziz ordered that a new alcazaba be built on the ruins of the original. He renamed the city and its fortress Izna Rand Onda. After the fall of Cordoba and the Umayyad caliphate, the fortified city and the surrounding countryside were usurped by my nemesis, Abu-Nur, who renamed the place Madinat Ronda. Abu-Nur improved the defenses and added the gate of Almocabar to allow easier entry to the alcazaba via the approach from Gibraltar. That gate is the largest, strongest, and most protected access to the city."

One of our servants knocked on the doorjamb to my study.

I was annoyed at the interruption. Joseph laughed as I furrowed my brow then ran my hand through my gray hair, all while shaking my head.

My servant hesitated, cleared his throat, then finally managed to speak. His voice was barely audible.

"There is a messenger from the alcazaba, Nagid."

"Well, don't stand there, bring him to me." My irritation had not abated.

The man who entered the study was dirty from the road, his clothing stained with dried mud. His shoulders slumped like a bag of wool balanced over the back of a patient donkey. His eyes were swollen and inflamed. His left hand trembled. He looked around the room furtively, then looked at me and frowned.

I understood he was reluctant to speak with Joseph in the room.

"My son repeats nothing said in this room. What is your message?"

"My apologies, Ha Nagid. I have been riding hard, day and night for three days, to report to Caliph Badis about events in Baeza and Úbeda. When I finally arrived at the palace, I was told he was indisposed. I was sent here to report to you."

I glanced at Joseph, then mouthed in Hebrew "drunk," indicating Badis's condition.

"So, tell me your news. I assume you were told to do so at the alcazaba."

"Yes, Ha Nagid. The governor of Baeza and his tribe are raiding the territories of Úbeda. He has made your duly authorized tax farmer, your friend Shlomo ben Hasham, a prisoner."

I immediately shouted for my house steward, who appeared in the doorway in less than a minute.

"Run to the barracks and tell Colonel ibn Hakim to come to the house immediately." I turned to the messenger. "I thank you for your loyal service and dedication. What is your name?"

"I am Ezra ibn Dunash, Ha Nagid, at your service."

"And your home is where?"

"Úbeda, sir."

I reached into the inner pocket of my robe and handed the man a leather pouch filled with coins. While we waited for the colonel to arrive, I inquired of the messenger's family, trying to make him more comfortable. After a short time of uncomfortable silence, I addressed him again.

"The colonel will arrive shortly, Ezra ibn Dunash. Please tell the servant, the one lurking there in the hallway, to take you to the kitchen to be fed. After I give the colonel his instructions, he will take you with him to the barracks where you can rest. To ensure your safe return home, you will accompany us when we go north to deal with the renegade."

After the messenger left us, I turned to Joseph.

"This annoyance will take me away from home once again. I cannot allow this sort of insurrection to go unpunished. I must also rescue my friend Shlomo from the rebel's dungeon. I pray he is still alive."

"Of course, Papa, I understand."

"Another thought, Joseph. Do you think you would like to go along on this adventure? It will be safe enough. You will have the opportunity to learn more about what I do when away from home."

"Oh yes, Papa! I would surely love to be able to go with you."

He was excited, but perhaps a little anxious. We continued with the lesson we had been working on until Colonel ibn Hakim appeared in the doorway.

I thanked the colonel for coming so promptly and explained the situation in Baeza and Úbeda.

"I will require a full company, consisting of two units of heavy cavalry and a unit of mounted archers, crossbows, and slingers, a unit of light cavalry, and a unit of infantry. That amounts to twohundred men and their officers. You must also involve all the support people you think necessary to manage the supply train. I want everything ready to travel, with all the necessary supplies and wagons, at first light in two days."

"Of course, Ha Nagid; all will be ready."

"We will deal with the renegade governor wherever, and whenever, we find him. Just plan on supplies for the outbound trip. We will resupply for our return from the traitor's stores. I think we should be able to reach Baeza in six days."

"Six days will be an easy march."

Eighteen

THE MORNING BEFORE we left for Baeza, I gave Joseph his first horse, a gentle mare. The first day of travel with Joseph was clearly very exciting for him. He was full of unbridled joy for his first horse and for the adventure. When I gave him the mare, I told him:

"This animal is yours, Joseph, and you are responsible for her welfare. You know my groom, Simeon."

"Yes, of course, Papa."

"Simeon will be with us on this journey. Our purpose is to correct the actions of our former friend, now enemy, the governor of Baeza. Simeon's purpose, aside from taking care of my horses, is to instruct you on how to care for the mare. You must listen to him and do what he instructs you to do for her. He knows everything there is to know about horses and their care."

The mare wasnot big; she wasa full head shorter at the withers than my bay stallion. She wasa dappled gray with four white stockings. I patted the mare on her nose, soft and smooth to the touch, then I gave Joseph a lump of sugar.

"Give it to her with your hand open. She will carefully remove the sugar with her soft lips. Do you feel the hairs protruding from her nostrils and chin?"

"Yes, they tickle my hand."

The mare chewed the sugar with her eyes closed, then nudged Joseph with her nose, pushing on his chest, asking for more.

Riding next to me as we left Granada, Joseph sat on his mare proudly. Those people up and about early stopped to watch and cheer as we rode through the gate. We stopped at noon. The soldiers ate cold food prepared that morning. Everyone except our servants rested for an hour. As soon as Joseph and I dismounted, the servants spread out rugs and cushions and put up a silk canopy to shade us. Then they prepared food and drink. After we finished our meal, they whisked everything away. As soon as we got to our feet, they took up the cushions, rolled up the rugs, and took down the silk canopy. They stowed everything away in a large wagon, not resting until all the things necessary for our comfort were back in place. Then they took their positions riding on top of our equipment in the wagon as the column moved north. I did not notice if or when they ate.

Joseph was quite stiff and sore when we stopped for lunch. Once back on his mare, he seemed even more uncomfortable. He was unused to riding for so prolonged a time. As the afternoon wore on, the inside of his thighs, as well as his posterior, became increasingly chafed. He was excruciatingly uncomfortable, and not silent about it. I ignored his complaining.

When we stopped for the day, the servants set up my tent and started to prepare our evening meal. Joseph complained again to me about his saddle sores. I shook my head and frowned. Without saying anything, I took the jar of ointment one of our servants placed in my outstretched hand and gave it to my son.

"Rub this gently into the sore areas and stop being a baby. You've been bar mitzvahed; you are supposed to be a man. Act like it."

I waited, tapping a foot on the carpet covering the dirt floor inside the tent, until Joseph finished and pulled his pants back up.

"Are you done, Joseph? May I continue with my duties while you remain silent and put an end to your complaining?"

I called for one of the captains and, after conferring with him, instructed the man to send three of his most trusted and capable men to me. I had a mission for them. The men arrived and I dispatched them as spies to discover the exact situation we would face in Baeza.

I know Joseph tried his best to sleep on the ground with only a rug between him and the earth. I stretched out next to him and fell asleep almost immediately. Josephtossed and turned and moaned and rolled all night, dozing for short periods of time.

Long before dawn, the mosquitos attacked. Joseph's face, neck, and arms were soon covered with welts. He was scratching without relief. Of course, his scratching only made the bites worse.

Dawn finally arrived. Joseph was exhausted, still scratching at the mosquito bites which were now open and oozing blood. His saddle sores still screamed for attention, adding to his litany of discomforts.

The soldiers, servants, and I, all accustomed to campaigning, were quickly ready to travel. As the day wore on, Josephcould not resist complaining about his ailments and unhappiness.

"Stop whining, Joseph. Do you want all these men to think I am raising a sissy? I've heard enough of your complaining. Tonight, you will be tired enough to sleep on the ground. Look around you and enjoy what Adonai created.

"Look, there in the distance are the mountains with their highest peaks still covered with snow. Look at the beauty of the hills close by. Look at the plowed fields, the furrows that have already received the seeds from which the crops will grow. Look at the orchards, ablaze with flowers that will mature as fruit. And look at the vineyards; the buds are out and the leaves are growing. Notice, as we pass them, the sparkling, clear creeks carrying the water from the melting snow in the mountains. That waterflows to the rivers that irrigate the fields and grow the crops that bring us life. Look at the trees in the forests. Adonai provides them for us to use for lumber and fire. Look at Adonai's grass growing to feed the animals that he created for our use and enjoyment. See, off to the left there? Do you see the doe? Do you see her? Good! You must appreciate these blessings, Joseph and, pleaseAdonai, stop your whining."

Joseph, to his credit,didn't say a word of complaint all the remainder of that day, but in my tent that night he showed me his insect bites and saddle sores. They were more inflamed, some appeared to be infected, and Iappreciated how much pain they were causing.

He fought back tears, wiping his face with the back of his hand.

"I miss my mother and my comfortable bed."

"Rub more of the ointment on your sores and get what rest you can. Tomorrow I will send you home in a wagon with two soldiers and one of the servants. They will take care of you and make certain you arrive home safely. I'm afraid you are still too young and unused to the rigors of travel to learn firsthand about campaigning. After you get home,take time each day to ride your mare so you can do so for long periods without discomfort. We will try this again when you are older."

It was my very good fortune that Josephwas so miserable that I had to send him home early. I watched as the wagon left camp.

Two evenings after sending Joseph home, I stopped my army in an idyllic canyon in the Sierra Magina, where we made camp for the night. The clear waters of the Guadiana River, fresh with spring runoff, wound their way through the canyon. The evening was fragrant with the aroma of pine trees. The swift water passed over rocks, forming eddies, rushing through narrows, falling four feet over a small cliff, then spread out, widening and slowing. The sound created by the tumbling waterreassured the men of the tranquility of the spot. Iwas completely lulled by the charm and serenity of the place. Colonel ibn Hakim consulted with me.

"Ha Nagid, do you have a preference for where I should post sentries?"

"I don't think it necessary, Colonel. Let all the men enjoy this beautiful place and get a full night's rest. Our forces are more than adequate to deal with this insurrection. This is just another routine policing expedition."

I had no premonition of danger, a mistake I will never make again. I was unaware that Abu Nun, the caliph of Ronda, had encouraged the governor of Baeza to perpetrate the raids and looting.That Berber governor needed very little encouragement to raid and loot. Abu Nun knew I would be forced to respond to this breach of discipline and order. I was completely unaware that Nun's scouts were monitoring the progress of my troops. The wily devil had prepared an ambush. He hid the fourhundred men he commanded close to where we were camped, anticipating I would halt at that scenic and tranquil place for the night. Abu Nun's objective was singular: to kill or capture me.

I suspect Abu Nun did not arrive at this strategy himself. I have reason to believe he was encouraged to undertake the operation by Mu'tadid, the king of Seville. Mu'tadidhad the most to gain by eliminating me and weakening Granada.

Later that night the skies grew cloudy, threatening rain. The officers and Iwere in our tents, the soldiers rolled up in their cloaks. The camp was quiet. The occasional snore or stamping of a horse's hoofwere the only sounds penetrating the black night.

Abu Nun attacked, first with his heavy armored cavalry. They were ordered to rush through our camp, strike as many of my men as possible on the way through, then turn and sweep through again. The initial surprise attack was followed by archers and infantry.

Fortunately for me, the surprise attack planwas ill-conceived. The night was extremely dark because of the cloud cover. There was only a quarter moon, and it was hidden behind the heavy clouds. The darkness made communication among the attacking forces difficult, in some cases impossible. The obscure night also prevented the attackers from identifying their main target.

Colonel ibn Hakim reacted to the attack in a calm and efficient manner. He had drilled his troops on how to respond to this type of situation, and his orders were carried out without hesitation. A special platoon of Nubian infantry quickly formed a perimeter with locked shields around my tent. The rest of the Nubians positioned themselves with their shields and spears to confront the charging horses of Abu Nun's cavalry. Our archers, crossbows, and slingers split and ran to opposite sides of the camp, concentrating their fire on the enemy from both flanks. All this time, the enemy commanderswere shouting to their men:

"Identify the Jew's tent! Capture him! Kill him!"

Colonel ibn Hakim and his soldiers fought valiantly. The colonel deployed a tight circle of archers, crossbows, and slingers to reinforce the Nubians surrounding me. I searched out mystallion, who was tethered close to my tent. Our cavalry rushed to bridle and saddle their horses, not bothering with their armor. A contingent of cavalry and I were able to lead our horses to the river and into the current. The river was still running deep with the spring runoff. We swam to the far side, where we mounted our horses and made our way upstream. Ibn Hakim's rear guard protected access to the river so more of our men, with their mounts, managed to escape.

Because of the darkness, the enemy archers were unable to pick specific targets. They resorted to firing one volley after another. Arrows coming from the dark sky careened off the raised shields forming a roof over the heads of the soldiers, who crouched down when they heard the whoosh of incoming missiles. The small, round shields of the archers, crossbowmen, and slingers were not as effective. Many arrows and other missiles found targets. The enemy soldiers screamed with pain when wounded by our defenders. My soldiers were stoic, professional, proudly brave. They endured their wounds silently.

A shout went up from the enemy as we made our way across the river. The heavy armor worn by Abu Nun's cavalry, both horses and riders, made it impossible for them to follow. Some did try to respond to Abu Nun's screamed orders, but their horses sank into the mud at the river's edge. One man continued to urge his horse into the faster current in the center of the river. Both horse and rider disappeared under the water, never to reappear. The fate of that horse and rider was soon communicated to Abu Nun's men. None of the other riders were willing to venture into the current encumbered, as they were, with their heavy armor.

The almost complete darkness prevented Abu Nun's archers from being able to identify me, or those with me, as targets. Our highly trained and brave Nubian infantry were able to hold off Abu Nun's forces long enough for most of our cavalry, archers, slingers, and crossbow soldiers to escape via the river. With discipline and order, small units of Nubians, their brothers protecting their retreat, were the last to plunge into the water and swim to safety. I lost over fifty men, including Colonel ibn Hakim, who stayed to command and encourage those most loyal and brave soldiers covering our retreat into the river. We lost horses and arms, armor, wagons, and supplies, but most of us escaped to fight another day, and Joseph was safe. I vowed revenge.

Nineteen

AFTER MY ESCAPE from Abu Nun's ambush, I returned to Granada, obsessed with finding out how Abu Nun learned my route of travel. More importantly, I needed to understand how he decided on the timing and planning of the attack. I was determined to never again be caught in that sort of trap, or any other, for want of knowing my enemy. I was so very thankful I sent Joseph home when I did. The distraction of having to make certain of his safety could have proved fatal for both of us.

Badis paid an assassin handsomely, and it wasn't long until the rebellious governor of Baeza no longer posed an annoyance. With Badis's blessing, I organized a massive invasion of Ronda to extract vengeance against Abu Nun. Granada could not allow his treachery to go unpunished. Granada's army was much larger, stronger, and better equipped than Ronda's. The instigator of the ambush, Mu'tadid, was not in a position, or apparently of a mind, to offer significant help to his puppet. Abu Nun was left to his own devices.

Ronda was soon under siege. Abu Nun's pleas for help from Seville were ignored. It would have taken a long time to starve Ronda into submission, but with noviable options or help from Seville, and with defeat inevitable, Abu Nun agreed to a treaty. He gave up considerable territory,paida large fine, and signed a treaty as Granada's ally. I decided to leave him chastised but still in control of his caliphate. It isn't worth the time, energy, or resources to starve him out and get rid of him permanently.

Back home I was again with my family. Joseph joined me in my study.

"Even though Abu Nun can never be trusted, the treaty he signed is worthless, it is a necessary expedient to allow him to live, and most likely, to plot against us in the future. I will be careful to keep a close watch on him. Do you understand why compromises of this nature are sometimes necessary, Joseph?"

"Yes, Papa. It is necessary to balance the cost of any action against the possible benefit."

"Exactly." I smiled.

I wrote anotherlong poem to chroniclemy escape from Abu Nun's ambush and of all of Adonai'sblessings I have enjoyed. It took Joseph and my students four full days to make copies of the poem for distribution.The poem also praises Adonai for my birth, my childhood, and my parents. In it I offer thanks to Adonai for my education, knowledge, wisdom, eloquence, and fame. I give Adonai all the credit for my high position, accumulated wealth, and the ability to manage and control the Berber court I serve.

The poem goes on to praise Adonai and thank Him, promising to continue to glorify His name and all His accomplishments in poetry.I ask Him to erase my guilt and hear my prayers, hoping that my prayers will be agreeable. I also ask that the angels defend me, then I belittle my detractors and end the poem asking Adonai that my loved ones never be ashamed of me and that the years remaining to me before my death should be sweet.

I believed Badis and Mu'tadid had more in common than any differences between them. Both hadthe ultimate goal of making their caliphatepreeminent. Both enjoyedthe support of their citizens in their efforts to achieve that goal. Neither would ever acknowledge that any constraints could be imposed on their whims, or indeed any aspect of their behavior. Both were free to exercise any desire or passion. There was no one who could, or would, or dare to prevent them from doing anything they wanted to do.

Both Badis and Mu'tadid faced the constant threat of assassination. The most significant danger often came from people closest to them. Their courtiers were suspicious of everything and everyone, particularly their colleagues. The same courtiers were fearful for their own safety, even while much occupied with intrigue. All were insecure about their position at court and constantly worried about their influence, or lack thereof, with their caliph. Both caliphs knew that if they failed to completely humiliate and kill their enemies, often in the most gruesome way possible, they would be seen as weak and unable to act with decisiveness. Indecisiveness is a fatal flaw for a caliph. I think this knowledge was instinctive in both of them.

Both caliphs were isolated, alone even while amongst many. All governments require an organization of people capable and willing to effectively implement the decisions made by higher-ranking officials. This is especially necessary when, as it is in most cases, those making decisions are unable or incapable of performing the tasks and completing the work necessary themselves. Other hands are required to assume the workload in order to reach the desired policy outcome. Worker bees make the honey. No caliph can rule without a cadre of people willing and able to make certain his desires and decisions are carried out.

Perhaps my most important skill was my ability is to convince my caliph to modify a contemplated action, or decision, that might be harmful to the caliphate. Another of my most important strengths was my ability to discover where along the chain of command a problem existed and either repair or remove the weak link. I also had a well-developed intuition that enabled me to identify and appoint men of intelligence and skill. Men who understood how to make things happen. Under my administration, things got done. I believed that Joseph would be able to match my administrative abilities, but I was not at all certain that he would be ruthless enough or intuitive enough to take over all my responsibilities. I was certain he would never be a warrior.

Badis, aside from his drunkenness, frequently displayed signs of paranoia and inexplicable behavior, sometimes just for effect. These paranoid-induced or calculated displays, as well as decisions made without apparent thought or consideration, seemedto have increased in frequency of late. Mu'tadid's paranoia, on the other hand, was almost constant and clearly a manifestation of mental illness. I had recently heard a troubling story from a former vizier in Mu'tadid's court who fled to Granada to secure safety for himself and his family. He verified my belief thatMu'tadid convinced Abu Nun to plan and carry out the ambush against me.

The same escapee reported that Mu'tadid's own son feared his father was going to have him killed, so he hatched a plot to kill Mu'tadid first. Unfortunately for the son, Mu'tadid learned of the plot. He slit the son's throat himself. But he didn't stop with that horrific act. He gathered his son's friends, his servants, all four of his son's wives, and all of their children, including two infants, and proceeded to kill all of them. Some of his viziers, including the man who described these events to me, fearfully entered the room full of slaughtered family members. They found Mu'tadid standing with a knife held in his right hand, drops of blood sliding off the blade and splashing on the tile floor. Their caliph stared at them withred-rimmed eyes, his pupils wide, dark holes in his head. His clothing, his arms, and both hands were covered with the blood of his family. Everyone in the room, save Mu'tadid, shuddered in the oppressive silence.

Finally, Mu'tadid screamed at the men huddledtogether in the room.

"Wretches! Wherefore are you silent? You gloat in your hearts over my misfortune! Be gone from my sight!"

I knew that Granada would never be at peace unless it achieved dominance throughout Andalusia. This fit exactly with Badis's ambitions. The Zanhadja had no argument with the Zenata king of Ronda, prior to his attempt on me. Now it was clear to all of us that Mu'tadid was the instigator of the Rondan act of aggression.

It wasn't long before the Zenata rulers of Carmona and Moron joined forces and began initiating raids on Granadian holdings. I was convinced Mu'tadid had a hand in this as well. My response wastwofold. Iorganized and conducted counter raids into the territories of Carmona and Moron. I sent out troops under trusted generals to take plunder, annex territory, and exact tribute from the inhabitants of those areas ruled by the Zenata Berber al-Birzali and Dammon families, the rulers of Carmona and Moron respectively. Meanwhile I raised the necessary funds to recruit a whole regiment, a thousand Mamluk mercenaries.

Only purchased slaves couldbecome members of the Mamluk. An extremely wealthy Berber family from Jaen ownedthe particular regiment I hired. All the physical needs of these men were taken care of by their owners; they provided exceptionally good living conditions and a reward system so generous it enticedmany freeborn but poor youngsters to volunteer themselves for sale to gain membership to the elite organization. Forty-man units weredivided into four ten-man platoons. Five units form a company, and five companies a regiment. The same organizational system wasused by almost all Andalusian armies.

The Mamluks spend all of their time together. They are indoctrinated into the dictates of the code of *fursiyya*. That code emphasizes courage, generosity, fraternity, and obedience. Every new recruit is trained with extreme vigor and intensity in cavalry tactics, horsemanship, archery, hand-to-hand combat, swordsmanship, and the treatment of wounds. Only after they are proficient in all of these skills are they formally initiated into a unit and assigned to a platoon. They continue to train daily for the rest of their careers.

They are well cared for, even if they are wounded severely enough to no longer be fit for service. If still healthy, they are retired from active duty at the age of fifty-five. After retirement, many stay on and continue to be cared for. If they have saved enough, from the shares of booty they received as rewards, if they have family, and if they want to live with that family, they are provided with a modest stipend and allowed to live independently. However, most retirees continue to live with their platoon, where they train the next generation of Mamluks, the most elite and feared fighters in Andalusia. Few caliphates are wealthy enough to hire, and keep, a full regiment on the payroll for prolonged periods of time. Granada was.

I also hired a regiment of Almoravids. The Almoravids, also fanatical mercenary fighters, wereorganized and under the command of the Jazula Berber, Abd Allah ibn Yassin. This entrepreneur was able to convert whole captured North African Berber and Negro tribes into his warrior Islamic culture.

The two hired regiments bolstered Granada's regular army. We also had a full regiment of infantry that includedsix hundred Nubians bolstered by four hundred conscripts. Our regular army also included three regiments of light and heavy cavalry, and another regiment of mounted archers and slingers. These last four regiments weretribal Zanhadja Berbers, actually militia, commanded by their own chiefs, and called upon whenever Badis and I neededthem. When not in service to Badis, these tribal warriors often occupiedthemselves by stealing sheep and horses from neighboring tribes or conducting raids on the holdings of their Arab or Zenata neighbors.

Each regiment wascommanded by a general, who reporteddirectly to me. As general-in-chief of the army, I answeredonly to my caliph. In total I commandedsix thousand fighters. All well-trained, well-equipped, well-supplied, well-drilled, and well-paid. Granada was formidable.

The weak and ineffective King Indris II of Malaga ceded more portions of his kingdom to both Granada and to her slippery and fickle ally, Ronda. Abu Nun, encouraged again by the bribes of Mu'tadid of Seville, renounced the treaty I forced him to sign and initiated raids into Granadian territory. I responded to these incursions with only minimal retaliatory efforts. I was not yet ready for an all-encompassing war with Seville. I understood Mu'tadidwas working to build his army and his resources, all the while encouraging the small-scale irritants by Ronda and other small taifa. Despite my measured responses, Abu Nun continuedhis scattered raiding, but he was careful to avoid any significant battles with the forces I deployed to retaliate. The inevitable result was that the only people who sufferedwere those occupants of the towns, villages, and farms plundered by the respective sides.

Abu Nunopened a second front of attack, this time from his southern holdings, new territories acquired from Malaga. This was made possible because of the unstable situation in Malaga when King Idris II was overthrown and sent into exile. Abu Nun installed Idris III as caliph and grabbed a sizable portion of lands claimed by Malaga. Badis also responded to the chaos in Malaga by personally taking a regiment of Zanhadja to Malaga. His intention was to return Idris II to the throne.

While Badis was thus engaged,I departed to the north to take personal command of our Mamluk and Almoravid regiments. While I retaliated against the raiding Rondans, forcing them to abandon their gains and retreat, Badis was on his own facing Abu Nun in the south. I was concerned about how he was managing on his own.

I found out that my concerns were well-founded. Abu Nun outmaneuvered Badis. He concentrated a superior force to meet Badis in the type of mounted fighting the Berbers love. The resulting battle was indecisive, both sides losing many fighters, but neither could be said to be victorious. Badis lost heart for the endeavor and returned to Granada and his jugs of wine.

ThenAbu Nun installed acaliph of Malaga, who took the name Idris III. He was as cruel and aggressive as Abu Nun could hope for. He resentedBadis's effort to remove him and recognized the advantage of being an ally of Ronda, and thereby Seville. Mu'tadidwas now ready to act directly. He formalized his alliances with both Ronda and Moron. He sent emissaries to several other taifa states seeking an even stronger coalition against Granada.

Granada was facing a multifront defensive war. Our enemies were able to pick the time and place of attack. I recognized Seville was the real enemy, but a direct attack on Seville was not a viable option. Seville was too strong and too far away. If I did move against Seville, I would have been vulnerable to an attack from the rear by Ronda, Malaga, and other states that would quickly recognize our vulnerability.

Joseph and I were in my study.

"Joseph, if I attack Malaga, my army will be isolated from home by the snow-capped Sierra Nevada, leaving Ronda and Seville an easy route into Granada itself. Ronda has a formidable alcazaba perched on a sheer cliff, but the route to this fortress is not difficult. I will depart in the morning to lead our Zanhadja regulars and our mercenaries into Rondan territory, leaving an experienced regiment and solid commander to protect Granada."

When he learned the magnitude of the threat, Abu Nun dispatched an urgent request for support to Seville. Mu'tadid made the decision to finally confront Granada directly. He responded to the Rondan plea by ordering General Mukhtar, with two regiments of cavalry, to join forces with the armies of Moron, Carmona, and Ronda. He anticipated the combined armies would be able to crush us.

Twenty

GENERAL MUKHTAR, MU'TADID'S choice to lead his army, was confident, overconfident. My spies informed me that he commanded five regiments, all cavalry, except for one company of mounted archers and two companies of infantry. I knew he would be determined to fight on open ground. He wanted the cavalry battle so loved by both his Berber and Arab troops. After Badis's failure at Malaga, and the constant pressure of our having to respond to raids on our territories, he no doubt believed we were weary of fighting. I wantedhim to believe the Zanhadja were no longer invincible.

My army traveled the hundred kilometers from Granada to Antequera in four easy stages. From there, we moved southwest following a small stream to the village of Valle de Abdalajis, situated at the western edge of a broad basin stretching over fifteen kilometers long and six kilometers wide. I moved my forces east from Valle de Abdalajis to the opposite end of the valley. I wantedMukhtar's forces to be compelled to attack us while looking into the morning sun.

My spies reported that Abu Nun had gathered in all of his raiding parties and marched his forces northeast from Ronda. Mukhtar's regiments from Seville were augmented by units from Moron and Carmona. This combined army traveled south from Osuna to join forces with Abu Nun, just west of El Chorro. They camped, held a strategy session, and the next day circled south through a low pass in the mountains arriving at Valle de Abdalajis in the early afternoon, only a day after we left that place. They set up a base camp and prepared for battle. I received almost hourly updates from my spies about all these movements.

I stood outside my tent. It was early and the air was clear and crisp. The sun warmed my back through the bright, cloudless sky. The hills and mountains surrounding the broad valley were the color of a ripe lime, theverdant green of dense forests. The forests, and the animals within, would soon be nonparticipating witnesses to the clash of arms and cries of the wounded.

I had met with my generals the previous night and givenall the necessary orders for positioning our troops. The only discord during that planning session was the desire by each of the generals to have their regiment at the forefront of the battle. I ordered that the Nubian infantry be placed in the center front, three ranks deep. Mounted Mamluks were to be on the right and left flanks of the infantry. Our own and the Almoravid archers and slingers were assigned the fourth and fifth ranks behind the Nubians, six ranks of Almoravid infantry behind them. I split the Zanhadja cavalry units, both heavy and light, half on the far-right and half on the far-left flank. Each company, unit, and platoon wasgiven explicit instructions for the part they were to play in the battle, and the drum signals that would tell them when to execute their role. In the eventuality that things went badly, we had a plan and a route for an orderly retreat. I hoped for the best but planned for the worst.

My horse was brought to me. I rode to the top of the highest nearby hill with my ten- member bodyguard, four drummers, and ten messengers, all of the later mounted our fastest horses. The hill, which I chose the day before, provided a panoramic view of the battlefield. The messengers were used to relay instructions to my generals and colonels as the battle unfolded.

Mukhtar advanced with the sun in his face, his cavalry spread across the entire width of the valley, three ranks deep. The air shimmered with the clattering sound of the tools of war. Horses snorted and strained at the bits holding them back. Theywere warhorses, anxious to begin the charge that would fill the crisp air with battle cries, drums, and men and horses screaming in pain,all mixed with the smell of blood, feces, urine, and fear. Dust kicked up from the iron-shod hooves of the sweating, armored horses of the heavy cavalry, burdened with their armored riders. The leather-backed chain mail of horses and riders was hot enough to sear the skin. A slight breeze coming off the eastern hills carried away all but a small wisp of the dust rising from the horses' hooves. At a trumpet signal they were spurred into a trot. Mukhtar's foot soldiers broke into a run, doing their best to keep up.

When Mukhtar's forces were just five hundred meters from our lines, I raised my right hand. The drummers beat out the appropriate signal, repeated five times. The Mamluks chargedforward from both flanks, galloping directly at the center of the approaching line, but when they were just out of range of Mukhtar's archers, they whirled their horses, retreated, and reformed in front of the Nubian infantry.

Mukhtar, his Arab blood pounding in his ears, couldn't control himself. He screamed the command to charge and spurred his horse forward. The Mamluks executed a perfect retreat to their original positions on the flanks, allowing the Nubian infantry to take the brunt of the charge from the oncoming cavalry. They planted the butts of their large teardrop shields next to the butts of their spears, into the ground. As men fell from the onslaught, otherNubiansmoved in to fill the break in the wall, and the line was once again solid, immovable.

The charging horsemen were also met with barrage after barrage of arrows, slung rocks, and Greek fire grenades coming from the Almoravids aligned behind the ranks of infantry. The missilesstruck the charging cavalry before most of them could engage with the Nubians. Many fell wounded or dead from the steady barrage, but most continued the charge forward. The thunder of clashing lances and shields moved up my hill like a huge wave and engulfed me.

I gave the order, and the Mamluks responded to the drum signal by charging into the melee from both flanks. The fighting was now hand-to-hand. When the enemy was fully engaged, I ordered half of the Zanhadja cavalry from each flank, where they were hidden from view behind hills, to circle around and attack from the rear. The remaining Zanhadja were held in reserve, much to their disgust, but they followed my orders and remained hidden, separated from the battle.

The superiority of the Mamluk and Almoravids was soon apparent, and the Nubians fought even harder, determined to not be outdone. The regiments of Zanhadja Berbers circling around to attack from the rear were doubly motivated to match the intensity and determination of the mercenaries.

Mukhtarwent down. A tall Mamluk soon held his severed head high in the air. The intense fighting continued. Scattered but sizable units of Mukhtar's forces were able to gather themselves and fight their way free, but only those units with brave and competent commanders, who managed to maintain control of their men, escaped the slaughter. I released the reserves to participate in the mop up.

The enemy dead were counted at five hundred and twelve, including those wounded so severely they were dispatched as an act of mercy. The enemy wounded, those still able to walk, I ordered to be taken to Grenada as captives, along with the many unwounded who dropped their weapons and raised their arms. The walking wounded and captured enemy soldiers totaledjust over three hundred. I lost only seventy-two men. All of our wounded were well cared for, but another twenty eventually died from their wounds. I ordered that our wounded survivors be transported home by wagon.

The enemy's abandoned weapons, armor, horses, wagons, and all their supplies were gathered as booty, along with anything of value taken from the dead and captured. All the victors shared in the prizes except me. I let it be known that I would donate my sizable share to our wounded, and to the families of those killed in the battle.

The most important spoils distributed came from the tributes collected from the territories recently conquered and annexed by Mukhtar's army. They are now reannexed to Granada, along with many former Sevillian holdings. I convinced Badis to award colonels and captains, as well as generals, shares in confiscated farms and orchards. Some of these men became landowners for the first time.

The captured officers, those who came from families of substance, were ransomed. Those profits, along with the king's fifth of the booty from the battle, all went to Badis.

I wrote another epic poem about this victory, and after copies were made, I distributed it throughout the Diaspora. It told how Mu'tadid mocked Granada and its caliph. How we responded, taking back what Seville had taken, and exacted revenge for Seville's brutality. I described, in detail, how our army prevailed, with what I hoped werevivid descriptions of Granada's heroes and their deeds.

Abu Nun, the leaders of both the Carmona and Moron contingents, and their soldiers who managed to escape, retreated to their respective strongholds. One of the captured Sevillian officers, who had achieved his rank by virtue of ability rather than birth, was given his freedom, with the task of returning Mukhtar's head to Mu'tadid. I never found out whetherMu'tadid rewarded him for this task or had the brave man murdered.

Following through on this victory, I took the army, minus those troops assigned to escort our wounded, the enemy captives, and wagons full of booty back to Granada, and followed Abu Nun to Ronda. Once again, I besieged that fortress, but after only a week the weather changed, heralding a long winter. True to form, the Zanhadja chiefs were not willing to participate in a long winter siege. They had their victory and significant booty. They decided to spread out on the way home so they could collect more tribute from the towns, villages, and cities along the way. I was forced to abandon the siege and return to Granada. I fully realized I had achieved a great tactical victory but suffered a strategic defeat by not taking Ronda.

Joseph and I wereagain sequestered in my study.

"Unless I can bring all of the smaller states in as allies of Granada, or neutralize them in some other way, Granada will never be secure and at peace. Mu'tadid will continue to plot our demise. I have two choices, Joseph. The first is to build and maintain alliances that will, eventually, enable me to destroy Seville. The other option is to attack and kill all the leaders of the small taifa and absorb those lands. The latter is beyond our resources. Even if I had all the resources necessary, the task will be too difficult, too risky. The option of forming a coalition against Seville will not be easy, and will be even more difficult to maintain than to form. Any of the taifa who join my alliance will most likely desert the alliance as victory over Seville becomes more certain. The ultimate goal of any taifa is to retain its autonomy. They will not want to risk being absorbed by Granada, despite their natural antipathy to Arab Seville. All of these potential allies harbor a realistic fear of Granadian hegemony once Seville is neutralized. There is also the Berbers' natural laziness and inability to see and understand the large picture. You must never repeat this evaluation of our situation, Joseph, most especially not to Badis."

Joseph noddedhis head, fully understanding.

"My first task is to convince the independent rulers, their viziers, and tribal chiefs that this war needs to be fought to prevent the hated Umayyads from conquering and reuniting all of Andalusia. The major historical motivations for the Berbers to go to war is the potential for looting and plunder. I have to convince them that this war has to be different. Its goal is to stop the Arab Umayyads."

The caliph of Moron, and the chiefs of his tribal families, recognized the superiority of the Granadian military and my leadership. With my encouragement, they managed to conjure up memories of the humiliation of years of defeats by the Umayyads. It was to their advantage to rekindle their hatred of the Umayyad dynasty. They abandonedMu'tadid and joined my coalition.

Carmona, located only thirty kilometers from Seville,was not happy with Mu'tadid's leadership nor his megalomaniac and unpredictable behavior. They recognized my skill as a general and signed treaties to join our coalition, as did the leaders of Arcos. The potential reward for these Zenata Berbers, who were still leery of the Zanhadja, wassweetened by the possibility of their being able to appropriate the riches of Seville. They anticipated that Seville, after this most recent defeat, would be easier pickings than Granada had proven to be.

Huelva is a tiny village located at the confluence of the Odile and Tinto rivers in the delta that eventually opens to the Gulf of Cadiz.

It is about a hundred kilometers west of Seville. This town was my gate to the back door of Seville. Its Berber leaders couldn't resist the symbolic and religious sanctification of the alliance I offered. They were also, of course, interested in booty.

I was constantly on the lookout for a person with the necessary family background to installas the titular Hammudite caliph. Such a puppet caliph would serve as a person all of the Berbers could provide lip service to, and rally around, while still maintaining their independence. The King of Malaga would have been ideal, but he was already aligned with Seville and still nurtured a grudge against Badis and Grenada.

The head of a branch of the Hammudite family, not directly related to the Zanhadja, ruledAlgeciras, a tiny port city located at the tip of the straits of Gibraltar. I eventually managed to convince our new allies to accept this man as their caliph. To sanctify this charade, I arranged a solemn ceremony to invest the new caliph. I managed to convince the caliphs of Granada, Carmona, Moron, and Arcos to attend. The rulers who attended the festivities didn't come alone. Their families, their nobles, their tribal chiefs, and their viziers accompanied them. The kings of Badajoz and Huelva were unable to attend, citing ill health, but they sent high-ranking nobles and their entourages in their stead.

For a Jew to play such a crucial role in organizing and maintaining a military and cultural alliance that would assure the survival of so many independent taifa was a diplomatic success not previously matched. I basked in the glory.

Abu Nun, secure in his fortress of Ronda, decided he had to establish complete independence from both Granada and Seville. He was waiting for a clear indication of which of the two big powers would be successful before making any commitments. He knew the character of his Berber relatives. All of them worriedabout any single big state encompassing them. He also understood that the draw of easy plunder was too tempting for them to ignore. Abu Nun managed to convince his chiefs it would be wise to forego any temptation for easy pickings and to sit on the sidelines for the time being.

Twenty-One

WHEN I WAS in the field, all the officers knew and understood that I was in charge. However, I always took great care to let them know that I served only at the discretion of Badis. It was understood, but unspoken, that my decisions hadBadis's prior approval. The mercenary troops were clearly apprised that Badis, not me, was their employer. It was to Badis they owed allegiance. Since I am a Jew, there were always those who would resent my high office. If it could be hinted that any segment of the army was loyal to me rather than the caliph of Granada,it would be easy to make a case that the Jew was plotting to take complete control. The Berber chiefs, always looking for an advantage, would be quick to embrace that suggestion and to act on it.

Late in 1048 the newly installed Hammudite token caliph of Andalusia and king of Algeciras died. I was once again faced with a crisis. My response was a diplomatic stroke calculated to keep our nervous allies in the fold. I convinced Badis to spread the story that I was the one who wanted to punish Malaga and get rid of their caliph. I used many sources to circulate the rumor that Badis did not agree with this course of action, but the Jew had managed to convince him against his better judgment. As the only living and legitimate heir to the Hammudite throne, the caliph of Malaga now had to be recognized as the caliph of all of Andalusia. With his ego properly massaged, Idris III accepted the responsibility, though he certainly understood no power came with the dubious honor. For what it was worth, Malaga and Granada were once again allies, at least until a more attractive option presented itself.

Nissan 4797 (April 1049) found me once again in the field. This time I was leading an army to besiege one of the small peripheral fortresses of Ronda. Rondan tribal raiding parties were using the fortress as a safe haven from which to terrorize a number of Granadian and Malagan villages. Idris III assigned troops to our Granadian forces for this retaliatory mission. The fortress was besieged and bombarded.

After four days of siege activity, I called all my officers to my tent to outline my strategy for a final assault the following day. I had no reason to put my own men at great risk, so I decided to assign the Malagans to be in the forefront of the assault. I took great pains to emphasize the honor that would accrue to them by leading the attack.

"Because of their well-known bravery and fighting skill, I am giving our comrades from Malaga the honor of leading the assault."

The likelihood of harm to the Malagan commanders and soldiers no doubt outweighed their estimates of the potential for honor and loot. After our meeting, the Malagan forces deserted and returned home. No excuse for this perfidy was offered. I was not aware they had departed until I awakened the next morning.

I was upset when my deception failed. I seethed at myself for the miscalculation and decided to walk off my anger. I strayed from the camp, on foot, with only two bodyguards trailing me.

From the parapet of the besieged fortress, the youngest son of the fourth wife of the governor of that Rondan precinct gazed at our camp. He saw me stride out of my tent with two of my bodyguards rushing to catch up. Curious, no doubt, he continued to watch. At some point, he realized the tent must be my mine, as it was the most elaborate in the camp.

Could that be their general, the famous Ha Nagid? he thought. He continued to watch as I, head bent, striding purposely, lost in thought, came closer to the fortress, and further from our camp. The young man was the commander of a company of cavalry. An outrageous thought came to him. He called for the sergeant of one of his platoons, who happened to be just below him, leaning against the wall in the shade.

"Akim, come up here."

The sergeant groaned, then pushed away from the wall, walked the ten paces to the ladder-like stairway, and slowly mounted to the catwalk, joining his commander.

"Yes, ibn Fakir, what is it?"

"You see those three men?"

The younger man pointed at me and the two bodyguards.

"I think the man in front is the generalof the Granadians, maybe even the infamous vizier. Look at the cloak he is wearing and his armor. See how the cuffs of his sleeves glitter in the sunlight? I believe that is gold thread on his sleeves. Look at the color, how the gold shines in the sun compared to the white cloth. I bet you anything that is pure silk. And see the armor under the cloak? Can you see how shiny it is? That is an important man. I want you to get your platoon together with their horses and mine. If that man gets close enough to the fortress, we are going to rush out of the gate and snatch him. Go."

I was still absorbed by my frustration and anger at myself. Before long I was almost within range of an arrow. I looked up and saw where I was. I stood with hands at hips, looking at the fortress until one of my bodyguards shouted.

"Ha Nagid, ten mounted men just rode out and they are coming directly at us, fast. We must flee."

I was much too old to run fast, and the mounted men quickly overtook us. Both bodyguards had their swords unsheathed.They turned to protect me. I had neglected to take any weapons with me when I stormed from my tent. The young commander in the lead leaned over and took off the first guard's sword arm with a sweeping stroke as he thundered past. The next rider severed the same guard's head. The other guard was surrounded by four horsemen and soon dispatched. The commander's horse caught up to me. As he rode past, he grabbed me by the back of my cloak and dragged me up and over the horse's neck, wedging me against the pommel of his saddle. He pressed the point of a knife over my right kidney. I could feel blood oozing from the minor wound.

"I am told that a knife to the kidney is extremely painful. You will keep your balance and remain still. Do not struggle unless you want to feel the knife as it enters your body."

Someone from my camp witnessed the abduction and a shout went up. Men jumped into their saddles, grabbing whatever weapon was closest at hand. A ragged pursuit was launched, but the foray from the fortress wheeled and spurred their horses, heels flailing. As they approached the gate from which they had launched their attack, it groaned open and we galloped inside. The gate slammed closed, pulled by many willing, cheering men.

I was shoved from the horse. Wind-milling my arms to regain balance, I managed to not fall onto my rump in the dirt. I stood straight and tall. My captor dismounted and again grabbed the collar of my cloak.

"Look who I have brought!" he shouted. "Are you the great Ha Nagid?"

"I am Samuel ibn Nagrela," I answered.

The young man's father, governor of the precinct and commander of the fortress, pushed through the crowd of warriors that was pressing ever closer. The pressure from the crowd forced horses against both me and my captor.

"Get these horses out of the way and you men step back!" shouted the governor. "Fakir, who is this you have brought to me?"

"Samuel ibn Nagrela. He is the grandvizier, and general of the Granadian army."

The governor squinted and peered at me through cataract-clouded eyes.

"So, this is him? On your knees, Jew."

"I will not kneel to you, sir. Think for a moment. What am I worth to my caliph alive? If you kill me, all you will reap is the wrath of my army and that of my caliph. You and everything you hold dear will be destroyed. For your own good, I suggest you take the time to consider all the possible ramifications of killing me and hanging my head from the top of that gate, versus making ransom arrangements for my release."

The governor's son pushed his knees into the back of my knees, and I went down, my knees in the dirt. I immediately jumped back up and spun to face the young platoon leader.

"You are a brave young man, but do not think to humble me. You stand to gain much from my ransom, and only a slow death if you do me harm."

The young commander raised his sword over his head but was restrained by the hand of his father.

"No, Fakir, hold your sword. What he says make sense. Take him to the dungeons and lock him up. I have to consider what ransom we will demand."

I don't know why they failed to kill me as soon as they had me. But these men were Berbers. My mention of the huge ransom they could expect to receive for me was too enticing.

My remaining forces, after the Malagan desertion, consisted of four companies, two Mamluk, one Almoravid, one Nubian infantry, and an artillery unit with their machines. The four company commanders and the captain of the artillery unit huddled together even as the enemy platoon reached the gate with me. Before the gate was completely closed, they made the decision to implement the plan I hadoutlined to them the previous evening.

The Nubian colonel insisted his infantry, supported by the Almoravid archers, crossbowmen, and slingers, lead the attack. The artillery needed to concentrate their missiles on the gate through which I had beentaken and open a breach. Within minutes, the siege machines launched a furious and unrelenting bombardment of that gate.

The governor delayed selecting a man to go forth with a white flag to negotiate the ransom demand while he tried to decide how much Badis would realistically pay. As the messenger was opening a small, low, one-person gate to bring the governor's demand, the large gate through which I had been abducted was smashed, and the adjacent wall was breached. The Nubians attacked, forcing their way over the debris and into the fort. The Almoravid archers, crossbowmen, and slingers were close on their heels. The engineers followed and demolished portions of the wall on either side of the original opening, shoving the debris out of the way and enabling the cavalry to rush through. Once the cavalry entered, it took only moments to force the defenders to yield.

My bodyguard and ten Nubian infantrymen rushed into the governor's quarters, pushing their way past the guards who threw their weapons to the floor and sank to their knees.

"Where is our general?"

One guard gestured to a stairway leading to the dungeons in response to the shouted question.

The jailor fumbled with the key until the door was open. The rescuers found me sitting on the filthy floor, my cloak and armor gone. My white linen clothes were already rank and filthy from the accumulated muck in the cell.

I smiled and pushed myself up from the floor.

"Gentlemen, I prayed the noise of battle heralded your arrival. I am pleased to welcome you to this extremely humble abode. I am sorry I cannot move any faster. The ribs on my right side are sore from being bounced against the pommel of my captor's saddle, but I don't think anything is broken. Please lead the way into the sunlight; I am quite weary of these surroundings."

Two of the strongest Nubians supported me, each holding an arm in one hand, the other hand lifting under my armpit as we moved up the steep stairway. I looked back just in time to see one of my bodyguards raising his sword to strike the jailor.

"He is of no consequence. He was as kind to me as the circumstances allowed. Don't kill him."

They took me back to our camp and the warm bath and clean clothes waiting for me. While I cleaned myself, the fortress was sacked. All but a few of the defenders were killed in retaliation for their affront. Putting the life of the grandvizier of Granada at risk could not be tolerated.

Smoldering ruins and dead bodies marked my army's irritation and wrath at the temerity of those who dared to threaten the life of their beloved Ha Nagid. We entered Granada with twenty wagons full of plunder. Ten of those wagons were adorned with the heads of the young commander and those soldiers who snatched me. An eleventh wagon displayedthe severed head, and now totally unseeing eyes, of the young man's father.

When I wascampaigning, I always took along an extra pack mule to carry reference books and writing materials. On this campaign, despite the treachery of the Malagans, my capture, miraculous rescue, and my revenge on my captors, I continued my real life's work, work that I hoped would endure after my death. I was already in my late fifties, but during this campaign I completed the first draft of the *Sefer Hilkhata Gavata*, a compilation and explanation of Jewish law based on the writings found in both the Babylon and Jerusalem Talmuds, along with the written decisions of the most famous of the *Geonim*. Itis certainly my most intellectual book.

The *Gaon* is the head of the Babylonian yeshiva. Whoever occupies that post is generally considered to be the head rabbi of the Diaspora. In the *Hilkhata Gavata,* I also cite the *Midrash* and the *She'iltot of Ahai of Shabka*. After my return, I worked with Joseph to edit and polish this work. When it was completed to my satisfaction, I gave Joseph the responsibility of overseeing the making of copies. Many copies of this book were made and distributed. Its publication established me as an expert on the most complicated aspects of Jewish law. I wasresponsible for engendering requests for my rulings on specific points of law from Jewish communities everywhere. Throughout the Diaspora the name and accomplishments of Samuel Ha Levi ibn Nagrela, Ha Nagid,were becoming legend.

I also returned to Granada from that near fatal campaign with a new poem. In this poem, I praisedAdonai for my rescue, but ignored the love and respect my men demonstrated by their immediate response to rescue me. I regret I did not acknowledge my debt to those men in the poem. Perhaps I will revise the poem to do that. I do know that all of my soldiers benefited financially for their efforts. I kept none of the plunder from that campaign for myself.I distributed everything to the officers and men who rescued me, except of course the caliph's fifth.

Twenty-Two

A SIMPLE FACT accounts for the magnitude of academic study, learning, success at war, and creative productivity that I was able to accomplish. I almost never sleep more than five hours a night. This leaves me with nineteen hours a day to study, learn, plan, work, think, and write all this with the constant strain of palace intrigue. I also had to keep an often drunk and unpredictable master happy. I was truly blessed by Adonai with the ability to focus and concentrate my attention better and more completely than most men. My son Joseph, I am proud to report, never seems to forget anything he has heard, read, or seen.

Because of its importance to all Jews, I should say more about my *Hilkhata Gavata*. I am thinking about this now because this past week I told Joseph to dispatch eleven more copies of the work to my colleagues throughout the Diaspora. More copies are being made for further distribution. In this work I take care to emphasize the six principles I consider to be the basis of belief for all Jews. I expressed thankfulness that Adonai has no beginning and no end. I expressed my gratefulness that resurrection is certain, and that there is an afterlife. I am eternally pleased that Moses gave us the Torah, and that the Torah is truth and perfection. I believe the words of our sages are just, as is their lore. The study of the works of our sages is a pleasure. I think there are rewards in this world, and whatever comes after, for the pure and the just, and that the dead are recompensed for their sins but remembered for the good they do while alive.

After my death I have instructed Joseph to edit and publish three books of my poetry. They will be named *Son of Psalms*, *Son of Proverbs*, and *Son of Ecclesiastes*.

The *Son of Psalms* should include all of my autobiographical poems, 222 of them at last count. Many of these poems are long, over a hundred lines. I told Joseph to include a preface to this book that will provide the historical context for some of the poems. Most, I feel, need no introduction or explanation. Those tell the story of who I was and what I was thinking at the moment they were completed.

The *Son of Proverbs* will be a collection of aphorisms. Many of these are not my original creations, but I often repeat and use them for effect. Sometimes I add editorial improvements to these old sayings.

The *Son of Ecclesiastes* will include over four hundred poems, all of them my original work. Some of the poems should be included in this volume only because they do not fit the categories of the first two volumes. There are poems about solar and lunar eclipses and earthquakes. There are a number of poems that discuss various aspects of aging and death. Not surprisingly, these latter topics come to the forefront of my thinking the longer I live.

Throughout my life, I have been an active correspondent. I regularly exchanged letters with Jewish community leaders, institutions, and scholars wherever they could be found, as well as with dignitaries of other Andalusian, and a few Christian, kingdoms. I corresponded regularly with Jewish scholars living in Kairouan in Tunisia. That city, founded by the Umayyads over four hundred years ago, is still flourishing and is home to a significant Jewish population and some highly respected rabbis.

I also corresponded with scholars in Babylonia, Palestine, Sicily, and in several persecuted Jewish communities throughout Christian Europe. I even sent and received letters from as far away as England and India. When Rabbi Hushiel of Kairouan died, blessed be his memory, I sent requests for a memorial service to be held in his honor in Cordoba, Jaen, and other Jewish communities in Andalusia.

I admired Rabbi Hushiel greatly. I personally organized memorial services for him in Granada and Lucena.

My Jewish identity defines me. From itI derive my own relationship to the will of Adonai, the history of our people, and an appreciation for our prehistory. I have always celebrated the fact that we have our own special language, literature, wisdom, philosophy, laws, morals, and even our own astronomy and mathematics. Since our calendar is based on the phases of the moon, rabbis have to be experts at mathematics and astronomy. This is necessary to establish the proper times and dates of our holidays and holy days. I have mastered those subjects.

In my home our cuisine is kosher, traditionally Jewish. The Shabbat meal is usually *chamin*,a hot stew with beans and other vegetables, often including chunks of lamb. We also often have *pestelas*, a pastry topped with sesame seeds filled with pine nuts, a small bit of meat, and onion. *Sambusak*, a pastry filled with mashed chickpeas, fried onions, and several spices, is regularly served. Everything must be prepared ahead. Those foods destined to be consumed hot are left on the coals of Friday's fire. They simmer slowly until it is time for the dish to be eaten. I mention this now because it is almost time for our Shabbat meal. The aroma of cooking fills my house filtering into my study. My mouth is full of saliva.

When I am at the alcazaba or on a military expedition, it is essential that I undergo a self-induced metamorphosis. It is a requirement of my position as grandvizier to attend, and sometimes host, both social and formal gatherings. At these functions, I become a fully acclimated Berber, a participant in all their vices. Most of these vices are contrary to the teachings of Islam. Some of them ignore the teachings of Moses. I have written many poems praising wine, and its effects, both in Hebrew and Arabic. However, I take special care to warn Joseph about the dangers of overindulgence. I have written poetry praising the beauty of both the young boys and young girls who are servants at these orgies of food and drink. I also write of the children and women who are brought to these functions to entertain the men with other favors. To ameliorate this behavior, I have had many discussions with Joseph about the Torah's strictures against homosexuality and sex outside of marriage. I struggle with my own morality but justify my activities as essential for me to protect my people. Thankfully, as CaliphBadis ages, he is less inclined to these pursuits than he was previously.

My relationship with my wife is as traditionally Jewish as the meals we eat. I do my best to not demonstrate any annoyance with Rebecca, never anger. I do my very best to avoid arguing with her with anyone else present in the room, especially the children. I speak to her always with respect, and on some occasions, when we are alone, with tenderness and love. On occasion I will lay my hand gently on her shoulder as a sign of affection when one or more of the children are with us. I want them to understand that I love their mother.

I remember one evening, about a year after Joseph's marriage, I told him I wanted to give him advice about how to treat his wife. Without saying anything more I handed him a poem, entitled "Advice to a Husband." The poem suggests not to let your wife dominate you and rule you as a husband is supposed to; she is your woman and should not usurp the role of the husband.

I was determined to provide Joseph with all sorts of helpful marital advice that night. After he finished reading the poem, for a second time, he stared at me, not knowing how to respond. Saying nothing, I handed him a second poem whose advice was to not take a woman into your confidence, do nothing to harm or disgrace a friend, and to avoid taking drugs that alter your mind.

I continued my writing by describing how I made an ally of the taifaof Badajoz. Badajoz is a Berber controlled city-state at least eighteen days of hard travel from Granada. It is about two and a half days directly west of Merida, and over ten days northwest of Cordoba. Most importantly to me, and to CalpihBadis, it's only about a week of easy travel north and slightly west of Seville. As our ally, Badajoz providedanother front from which we can attack our enemy.

The king of Badajoz, Muhammad ibn Abd Allah al-Muzaffar, heldthe normal antipathy of all Berbers against the Arabs of Seville. He felt, and understood, the threat of Sevillian hegemony.

Nevertheless, I found it necessary to use all of my diplomatic skills, as well as buying the friendship of several highly placed notables in al-Muzaffar's court, to bring him into our Grand Alliance. Despite my diplomatic successes, I admit I wasstill ambivalent and distrustful of the motives and loyalty of some, if not all, of the allies I hadbrought in.

The Zanhadja and Zenata Berbers wereagain unified, but only for the time being. All proudly flewthe *Amazigh* flag. The design of this flag holds many special meanings to the Berbers. Its blue horizontal stripe represents the Berber tribes who originally lived by the sea; the green stripe represents those Berbers originating from the Rif and Atlas mountain ranges; and the yellow stripe recalls the desert dwellers. The red *Amazigh* symbol in the center of the flag represents the very human yearning for freedom of all peoples, arms open and reaching for the sky. It is sad that the trust and family the flag represents is so easily put aside when the Berber tribes, for whatever reasons, fail to remain unified.

Twenty-Three

BADIS WAS ALONG for the adventure. We led our army out of Granada, our citizens lining the streets and cheering. Once again, we were embarking on a campaign against Seville. This time, my strategy wasfor our attacks to be coordinated from three different directions. Al-Muzaffar, the ruler of Badajoz, agreed to invade Sevillian territory from the north and did so over two weeks previous to our departure. Initially, his army met little resistance. They overran villages and towns, capturing fortresses as they moved south. Their successes garnered much plunder and resulted in a continuous column of wagons returning to Badajoz. Carmona's role was to attack Seville directly from their city's stronghold. My spies reported that they initiated that three days before we left Granada. Badis and I advanced from the southwest, passing south of Antequera and north of Malaga. We contactedMu'tadid's forces just south of Utrera.

The Sevillian commander wasnot much of a strategist. I enticed the Sevillians, their army again almost exclusively composed of cavalry, into a trap. I deployed our troops in small units, apparently separated from support, while I positioned reinforcements carefully hidden from the Sevillians. This induced the Arabs to attack with their typical and now familiar abandon of reason. I took advantage of the Arab propensity to satisfy their urge for honor, their machismo. Their reckless,headlong, attacking behavior reinforcedtheir concept of bravery. The trait wasnot different amongst the Berbers, but the later now recognizedthe success of my strategies. The Arabs charged, oblivious to everything, into my infantry anchored by the Nubians. These stalwarts, after years of experience, training, and success, no longer consideredcharging cavalry anything to be feared.

Once the Arab army was committed to their charge, I ordered my hidden reserves to quickly join the units used as bait. The Nubians formed up as Iinstructed them. They were protected behind their mobile fort of shields, undeterred by the screams of the oncoming horsemen. They aimedtheir long spears, the butts firmly anchored in the ground, at the unprotected undersides of the charging horses. After hitting their marks or shattering their spears, the Nubians used their javelins to devastating effect. They were no less effective when they resorted to their swords. Behind the ranks of infantry, I deployed three rows of archers, crossbowmen, and slingers. The first of these ranks fired their missiles then knelt down to reload while the next rank fired; by the time the third rank fired,the first wasready with their next round. To my great surprise these tactics worked as perfectly as they had previously. The Sevillians learned nothing from their previous defeats. We rained down barrage after barrage on the attacking Sevillian cavalry, inflicting considerable casualties before most of them got close enough to engage our infantry.

The forces clashed. When the enemy was fully engaged, I unleashed my cavalry, still hidden on each flank. By this time the archers, crossbow soldiers, and slingers were able to pick individual targets, their missiles even more effective. Swords flashed, and javelins, arrows, crossbow bolts, grenades, and stones filled the air. Arms were severed, or nearly so. Terrible wounds were made to the face, neck, hands, and legs until torsos were exposed. Then came the killing thrusts. The air was again filled with the noise, and awful smell, of conflict. The entire battle lasted less than an hour and a half.

The Sevillians were overwhelmed. They lost more than half of their army, killed, wounded, or captured. After what was left of the Sevillian forces fled the field, my men gathered the plunder and dispatched those enemy fighters so severely wounded their recovery was doubtful. We moved on to lay siege to the alcazaba of Utrera.

While Badis lounged with his tribal chiefs in his huge pavilion, partaking of only the best of the local wines, I supervised the placement of the siege machines and initiated bombardment of the fortress.

Once I was satisfied with all the arrangements for the siege, I retired to my tent. I had my books to study, poems to write, and correspondence to attend to. Meanwhile the walls of the alcazaba were gradually, but inevitably, weakened, and the water supply of the besieged fortress dwindled. My intellectual pursuits were interrupted by a meeting with a unit of engineers. I gathered them around a map detailing the plan of the alcazaba.

"I want you to tunnel under the section of wall you think is most vulnerable."

One of the officers put a finger on the map.

"This section is starting to crumble already. It appears to be a combination of stone and bricks, but not well integrated."

"Good, let's target that section then. Any questions? No? Good, get on with it and tell me when the powder is set and ready to detonate."

On the road to Utrera the army camped for one night at the ruins of an ancient fortress. I noticed that as I gained in years, I became more retrospective. That particular night I felt depressed and was moved to compose a poem I entitled "I quartered the troops for the night." The poem gave vent to the emotions I experienced thinking about all the people who dwelt, fought, and died in that place. I wondered what happened to the inhabitants of that place, who, by now, are all long dead. What were the lasting effects of their lives, and what, if any, will be mine?

While we were occupied with the siege of Utrera, Carmona, still a loyal ally and the third aspect of my strategic planning, maneuvered ever closer to Seville. The strategy was to use Carmona and Badajoz to draw Mu'tadid's resources away from my front. For a while this strategy worked well. Initially, the army of Badajoz met only token resistance and was able to advance, but Mu'tadid sent reinforcements, led by one of his best generals, and the Sevillians were able to win some confrontations.

Next the wily Mu'tadid played a different card. He still had great influence with the king of Malaga, that same fellow we made the erstwhile caliph of Andalusia. Mu'tadid reminded that false friend that Badis had wanted him dead and convinced him I had tricked him into believing otherwise. He managed to convince Idris III that, if the truth were to be known, Badis and his Jew chiefvizierhad never been his, Idris's, friends. With considerable effort, and the application of appropriate financial incentives, Mu'tadid encouraged Idris III to attack our forces from the rear, a strategy Mu'tadid had used previously when he incited a rear attack by Ronda.

Badis was infuriated by this turnabout. He was the one who made IdrisIII the caliph of Andalusia, even if the title was little more than an honorific. To meet the Malagan threat, and to punish the ungrateful caliph, Badis ordered me to withdraw the army from our siege. He was determined to confront and to crush this newly crowned caliph. Idris III had very little time to gloat over his success at relieving Seville. He fully expectedMu'tadid to attack and trap our army between them.

Mu'tadid cared little, if at all, about the safety or ambitions of Idris III, or indeed of the fate of Malaga. Malaga's rear attack and our response made it possible for him to redistribute what remained of his army to confront Badajoz and Carmona. With overwhelming numbers arrayed against them, both Badajoz and Carmona were forced to abandon the war and return to their respective strongholds.

Idris III was deceived. He fully expected Mu'tadid's support and counted on that support to reclaim at least some of his lost territories. But Mu'tadid achieved his short-term goal. Idris III was still flush with his early victories. Being a Berber, he knewthe Berber nature. He managed to convince himself that although Badis might easily win a few skirmishes, he would stop to allow his troops to pillage and plunder. Badis certainly wanted to follow that scenario, but Imanaged to convince him otherwise.The time had arrived to deal more permanently with the treachery of Malaga and its caliph.

One by one, our army attacked and subdued villages and towns belonging to Malaga. In each conquered location, I was able to identify people I felt could be trusted. Many of these men happened to be Jews. Badis and I installed them in office with the responsibility of representing Granada and administering the conquered territory. Before leaving, we exacted tribute from the conquered peoples. We use those resources to pay our mercenaries and swell Badis's coffers. I also installed tax collectors in each precinct to continue to divert the flow of wealth from Malaga to Granada, providing my caliph's personal fifth of everything collected.

The Malagan kingdom was decimated. The erstwhile caliph of Andalusia was now boxed in and sequestered in the formidable alcazaba of Malaga. That fortress consists of three circuits of defensive walls with over a hundred towers, sited on the top of a mountain overlooking Malaga's port. After less than a month laying siege to his fortress, we discovered that Idris III, the bully, was also a coward. He was not prepared emotionally to withstand a prolonged siege, particularly one that would inevitably end in his death. He sent emissaries to beg Badis for peace and for his life, ceding everything taken from him. I weighed the cost in resources and manpower to continue the siege and convinced Badis that revenge, and the complete absorption of Malaga, wasn't worth the cost of men and resources it would require.

Moreover, I was tired. I was feeling my age. For the last two weeks of the siege I was troubled by a persistent cough that drained me of energy. The rigors of this particular campaign were no more strenuous than any of those preceding, but this time they exhausted me.

Badis, true to his nature, was bored with the siege. He readily agreed with my assessment of the situation, and we returned home with many wagons full of plunder. The economy of Granada was given a huge boost by the infusion of appropriated wealth, and my personal financial situation, if not my physical health, increased significantly. I possessed additional estates and put them in the care of my brother-in-law, Rabbi ben Judah.

One of the estates I acquired from Malaga wason the sea, with a beach only steps away from the main house. After Passover, I took my family with me to visit the property for the first time. It wasone and a half days of easy travel almost directly south of Granada, through the western slopes of the Sierra Nevada's snow-capped peaks. We arrived at the estate, perched on a small plateau, with olive orchards, orange orchards, and vineyards. The vineyards wereon sandy soil and producedan extremely pleasant white wine. From the house, there wasa path down an easy slope to a small beach with fine gray sand.

Rebecca and I stretched out on the warm sand, our shoulders touching, watching our children cavort in the small waves caressing the shore. The warmth of the sand and the soft smell of salt water and marine life soothed us. I decided this place would become our family's seaside retreat.

We entered the winter of 4799 (1050) with Seville still posing a threat. Mu'tadid, despite losing every direct confrontation with our forces, was still able to marshal fighting strength and resources. For the time being, however, we were at peace.

I spent a significant portion of my adult life in service to CaliphBadis. On many occasions, I was able to save the caliph's life by smelling out, unearthing, and quelling plots against him. I enhanced the caliph's position and reputation by making Granada the largest and most powerful taifa in Andalusia. I enabled, and even encouraged, Badis to indulge his every whim, while I concentrated on making certain the caliphate functioned smoothly and was in sound economic shape. I did everything within my considerable power to encourage trade and commerce.

I wanted Joseph to understand that the real strength of Granada is, and will always be, based on strong and reliable financial resources. I know Joseph has no enthusiasm nor talent for war. I doubt he could bring himself to actually kill another human, or in fact even an animal, unless he was starving. That is no doubt a good thing in the eyes of the Lord. I hope he will be able to provide the level of support the kingdom requires from a chiefvizier. I know he is more than capable of being an outstanding financialvizier. I must do everything possible to make certain he fills that role if none other.

I understoodand acknowledgedthat Badis wasa despot. Any hint of disloyalty, even by the most highly placed tribal chief or vizier in his court, was addressed with immediate and often brutal execution, frequently by his own sword. I had tobe constantly on guard and mindful of the possibility of any adverse rumor about me reaching the ears of the caliph. This level of psychological pressure sometimes requiredemotional release. I foundthis release by writing seditious poetry.

One evening while we sat in my study, I handed Joseph a new poem. He read it, looked up at me, then read it again more carefully.

"Papa, this could get you killed."

"Yes, I know, but I must allow these thoughts out. I want you to find a safe and secure place to put this poem; no copies are to be made until after I am long gone. Will you do this for me?"

"Yes, of course, Papa. I have a secret place where I secure sensitive documents. I will add this one."

"Good, now please read it aloud. I may want to edit it."

The poem asked if my caliph made me bitter by criticizing some of my actions, then drew an analogy of me wanting to respond to his criticism by talking about the difficulty in putting together the shards of a broken jug. Joseph and I sat in silence for a time while I considered the words of the four-line poem. The candles in the room flickered. Our shadows on the wall oscillated even though we were both immobile. I finally nodded my head.

"No . . . it is what I want to say."

Iwasoddly tired, so I got up and moved to the couch to lay down. Ihadlost weight in the last couple of months. I knewmy face wasgaunt, my brow permanently furrowed. I rolled to my side on the couch and reached into a deep side pocket of my long brocade cloak. I was forced to kick impatiently in my efforts to free the tangle of the cloak from my legs before extracting two more sheets of folded paper. I held out my hand, extending the papers to Joseph.

"What is this?" heasked.

"More of the same. Read aloud, if you will. They express thoughts you must take to heart. My time is fast approaching, Joseph. These military campaigns take a huge amount of my energy and have now affected my health."

I was overcome by a fit of coughing. Joseph jumped up to come to me, but I waved him back to his chair. I took a slow, deep breath before speaking.

"I'm sorry, Joseph. This cough does not improve. We are approaching the time when you will have to take over for me. It will fall to you to protect our family and our people."

"Nonsense, Papa, you are still strong. You are just overtired. You need to sleep more. If you follow the instructions of your physicians, you will recover your health as you have always done. I pray every day to Adonai that he will help you regain your health and strength so you can continue to protect his people."

I looked into my son's eyes and saw he was seriously concerned about me. Another fit of coughing engulfed my body, jerking me forward with each expulsion of air. The cough produced no phlegm, but I felt as though I was coughing up the tissues of my lungs. I willed myself to stop.

"Read the poems aloud, Joseph."

Joseph unfolded the paper. The five-line poem talked about how a caliph can force you to some action that could prove fatal, then rescue you from the danger he forced you into.

"Papa, this is more dangerous than the first. God forbid the caliph ever sees or even hears about this. We must destroy these poems."

"Yes, Joseph . . . I understand your anxiety." I paused and took four deep breaths. "If as you say, you have a place to keep these well-hidden, nothing will happen. I must be able to rid my mind of these thoughts, and writing them down is the best way for me to accomplish that. Go ahead and read the last one."

Joseph shook his head at my obstinacy then read the third poem aloud. It was another five lines speaking to the volatile nature of the caliph and how he could strike out at his most loyal friend when angered or in a sullen mood. How his moods were like the responses of a spoiled child.

Joseph refolded all three pages of poetry and put them inside his tunic next to the bare skin of his chest, then patted the tunic that concealed them.

"No one must see these. Papa, I will guard them with my life."

I held up my hand, engulfed with another fit of coughing.

"Do you . . . understand why . . . I have shared these thoughts with you, Joseph?"

"Yes, Papa, I understand, and I take these thoughts of yours to heart, as I do all you have taught me."

"Good. If you want, after I am gone, you can add these to your anthologies and distribute them throughout the Diaspora. But only do so if you feel safe from recrimination."

Twenty-Four

WHEN JOSEPH WAS sixteen years old, I sent him across the Mediterranean Sea, then on a long trek through the desert to Kairwan in Tunisia. His education was progressing well, but I thought he needed to be exposed to different ideas, different methods of learning, different thinking. So, I sent him to learn at the yeshiva of Rabbi Nissim. I considered Rabbi Nissim to be one of the most learned rabbis throughout the Diaspora. Rabbi Nissim was also my friend and colleague of many years. Although, at that time, we had never met face-to-face, we conducted an intense correspondence regarding the proper interpretation of passages from the Torah. After Joseph entered his yeshiva, we corresponded frequently about the progress Joseph was making with his studies.

Three years later I received a letter from the rabbi telling me that Joseph was the best student he ever had, and that he hadlearned as much Torah and Talmud as he, Rabbi Nissim, could teach. It is time for Joseph to return to Granada.

"Ha Nagid, both you and I are reaching the end of our years. Joseph is now ready to learn everything else he needs to become your successor. On a happier note, your son has formed a lasting friendship with my daughter, Sarah, and I, with your permission, will offer her to him as his bride."

I, of course, was more than pleased to have our two families united by marriage. I wrote immediately suggesting Rabbi Nissim join Joseph on his journey home and offered him a well-paid position to teach in my yeshiva.

My offer was accepted, and the rabbi agreed the marriage should take place in Granada. Rabbi Nissim, and his entire family, accompanied Joseph on the long sea voyage to Malaga, and from there, by mule-drawn wagons, to Granada.

Soon after their arrival in Granada, the wedding was held, and our two families were joined. To make it easier for everyone, I moved myyeshiva from my house to a much more commodious venue, a house in the Jewish section, and I made a gift of that property to Rabbi Nissim.

Not long after Joseph's wedding, a renowned Arab scholar by the name of Haj Amin el Badr returned to Andalusia from a pilgrimage to Mecca. It seemedhis primary mission in life was to convince Badis to get rid of me as his vizier. Badis refused, as he had refused all previous attempts to force me out of my office. El Badr started preaching in the largest mosque in Granada, hammering at the idea that it is not possible to trust a nonbeliever. He finally managed another audience with Badis, claiming he had a solution to the Jew problem. He proposed to convince me to convert to Islam.

Badis was delighted at the prospect of relieving his boredom by having el Badr and me debate the merits of Judaism versus Islam. He ordered that el Badr and Iconduct an open debate in his throne room, in front of all those nobles who wanted to attend. He made it clear that this would be el Badr's one and only opportunity to convince me to convert. I insisted that Joseph be present and that he be allowed to make careful notes of all that transpired.

We entered the alcazaba through the gate at the foot of a tower. The access to that gate is from a walkway that goes up a slight slope then makes a right-angle turn. That configuration prevents the gate from being seen from outside the walls. We passed through the gate and entered the large inner, closed space,vaulted, with many turns.Openings high on the walls allowed defenders to fire arrows and crossbow bolts. We emerged through an archway into the large courtyard called the Place of Arms. Defenders controlledall access to this courtyard where, during peacetime, troops practice marching and maneuvers. In case of an invasion, any enemy that managed to reach the courtyard could be attacked from the top of the surrounding wall and from the tower. Both of those areas were only accessible via a narrow, steep, and vaulted staircase, easily defended.

The massive stone inner walls werefaced with Granada's brick, red in the bright summer sunlight, dark and ominous in the shadows. We passed through alternate heat and cool, sunlight and shade. Only the sound of our footfalls echoing through the passagewayswas heard. No other people were seen, no other sounds were heard. I smelled orange blossoms but didn't see any orange trees. I smelled spices being toasted but no kitchens or workers were visible.

Leaving the Place of Arms, we walked through a pointed arch embellished with vertically juxtaposed prisms. Next, we entered the Baraka, the blessing hall. This hall was rectangular in shape, about twenty meters long but only slightly over four meters wide, with a high vaulted ceiling. A plain low plinth servedas the foundation for the walls, all of which wererichly decorated with painted plasterworks. At both ends of this hall werealcoves with tiled plinths embellishing the columns that supportedstilted scalloped arches ornamented with highly decorated pendentives. The pendentive is a construction where the curved triangle of vaulting is formed by the intersection of a dome with its supporting arches.

Finally, we entered the throne room through a double arch. The room was already crowded with nobility and administrators. I was aware of the sound of many guttural, hushed voices. The sound seems strange because my earswere, by then, accustomed to the muted sound of our footsteps along our route. I specifically designed this room to create awe, and it does.

The room wasexactly eleven long strides square, but the ceiling soaredfar above our heads. The floor wasbrilliant white marble and wascovered in brightly colored silk and wool rugs. Scattered around the room werepiles of cushions, also covered with ornately decorated silk weavings. Some of the areas on each wall werehung with tapestries, heavy wool rugs with sumptuous colors and intricate designs. Huge ceramic vases decorated with cobalt blue, manganese-black, iron-green, copper-red, tin-white, and lead-yellow designs were scattered around the hall.

Each wall containedthree arches, the center arch being the largest. Each of the eight smaller arches openedto niches through the two-and-a-half-meter thick wall. All the niches extendedthrough the wall and endedas balconies. Both center arches weretwins, with two lattice windows located near the top. The arches, the walls, the niches, the balconies, everything in the room wascovered with decorative inscriptions. These werepoems, or excerpts of famous poems, thatpraisedAllah or the caliph.

In the center of the wall to my left there wasan arch over the platform, covered with huge cushions, thatservedas a throne. The platform wasraised half a meter above the floor, accessed by two steps. It was unoccupied. The arch over the throne platform wasdecorated with a molding framing the opening. The wall behind the platform containeda quote from the Qur'an:

Help me Allah stoner of the devil.

In the name of Allah who is merciful and has mercy.

Be, Allah, with our Lord Mahomet and his generation, accompaniment and salvation.

And say: my help of Allah's rage and of the devil that permits breakage of hell;

And save me from evilness of the jealous when he is jealous

And no other divinity lives than Allah's to who eternally praise

The praise to the Allah of the centuries.

Most of the room wasin dim light. The lack of sunlight madethe room cool on the hottest days, but the latticework on the openings allowedfiltered light into the room. The light from several of the lattices wasfocused on the platform throne. The effect wasto surround the seated caliph in diffused light, which addedto his power and mystery.

Above the arch over the throne platform wasa paneled ceiling embellished with ribbon bow motifs and painted stars. The walls of the room, surrounded by a glazed tile plinth, weredecorated with carvings of a wide variety of fruits and vegetables combined harmoniously with geometrical designs. Scattered on the walls, embedded in the geometric designs, were inscriptions. *There is no victor but Allah* is repeated several times. *Rejoice in good fortune, because Allah helps you. Be sparse in words and you will go in peace.*

These sayings are an elaborate form of propaganda, designed by me, to reflect the power and might of the caliph.

The murmuring of many voices stopped abruptly as Badis entered the room. He wore a turquoise-colored outer silk robe decorated with intricate designs made of gold thread on the collar and cuffs. Under the robe were pants and a shirt of brilliant white silk, and on his head, a silk turban matching the cloak, also decorated with gold thread. Without speaking, he ascended the platform, sat crossed-legged on his cushions, and nodded at el Badr.

Without preliminaries, el Badr started the debate by pointing out that the Qur'an clearly states that Jews are money grabbers.

"How can a money grabber be trusted to control the finances of the kingdom?"

"Highness and notables of the land. Our Holy Torah forbids the charging of interest on loans to our people," I answered.

"But Jew, we are not your people," el Badrsaidwith a laugh.

"Your Highness, I had not finished my answer. Our Holy sages tell us in the Talmud that it is a far worse sin to charge interest or deal falsely with non-Jews." I proceeded to quote from memory the various passages from the Talmud that make this concept clear. I ended my response with the clincher:

"Our rabbis strictly enforce this rule of law, and Haj Amin el Badr has benefitted from this directly. He borrowed the funds necessary to make his recent pilgrimage to Mecca from the money lender, Yehudah. He was not charged interest. I am also told he has not yet paid back all of the borrowed funds."

El Badr seemed confused.

"Your Highness, the Jew has cleverly confused the issue. I request that the debate be halted for today and be resumed tomorrow, allowing me time to verify his statements."

Badis, with a wry smile on his face, nodded his agreement, stood up, and left the room.

The audience of nobles was stunned. They expected something dramatic but had witnessed only an initial salvo.

The following day Joseph and I followed the same route, but I felt something ominous. As we entered, I made my countenance calm, serious, and unworried, no outward signs of nervousness. This time the cacophony from those gathered in the throne room was louder, more intense. Badis entered,dressed in royal blue, and again the audience went silent. Badis did not smile, just waved his left hand at el Badr, who openedthe second day with:

"Is it not written in your Torah that a prophet from your midst will be chosen by God and that you must heed his words? Whom else can this be but Mohammed?"

El Badr continuedto stand, smiling with satisfaction. I got to my feet and straightened to my full height.

"That is a total misinterpretation. Our scholars have pointed out that the Torah says, 'Just as I Moses am from your midst so will our Lord bring forth additional prophets from your midst.' This is the direct quote from the Torah. I submit that your sainted prophet Mohammad did not receive the prophetic tradition in a direct line from the prophets as Moses foretold. He did not come from our midst. Moses was our prophet, and we believe in him because of the miracles he performed leading to our exodus from Egypt, and because he was the one chosen by God to receive the Ten Commandments on Mount Sinai. The Torah also commands that we Jews not add to what is set as law in the Torah, nor delete from it. Your prophet ignored portions of the Torah that contradicted his message, just as the Christians have done. We do not accept any revisions to the Torah."

El Badr sneered, his face reddening as he struggled to contain his anger and frustration. I allowed only a hint of a smile and stood calmly, waiting. Badis smiled broadly, leaned forward, and rested his chin on his left fist as el Badr responded.

"So, Jew, if yours is the true faith, why and how did Islam become the dominant religion of the world? Why does a mosque now stand on the very ground where your temple was? Why have so many Jews converted to Islam?"

Only the sound of many men inhaling deeply was heard. All heads shifted to look at me. The anticipation was palpable. How could the Jew possibly respond to this?

"Islam has spread among the multitudes. I cannot deny that fact. This must have happened because God willed it so. We believe that God wishes that monotheism be spread amongst all nonbelievers so that when the Messiah does arrive, it will be easier for all to accept him. Your Prophet did not accept the Christ as the Messiah, nor do we. We Jews were expelled from our homeland because we sinned against our Lord and his Torah. When we all return to God's commandments and repent, he will restore his people to Zion. This is what we believe."

"This Jew is too clever, Majesty. He has answers for everything. I ask a favor. I have brought with me a former Jew by the name of Abu Sufyan. I ask this man be allowed to debate ibn Nagrela.I think, YourHighness, that it will take one cunning Jew to outdebate another Jew."

"Where is this man?" asked Badis.

A short man in a common wool cloak pushed forward from the back of the room.

"I am Abu Sufyan." Hebowed low to the caliph. "May I speak, Majesty?"

Badis gave permission with a wave of his right hand.

"Your Highness and gathered nobles, when a Jew is faced with death, the Torah instructs that he must convert, because to preserve a life a Jew may ignore any prohibition of the Torah. The only exceptions allowed are that one must die rather than commit murder, lead an amoral life, or worship idols. Islam is not considered idolatryby the Jews, so if you order ibn Nagrela to convert, he is not being ordered to commit murder or compromise morality. He must convert or be put to death."

"Great Caliph," I said, gathering my thoughts, "I am attacked by an apostate Jew who converted rather than be executed for being a thief. I ask that I be allowed to go to my home and pray to our common God for guidance before responding."

Badis agreed.

"We will resume this tomorrow after the noon meal."

As soon as Badis left the throne room, the place erupted with sound.

On the walk home, I was deep in thought. Joseph dared not ask how I planned to respond. Would I risk death by refusing to convert?

All that night I prayed after consulting with Rabbi Nissim. We considered several ways to respond to the argument raised by Abu Sufyan.

Badis spoke to open the proceedings.

"Ibn Nagrela, based on what we heard yesterday, I believe you must accept Islam with a clear conscience, or I will be forced to order your execution."

I stepped forward and spoke directly to the caliph.

"My caliph, the Torah tells us that in times of persecution, we may not abandon Torah to save our lives. It is obvious to me that we Jews are facing a time of persecution."

Abu Sufyan jumped off the cushion he was sitting on.

"There is no truth to that statement," he shouted. "Nobody in Granada is preventing the Jews from practicing their religion. The truth is that the people do not want the right hand of the caliph to have influence over their lives if he is a Jew. They fear he will favor his own people over them."

I turned slowly to face my accuser.

"Even if I agree that you are correct, and also believe that my people will not be persecuted in the near future, I still may not convert. If I accept Islam as my religion, I will be rejecting the Torah. Moses told us the Torah is eternal. There are many passages in the Talmud describing self-sacrifice. How can I do less than Rabbi Akiba or Daniel, who was thrown to the lions?"

Once again, I addressed Badis.

"As Ha Nagid of the Jews, and as your vizier who has always supported YourHighness, my conversion would be an embarrassment and a sin for all generations who follow. Your Highness knows that for the past many years, first for your father and now for you, I have devoted my life, my brain, and all my energy to you and to your caliphate. My guiding principle has always been the best interest of the caliphate. No, YourHighness, I am prepared to die here and now rather than convert."

My heart beat so strongly in my chest I feared those close to me could hear it. I managed, somehow, to keep my face calm, serene, althoughI felt a slight tremble of my lower lip. I prayed to Adonai that nobody else, especially Badis, noticed that tremble.

Badis was immobile, his chin again rested on his left fist. He slowly moved his eyes around the silent room, then stood up and stared at each of the nobles and tribal chiefs in the room until theylooked away.

"Ibn Nagrela, you have convinced me and all of those present." He looked again around the room and held each person's eyes until they nodded agreement. "You have remained true to your people and to your religion, and have answered all of the arguments of your accusers. I have complete faith in you. You have served me and my caliphate well and, I am certain, will continue to do so. I order that Abu Sufyan and Haj Amin el Badr both be imprisoned and locked away to ponder the danger of attacking my most trusted servant."

I smiled with relief.

Two weeks later, I was stronger. I coughed only occasionally and less severely. I asked Joseph to ride with me to attend a sale of mares. As we rode to the alcazaba, I explainedwhy.

"Badis plans to attend this sale. He specifically requested that I join him and bring you along. I don't know why; perhaps we will find out."

We rode up to the alcazaba, where the caliph was waiting for us. We found him sitting calmly on a prancing white stallion. The animal was incapable of standing quiet for even a moment. The three of us, accompanied by a platoon of marching Nubians and ten mounted bodyguards, made our way out of the alcazaba then through the streets of Granada. It was midwinter, the air clear and cold. The sunlight was bright, causing all of us to squint, but its rays did little to warm us. The snow-capped Sierra Nevada sent gusts of cold wind to whip our cloaks and threaten the turbans on our heads. We were headed for the horse farm, only a short distance from the city.

While winding through the streets, we came upon an Arab merchant sitting in the sun, basking in the reflected heat from the brick front of his leather goods shop. As we passed, the man directed a string of vile curses at me. The mildest was "dirty Jew." Without stopping, Badis twisted in his saddle to look at me.

"Say the word, ibn Nagrela, and I will order that scum beheaded this instant."

"No, My Lord, his words mean nothing. Words are incapable of causing me harm. I will take care of this incident, please trust me to do so."

Badis stared hard at me then smiled.

"I understand. I have seen you take retribution, Nagrela, and I know you are capable of swift and violent action. Good . . . people in our positions cannot afford to show weakness. I will trust you to make certain this incident is not repeated."

The whole day Badis said nothing to indicate why he requested that Joseph join us.

Three weeks later, Badis, Joseph, and I, again accompanied by guards, were in a similar procession, this time on our way to a party hosted by one of the tribal chiefs. Badis insisted we pass by that same leather shop. Before turning the corner nearest the shop, Badis reined in his stallion, on this occasion a magnificent black, to a slow, high-stepping walk. As we came abreast of the merchant, again in the sun, again leaning against the brick wall of his shop, the man jumped to his feet and ran alongside my horse, holding on to my right stirrup.

"This man is a saint," he shouted. "A jewel amongst men. Praise Allah Granada has been blessed with so wise and forgiving a grandvizier, and so great a general. And Allah praise our blessed CaliphBadis for the wisdom to honor and promote this man."

Surprised, the caliph turned to me.

"How has this transformation come about, vizier? What did you do to this fool?"

"The wisest of our rabbis tell us the surest way to defeat an enemy is to convert him into a friend," I smile.

"And how did you accomplish this?"

"His young son was very ill. I sent a physician who cured the boy. The man's business was failing, and he was deep in debt. I gave him a no-interest loan. His daughter is of an age to marry. I supplied her with a dowry."

Badis laughed, shook his head, and spurred his stallion forward.

This story has become another legend. Unlike most legends surrounding me, this one is true. Joseph told me that on that day he was very proud to be my son.

Twenty-Five

ON NUMEROUS OCCASIONS CaliphIdris III of Malaga proved to be treacherous and lacking in moral character. He was our ally, but for how long? I was acutely aware that Idris was not a man to be trusted. He wouldcertainly betray Granada the first time it appearedadvantageous for him to do so.

I worried about a multitude of possible threats to the caliphate. One of my constant concerns was the possibility of someone using poison to eliminate me, or even worse in my mind, CaliphBadis. A plot could be promulgated by high-ranking Granadian functionaries, but this was not a huge concern, although vigilance was essential. Poisoning was the most likely method to avoid exposure for any person or persons contemplating such an action. For this reason, I made it known to all the physicians in the city of Granada and its territorial holdings, that if they knewof any new poisonous substances, or if they heardof or developedantidotes to any poisons, I wasto be informed immediately. This morning, a physician from Jaen showed up at our door. I ordered that he be admitted to my study.

After the physician told me why he had come, I sent a servant to tell Joseph to stop whatever he was working on and come immediately to my study. When Joseph arrived, I turned to the physician.

"This is my son, Joseph. Joseph, this is the physician David ben Noah of Jaen. Dr. ben Noah has come to us with interesting information. Please, ben Noah, tell us again about what you have discovered."

"Of course, Ha Nagid. The powder is made from fruit pits—cherries, apples, apricots, any or all of them. The pits are crushed into a fine powder, a very fine powder. When you have a full cup of the powder, you add hot water and, while keeping it warm, stir until the powder is in solution. The water must not boil, however. After the powder is completely dissolved, you spread the liquid in a shallow container and allow it to evaporate. It can be put out in the sunlight to hasten evaporation. The powder that remains after the liquid evaporates is the poison. If the poison is mixed with wine or vinegar, it will emit a gas that is also poisonous."

"And you have some of this powder?" I asked.

"I have it here," said ben Noah. He extracted a small glass container with a cork stopper from the pocket of his cloak and handed the flask to me.

"And what is the antidote for this?"

"There is no known antidote, Ha Nagid."

"No antidote?" I furrowed my brow and rested my chin in my hand, unaware I was imitating Badis until Joseph cleared his throat.

"How fast does it act?"

"That depends on the size of the person and upon the amount consumed or inhaled. One fourth of the powder in the flask you are holding will kill a horse."

"Thank you, ben Noah. I assume you are doing experiments to find an antidote to this poison?"

"Yes, of course, Ha Nagid, but so far none of the antidotes have an effect, even when given to a test animal prior to exposure."

"Well, I want you to continue to work on the antidote." I handed the physician a pouch of gold coins. "This should enable you to continue your research for the antidote. Please keep me informed of your progress on a regular basis. Is there any way to detect this substance so a person wouldbe able to prevent its use?"

"Yes, Ha Nagid, it seems that about one in every three persons can smell it. They are able to detect a faint odor similar to the smell of almonds. It would be wise to have someone with that ability available to smell food or beverage offered by someone you do not know or trust."

"Is it safe to sniff this?"

"Yes, as long as it is still a dry powder."

I removed the cork from the flask and sniffed tentatively at first, then more strongly, then replaced the cork stopper.

"I smell nothing," I said and handed Joseph the flask.

Joseph removed the cork, took a sniff.

"Yes, I smell almonds, it seems to be a bitter scent, but still of almonds."

I smiled broadly.

"From now on, Joseph, you will give the smell test to everything on my plate before I take a bite," I teased.

"Even food my mother prepares?" Joseph responded, serious, worry on his face.

I laughed.

"Especially food prepared by your mother." I reachedover and pattedhis shoulder. "I'm teasing you, Joseph. You take everything so seriously, therefore it amuses me to tease you. Put the flask away in your safe place."

Two weeks later, as we were finishing our evening meeting, I turned to Joseph.

"Before you retire this evening, Joseph, please bring me the flask the physician ben Noah brought to this house."

Joseph looked at me, raised his eyebrows, and waited.

"Never mind, that is all you need to know for now. I have a plan I must discuss with the caliph. Just please bring the flask to me in my study this evening."

"Of course, Papa."

He did as I requested, but even when my son withheld the flask for a moment, with a questioning look on his face, I told him nothing more about what I wanted the poison for. The evening of the following day when I handed the flask back to him, about a third of the powder was gone. Once again Joseph gave me a questioning look.

"Badis agreed to my plan with considerable enthusiasm. He gave me a solid gold wine cup, exquisitely decorated. He also provided a small cask of his very best wine. We are going to send Idris of Malaga the cup and the wine as a special present."

"And the poison that is missing from the flask?"

"That has been dissolved, and all the liquid is being evaporated from the cup. When all is ready, I will send the gifts to Idris as a token of our appreciation for all he has done as our much-valued ally."

"And who will you send to bring him these presents?"

"Our king has suggested Ishak ibn Mohammed, chief of the Bani tribe."

"Ishak ibn Mohammed? Isn't that the same man you told me about a month ago? He has been whispering evil about you."

"Exactly so."

Joseph shook his head.

"And the caliph has approved this plan, and even recommended ibn Mohammed for the task?"

"Yes. This is yet another harsh lesson for you, Joseph. Say nothing. Watch events as they develop. You must observe what people say, and more importantly do, as the plan unfolds."

As he was instructed, ibn Mohammad delivered the gold cup and the cask of wine to Idris III. I heard some time later, from a tribal chief who was present, that ibn Mohammad gave Idris his testimony as to the fine quality of the wine.

He said to Idris:

"I was summoned to CaliphBadis, and he told me he wanted me to bring to you two very special gifts. He handed me the gold cup you now hold in your hand. I think you must agree it is one of the finest, if not the finest, such drinking cup in existence. The decorations are exquisite. My lord, CaliphBadis also gave me a taste of the wine in this cask I'm holding. He told me it is the finest Granada has to offer. I agree, it is the best I have ever tasted."

"Well then," said Idris, extending the giftedgold cup he was examining, "let's have a taste of this jewel of the winemaker's art."

Ibn Mohammad poured some wine into the cup. Idris raised the cup to his lips and sniffed, then sniffed again, inhaling deeply.

"It smells of almonds."

"Yes, Excellency, I have been told as much but could not detect that smell when I was given a taste."

Idris became pensive, perhaps thinking back to his own long history of treachery. He took another, longer and deeper, sniff of the cup and wrinkled his brows. Then held out the cup of wine.

"Ibn Mohammad, I want you to drink from this cup. Tell me if it is the same fine wine you were given prior to coming to me."

"Yes, of course, Excellency, as you wish."

He took a sip of the wine then gazed into the cup.

"Not quite as I remember it but still very good, Excellency."

"Drink the whole cup. We will fill it again, then I will drink."

Ibn Mohammad shrugged and finished off the contents of the cup before handing it back to Idris. Idris took the cup then turned it slowly again in his hand, examining the intricate carvings. He looked inside the cup, then studied ibn Mohammad, who seemed to be getting dizzy. Idris waited . . . unsmiling.

Ibn Mohammad sank to his knees and bent over. He tried to push himself upright again with both arms. He managed to get up on one knee then collapsed, rolled to his right side in the fetal position, and died. Foam came from between his lips. The nobles of Idris'scourt who witnessed this charade rushed to their caliph.

"How did you know?" asked one of them.

"I didn't, but I suspected. This is the work of the Jew, I'm certain of it."

Idris was not aware of the deadly toxic fumes released from the poison by the wine. That afternoon he complained of being weak and short of breath. He seemed confused and kept dozing off. He roused with a start, then exploded into a rage, ranting at a blameless servant for no discernable reason. The next morning, he was slow to awaken and seemed even more confused. His skin was a bright pink. He was breathing very fast, almost panting, while at the same time complaining that he couldn't catch his breath. That afternoon, despite frantic attempts at treatment by his physicians, he was comatose. One of the physicians reported he smelled bitter almonds on his ruler's breath. Late the next morning, he died.

Granada's complete takeover of Malaga was initiated the day after word of Idris'sdeath reached us.

CaliphMu'tadid of Seville was still plotting and planning. He was ready to set in motion his strategy for the coming summer's military campaign. My spies informed me that he would instigate the invasion of Granadian territory by the caliphs of Moron and Arcos. He promised them financial, military, and logistical support. They were to attack Granada in early spring as soon as the weather permitted.

Mu'tadid correctly anticipated that CaliphBadis would respond to the attacks as usual, by retaliating and invading Seville's lands. Once Granada was committed, Mu'tadid arranged for Ronda to attack our forces from the rear. This time he swore he would follow through on his promises. He planned to send two regiments of his army to support Moron and Arcos, and three regiments to support Ronda. He had already sent considerable gold and silver, as well as the promised logistical support in the form of long lines of mule-drawn wagons loaded with provisions, arms, and supplies, to Ronda.

I allowed events to proceed with the assumption that Mu'tadidwould become overconfident and make a mistake. I could take advantage of Mu'tadid's previously tried and proven strategy of getting Granada to commit, then attacking us from the rear. We were soon fighting on two fronts with significant numbers against us on each. Both sides managedto avoid large confrontations, but continuous small encounters occupied the armies. The usual outcome of these skirmishes was that Granada's forces retreated, but we always pulledback disciplined and in good order. During this whole summer, neither side was willing to fight a pitched battle, so neither side suffered devastating losses.

I engineered the strategy of orderly retreat by convincing Badis the combined forces of Seville and her allies outnumbered our forces significantly. I explained that Granada could easily lose an all-in confrontation. Any reinforcement I could send from Granada was likely to be ambushed along the way. The wisest course was to avoid any significant large-scale clash, abandon those territories we lost, and retreat to Granada while conserving ourown resources.We wouldbenefit by sapping the will of Mu'tadid'sallies, who expected quick and easy success. I proposed to use what was left of the fall, and the fast-approaching winter months, to rebuild our strength, remobilize, and be in a position to exact vengeance early the following spring.

Somewhat surprisingly, Mu'tadid seemed content with the outcome of the summer campaign. He recalled most of his troops, leaving only token forces with his allies. What I didn't realize until recentlywas that Mu'tadid's grand strategy had never been a final and extremely dangerous confrontation with Granada. His strategic goal was to expand and consolidate Seville's territories.

Twenty-Six

THE MUSLIM CELEBRATION of the birth of a newborn male is very similar to our Jewish custom. The circumcision ceremony is a great celebration, especially so for a monarch. Mu'tadid's third wife was only fifteen years old when she gave birth to a son. The caliphs of Mu'tadid's erstwhile allies, Moron, Arcos, and Ronda, were all invited to the circumcision. All three rulers arrived on the same day with their entourages. The three processions entered through the main gate into Seville within an hour of each other.

Mu'tadid himself welcomed each of the three when they and their entourage arrived.

"Welcome, brother," he told each. "I am extremely pleased that you came to honor us and celebrate the birth of my newest son. I have recently renovated my sauna, and I suggest that after all three of my caliph allies are here, you relax and freshen up by taking a relaxing steam bath. I am certain you will have much to discuss while you enjoy the facility. I am very proud of the work done on the bath, although, despite my orders to have it completed before your arrival, my stonemasons are still completing some final tasks. If the construction noise disturbs, all you need do is say so to the attendants. The workers will cease their labors immediately."

The three caliphs all readily agreed to the steam bath, looking forward to the relaxation it would provide. Mu'tadid made certain they were supplied with the best his palace had to offer in wine and snacks.

"Take care not to overindulge," he smiled. "This evening there will be a grand banquet, and many delicacies are being prepared, as well as the finest wines my caliphate can produce."

The three paid no notice of the masons working at the entrance to the sauna until one of them noticed that the entrance had been walled shut. Within moments the amount of steam in the room increased, along with the temperature. Their frantic shouts and pleas were not answered.

Nobody could say how long it took for the three to die, but Mu'tadid was in no hurry to check on them. He was too occupied with the murder of their entourages. Not one person, male, female, or child, was left alive. Late the next morning, Mu'tadid had the sauna reopened. He added the parboiled heads of the three kings to the collection of pickled heads he kept in his bedroom.

That same morning Mu'tadid dispatched a regiment of troops to Ronda, where they joined forces with the Sevillian soldiers already stationed there. The Arab population of Ronda immediately joined the Sevillian forces, and the Arabs slaughtered every Berber not wise enough to calculate the odds and flee, including many women and children. The caliph of Ronda had left one of his sons, the heir-apparent to the throne, in charge while he traveledto Seville for the festivities. The young man attempted to escape by rappelling down the cliff on which the alcazaba perched, but the rope slipped loose and he fell to his death.

Arcos was next to be brutally violated and annexed to Seville. The Berber rulers of that city-state, and their followers, were only able to mount a quickly suppressed token resistance. Mu'tadid installed his own people to administer the two taifa he annexed.His generals took command of their remaining armed forces and mercenaries.

When I was first appointed general-in-chief of Granadian forces, I looked forward, with excitement and anticipation, to taking the field each spring for a summer of campaigning. The garnering of more territory and wealth for my caliph and for his caliphate motivated me. It wasa fortuitous incidental that I acquired more wealth and honor for myself and my people.

In 1054 I celebrated my sixty-first birthday quietly, at home. I noticed large, persistent, dark, puffy bags under both of my eyes. My beard and hair, both long and gray, had become thin and wispy. My shoulders, once square and proud, slumped forward. When at work at my desk, I had to hunch forward, squinting and peering to see the words I wrote or read. I believed I had shrunk at least three centimeters in height. When I strapped on my armor and took up my weapons, I struggled under their weight.

The spring of 1054, Badis stayed home. He was drinking heavily and amusing himself with untold numbers of new additions to his harem. My health improved and I took our forces to unite with the armies of Carmona and Moron. The previous winter, I worked diligently to bring more of the Berber kingdoms into our grand alliance. Those that did not join the alliance seemed to believe Mu'tadid's takeover of Ronda and Arcos was unrelated to them and that the current raids into the territories of Carmona and Moron were only the normal activity of stealing sheep and horses. They didn't think the raids were anything more nefarious. I was frustrated. It did not enter their consciousness that Mu'tadid's true intent was to build an empire.

I was able to unite and integrate our forces with the troops and officers sent by our allies, Carmona and Moron. Those two caliphs fully understood the threat. I was able to deploy my Zanhadja troops, along with our mercenaries and my Zenata allies, with enough skill to engage Mu'tadid's various raiding parties in many small-scale skirmishes. In each instance I made certain I always had the preponderance of numbers. Thus, my troops were successful in all these confrontations. With the help of our allies, we drove the Sevillian forces out of most of the provinces of Carmona and Moron and returned those territories to the rule of their original Berber families.

Mu'tadid seemed content with his minimal gains. He didn't exercise a plan to take over Moron or Carmona, assuming he had such a plan. I was successful by making certain that two of his former

Berber allies wouldbe unlikely to change sides when next offered the choice. They werein our debt.

Before I embarked on this campaign, Joseph selected those servants who most valued and cared about me to accompany me during the campaign. I did not interfere when I overheard him instructing those loyal people.

"You must make certain that every possible creature comfort is provided for Ha Nagid. Aside from the obvious challenges and dangers of fighting battles, he will have to endure the added stress of exposure to the elements. I know campaigning often requires long days of travel under trying and dangerous conditions. I expect you to make every effort to see that he rests frequently and does not overtire himself. If he does, he will be more likely to become ill. Make certain he eats a balanced diet, with plenty of vegetables, and drinks more water than he does wine. I am relying on you to bring him home in good health."

However, during the campaign, my health deteriorated. First, I suffered from recurring boils. Next, I contracted an upper respiratory infection that initially responded to treatment then reoccurred three separate times. Most recently I wasconfined to my mattress on the floor of my tent, suffering from a fever so severe it induced a bout of delirium. My physicians feared I was dying and sentfor Joseph. After three days and two nights of hard riding, changing horses every ten kilometers, Joseph reached my encampment to find me sitting on a rug on the floor of my tent,writing a poem at my campaign desk.

Even when bedridden, I am compelled to work. I am afflicted with the inability to turn off my mind. Even when dreaming, I am mulling over a problem of diplomacy, palace intrigue, military strategy, the solution of a complex Talmudic question, or how to best express a poetic thought. I especially love to compose acrostics, the first letter of each line forming a word or phrase. I am particularly enamored of the *muwashat*, the girdle poem, with a two-line opening girdle followed by the first strophe rhyming three times, and the second strophe also rhymingthree times but encircled by the first opening girdle. The difficulty of expressing an idea or concept while finding Hebrew or Arabic words or expressions to fit this complex poetic structure is exactly the kind of mental gymnastics that most appealto me.

I apologize to the reader of this account who is not interested in, or familiar with, the exacting rules of poetic expression. They were drummed into me from an early age. Joseph, I am sad to say, can correctly identify the various poetic structures in mine, or the poetry of others, but he lacks the knack of composing his own poems, at least poems that have real merit. He seems to be satisfied with making copies of my efforts and the work of other poets that he admires.

Joseph stayed with me for the remainder of the campaign. I was almost fully recovered when we received intelligence that Mu'tadid's forces had feigned retreat but circled around and raided north of Malaga. His troops were causing havoc in some of the new Granadian territories we had taken from Malaga. I wanted to send Joseph home, but he convinced me that although he wasno warrior, he could be of service. He wanted to make certain I waswell cared for and did not suffer a relapse. I relented, allowing him to stay with me so he was able to witness me, the general, in action.

The Sevillian generals were still reluctant to engage in any pitched battles. They were specifically instructed to follow this tactic by Mu'tadid. Mu'tadidwas no fool. He recognized my skill and reputation as a fighter. Our scouting parties, backed with light cavalry, mounted archers, and slingers, fought a series of skirmishes while pushing Mu'tadid's forces back into Sevillian territory. I followed with the rest of my army to take possession of the towns, villages, and fortresses. Most offered only token resistance.

I enjoyed myself. The physical challenges of being in the field made me stronger. One day we were following a small unit that had dispersed after a short encounter. They retreated to the village of Ard-Allah, the land of Allah, known as Ardales in the common language of the Andalusians. The white-washed houses of the village huggedthe base of a huge rock on top of which wasperched a small alcazaba that provided protection to the soldiers we were chasing.

We occupied the village. After questioning several of the villagers, I was able to identify the most respected man.

"What is your name, sir?"

"Mohammed, Excellency."

"Well, Mohammed, you are to go up to the alcazaba and tell the defenders that if they do not surrender before tomorrow morning, the village will be torn down, the inhabitants will be taken as slaves to Granada, and the alcazaba will be bombarded, continuously, until they surrender or are starved out. Any survivors will also be enslaved. If they give up, they will be disarmed but set free, and the still intact village will enjoy the protection of Granada."

The defenders of the fortress followed my emissary back down the mountain and surrendered their arms. I kept my word. None of the soldiers were harmed and the village was spared. We didreprovisionmy army from the stores in the alcazaba, from the homes in the village, and from surrounding fields and pastures.

That same evening, I started coughing again. Joseph allowed into my tent only those officers we could fully trust to not disclose I was ill. I gave orders that the army needed to rest and refurbish itsarms. During the next five days, I gradually recovered and stopped coughing.We continued our march toward Seville.

The plunder was good, and I extracted tribute as we moved through Sevillian territory. Our army and our allies were happy to be gaining wealth with relatively little effort and practically no danger.

Two days later my coughing resumed. I wasnot able to shake the remnants of whatever respiratory infection had inflicted itself on me. The coughing sapped my strength and resolve. I deemedour retaliation against Mu'tadid sufficient, so I turned my army south then east to reoccupy Malaga. There was no opposition as we entered the city and took back the alcazaba. I installed people loyal to Badis to administer Malaga. The leaders of Malaga were humiliated, left devoid of power, their treachery avenged. We returned to Granada before Rosh Hashanah anticipating a peaceful fall and winter and an opportunity for me to rest and recover my strength and health.

When campaigning I worried first and foremost about the wellbeing of my troops. I was responsible for the welfare and supply of the thousands of men who depended on my attention to detail. I had to make certain I provided everything my soldiers needed in the field and on the march. Adding to all this, I had to deal with the arbitrary moods and desires of a capricious caliph.

Joseph and I were again together in my study.

"Joseph, I am so very happy you have no aptitude nor skill as a general. It has been my curse. You will be able to function well as a grandvizier, but I am pleased you will not become a general. It is too difficult."

I was tired, bone-weary tired. Again, I was ill with a severe cough and fever. I took to my bed. A parade of physicians came, administered their remedies, and departed. After four weeks, I regained strength, but only after my Rebecca sat with me and spoon-fed me bowl after bowl of rich chicken soup, her remedy for all ailments. After I was able to get up and move around on my own, I resumed all of my normal activities, including daily training with my sword. After just five or so minutes of exercise, however, the cough returned and I had to stop, catch my breath, and rest before resuming. After watching this display of my continued weakness, Joseph pulled me aside, out of the hearing of servants and my sword instructor.

"Papa, I am very worried about you. You must know how weak and ill you still are. If you were to go into a battle where you have to defend yourself, you wouldsurely be killed. You have generals. You educated and trained them. Please, allow them to take over for you. They can protect Badis and his caliphate. Each morning when I come to you, the bags under your eyes grow larger, your shoulders slump more, your posture gets worse. Please, it is enough."

One aspect of Mu'tadid's conquest of Ronda troubled me. I harbored no good feelings for the Rondan hierarchy, but the manner in which the kingdom was brought down was troubling. All of the Berber-controlled taifas, including Granada, werehome to significant populations of Arabs. These populations thoughtof themselves as a persecuted minority. At least the Arab intellectuals with whom I communicateddidfeel somewhat persecuted. Mu'tadid's successful takeover of Berber governments was significantly aided by an immediate revolt of the Arab populations residing in that place. They opened the gates of Ronda's alcazaba to Mu'tadid's forces and, once Mu'tadid's forces gained control, the Arabs killed every Berber they could find. This fact was even more troubling to Badis than it was to me. Granada's population included significant numbers of Arabs.

I was called to the alcazaba. I took Joseph with me. I knew Badis was, as usual, drinking steadily, although his tolerance washuge. We were ushered into his presence. He was slumped on his cushions, his eyelids half closed. When we were announced, he put aside his cup, roused himself, sat upright, and dismissed everyone else in the room. When the room was clear, with no slurring of speech and considerable glee, he revealed a plan he had concocted on his own.

"You know the problem, Nagrela. In every city and town of the Zanhadja, there is a fifth column of enemies and schemers who live, and I don't need to tell you that they live well, under our protection. But they resent us nonetheless. They pose a significant problem, as we have seen with what happened in Ronda. I have a brilliant solution. On a certain Friday, I will make it known that I will review and inspect all the troops you leave to garrison Granada. This will allay any suspicions about the reason for so many armed soldiers walking the streets. The devout and responsible Arabs will all be at prayer in the mosques. I will have the soldiers block all of the exits then send in units to kill those Arabs trapped within. What do you think, Nagrela, a brilliant plan, no? I will execute this plan while you are gone campaigning so no one can blame you."

"Ah, great Caliph. It is indeed a brilliant solution to the possibility that our Arab citizens, although they have always supported YourMajesty, will rise against us if the opportunity presents itself."

I was buying time, frantically trying to think of some way to dissuade Badis from killing a significant number of loyal Granadian citizens. I knew thatif Badis carried out his scheme, he would surely convert a host of Arab families into resolute enemies thirsting for revenge.

"I have not heard any rumors that our Arab citizens would contemplate a rebellion of this sort, despite what happened in Ronda," I temporized. "You know I have many spies who report anything of this nature to me immediately. Do you have any reason to believe those Arab friends who attended the gathering you hosted last week would even consider such an action?"

"You speak nonsense, Nagrela. Arabs have butchered Berbers for centuries. Many times, this has happened when to all appearances Arabs and Berbers were living together in peace."

Badis stared at me, then at Joseph. He set his mouth with the commissures of his lips pulled down. He squinted his eyes.

"Do I detect that you are in opposition to this plan, Nagrela? Do I have to worry about your loyalty? Do you propose to defend the Arabs who have always been the enemies of the Zanhadja? Can I no longer trust you?"

"Please, Majesty. I am now, and will always be, your loyal servant. I think only of the possible long-term effects of an action of this magnitude. Granada already has plenty of enemies. I have always counseled you to destroy any rebellion instantly and completely. I will never abandon that position. I cannot help but think, however, that the action you propose should be carefully thought through and all ramifications be considered. This, I think, is essential for the security of your caliphate."

Badis reached back with his right hand. A servant immediately placed a cup of wine in his hand and retreated back, out of sight. He took a slow drink from the cup, peering at me over the rim. I had not been aware of the hovering servant. I raised my eyebrows.

"Don't concern yourself, Nagrela, this man is quite deaf. He overheard nothing. This solution is one I have arrived at without your counsel. I understand you are uneasy about that fact. However, it is a good solution to the problem we have of harboring potential enemies in our midst. I do not want to hear any more of your whimpering. I will give the orders so this will happen. Do not interfere or you will regret it."

All was said with a calm voice and measured, distinct words. Then he staggered to his feet and shouted, his words slurred together; I could not decide if from wine or anger.

"Do you hear me, vizier, or do you no longer wish to be vizier? Possibly you want to join forces with your oh so intellectual Arab friends?"

I raised both arms over my head.

"Your Majesty knows what is best for his caliphate. You have my unquestioned loyalty and support for whatever you do, Highness. I am certain you have given the matter much thought. I do not presume to second-guess you."

The Berbers, as I have repeatedly mentioned, are mostly uneducated and crude. They came from a warrior tradition that made them outstanding fighters. They resented urbane, educated Arabs and felt uncomfortable when in the presence of those intellectual discussions that the Arabs love. This discomfort fed their memory of every slight, treachery, injury, double cross, and death any Berber had ever suffered at the hands of an Arab throughout their detailed and minutely remembered history.

"I should think not. You and your son are dismissed. I do not want to hear any more of your reservations," Badis interrupted my thoughts.

"Of course, Majesty."

I motioned for Joseph to follow me through the doorway. We both backed away. It is the worst kind of offense to turn one's back on any caliph, but especially Badis. I once witnessed the flogging he administered to one of his tribal chiefs who made that mistake. From beneath my lowered eyelids, I saw Badis sway and fall back onto the cushions that constitutedhis throne. He shook his head, trying to clear it, then slid around on his backside to find a more comfortable position in the nest of embroidered silk brocade pillows. He held out his wine cup to be refilled.The same servant who had been quietly hovering behind the curtain in back of the platform again materialized and poured more wine into the cup, then retreated to his post.

When we were safely away from the palace and walking home, I took Joseph's arm and pulled him close so I could whisper in his ear.

"We must come up with a way to warn the Arab community. It is imperative that we not leave any evidence that the warning came from our house. Start thinking, Joseph. How can we accomplish this?"

I was scheduled to leave with a small detachment to deal with a group of marauding Berbers who invaded from the north to steal horses and sheep. Joseph and I presumedBadis's plan would be put in motion soon after I left. Badis wasnot the kind of person who could or would wait to do something once he made up his mind. He wasunlikely to forget something as basic to his personality as the hatred, the feelings of inferiority, and the envy he harbored for Arabs.

Joseph and I were again in my study.

I was in my chair, leaning forward, both elbows on my desk, holding my head. My turban lay on the floor where I caused it to fall. Wisps of gray hair protrudedfrom between my fingers. I wastroubled and wantedJoseph to understand the magnitude of my depression.

"Have you come up with a solution, a way to warn our Arab friends?" I asked.

"No, I have not . . . but if we warn them and Badis finds out, he will likely murder both of us. Even if he allows me to live, only because he considers me insignificant, he will strip the family of our wealth. He might take retribution on the whole Jewish community. I believe his prejudice against Jews is only slightly less than he directs at the Arabs."

"That is true, Joseph, but to murder most, if not all, of the Arab population of Granada without reason would be a terrible act, an immoral act. It is the very type of act expressly forbidden by the Torah. We must do something to prevent it from happening. Badis must be saved from himself. This is an ill-conceived idea hatched from a brain befuddled by wine. The Badis I thought I knew is too shrewd to concoct such a terrible thing. It is his overindulgence of wine talking. Are you still friends with the son of Abu Ishak ibn Talib? I seem to remember that the two of you were close as youngsters."

"Yes."

"We must warn him of what Badis plans. When you and ibn Ishak were children, did you not create a cipher to send secret messages back and forth?"

"We did."

"Do you think ibn Ishak will remember the cipher?"

"Yes, it was quite simple. I think he will."

"You must let him know what the caliphplans, butuse your cipher. Do not meet him in person. It will be a disaster if someone witnesses a meeting. I have a man I can trust to deliver the message. You must instruct your friend to make it appear that the Arab community suspects something is wrong when they see so many armed soldiers on the morning of their Shabbat. They must express skepticism of the excuse of a troop review. They can give this as the reason they avoid the mosques. I will also plant rumors amongst the garrison troops so the Arab soldiers get wind of the plan and warn their families."

"We will not be able to save them all, Papa. The most devout will not fail to go to the mosques to pray."

"No, some will certainly be murdered, but we must do what we can despite the risk to ourselves. Adonai demands it. There is no excuse for us to allow the murder of innocent people when we have the power and the obligation to prevent it."

Joseph did as I asked. He put the details of the plot, and my suggestions of what to do, into a cipher message. I prayed to Adonaithat his childhood friend would recognize the game and be able to decode the message, warn his own father, and spread word throughout the Arab community. They neededto pay close attention to any increase in the numbers of armed soldiers on the streets on any Sabbath day. We didnot know when Badis wouldset his plan in motion. They neededto question the soldiers about why they wereso numerous and why they weremoving about the city with full armor and weapons. This wouldgive credence to the idea that the Arab population had a premonition that something bad was about to happen. It wouldexplain their apprehension about congregating in their mosques in the usual numbers.

The cipher message to Joseph's friend, and the spread of rumor among the garrison troops, accomplished most of what we hoped for. However, more than a few Arabs ignored or didn't believe the warnings. Two weeks after I left Granada,Badis's troops closed off the mosques that were only partially filled with worshiping Arabs, along with a few devout Berbers. Inside, his mercenaries attacked with sword and knife. The screams of the slaughtered were heard throughout the city. It took weeks to clean the floors and walls of the mosques before anyone returned to listen to the few remaining imamsand to pray. Badis was furious that his brilliant plan did not produce the complete annihilation of the Arab population. Some of the survivors were brought in for questioning; some were tortured. Although he might have had suspicions, he did not find evidence to associate the failure of his plan to me or to Joseph.

Twenty-Seven

THE WINTER OF 1056 I was tired, tired of living, tired of campaigning, tired of fighting, tired of being responsible for correcting Badis's poor judgment and failings, tired of the responsibility of protecting and advancing the lives of the Jewish people. It was fortunate that I no longer had to deal with the machinations and plotting of so many of my historic enemies. Yaddair was dead, as were Boluggin, Zuhair, Ibn Abbas, and the caliphs of Carmona and Ronda. Mu'tadid was ineffective. His behavior was more and more erratic, more and more crazy. He was also in failing physical health.

I focused my thinking, and therefore my poetry, on the physical afflictions of advancing age and the inevitability of death. My health was a major preoccupation. I was ready to leave the corridors of power. Each day I turned over to Joseph additional duties, responsibilities, worries, and tasks. Joseph would and could assume the role I chose for him.

One good thing did happen this winter. Yacob ben Rabbihi came to our front gate and begged to talk to me. Rabbihi was one of my favorite students, but he plagiarized an obscure piece of commentary in an analysis he wrote as an assignment. I, of course, recognized the copied passage as soon as I read it. My response was predictable, final, and required. I expelled the plagiarist from the yeshiva. On the cold day he arrived, I sent Joseph to the gate to ascertain what the man wanted.

"Joseph, thank you for speaking to me."

"Yacob, what is it that you want to talk to Ha Nagid about? He has no wish to see you."

"I understand, Joseph, but I have been wandering Andalusia since I did that one unforgivable deed. Now I have accomplished something I pray will allow Ha Nagid to forgive me."

"What?"

"Before I fell from grace, I was privileged to copy small sections of Ha Nagid's work that he titled *Minor Kobelet*."

"Yes, that manuscript was lost in the ambush by Abu Nun when Father had to escape into the river."

"I know, but a year ago I met the man who recovered that manuscript. He represented it to me as his own work. I told him I was very interested in the subject and begged him to allow me to study it. He agreed but would only allow me to access it in his presence. Each day I would memorize a section of the text, then I would write down what I had memorized when alone in the evening. It took me over a month to transcribe the entire manuscript."

He reached inside a pouch attached to the belt around his waist and extracted a sheaf of papers. He held them out to Joseph. He took them, examined them, and immediately recognized my phrasing and Yacob's calligraphy.

"Your calligraphy skills are still intact, Yacob."

"It was for those skills that Ha Nagid first accepted me as a student."

"Well, I'm certain he will want to examine this. Follow me."

Joseph brought him to my study but instructed him to wait outside the doorway while he told me the story and showed me the papers. I looked at them for several moments then nodded. I read more slowly, while alternating smiling, nodding, and frowning. I was conflicted.

"Yes, Joseph, this is it. So, the prodigal has returned and offers this gift in hopes of forgiveness?"

"Yes, he told me as much."

"All right, bring him in."

Yacob entered the study. I stood up from my desk, took two steps forward, and embraced him.

"Yacob, you have returned to me a work I thought was lost forever. If you will forgive my harsh response to your mistake, I will accept you back into my yeshiva. Your first assignment will be the task of making ten copies of this work."

"Thank you, Nagid, it is more than what I dreamed or hoped for. You will never have cause to doubt me or regret this decision."

Joseph told me later he was very surprised at my reaction.

"The father I know is quick to anger, unforgiving, vengeful, and holds grudges, sometimes beyond reason. Perhaps your advanced age has caused you to mellow," he teased.

"My joy at being reunited with a work I had thought lost forever is obvious. That is what induced me to give Yacob ben Rabbihi a second chance."

"This is the first time I ever knew you to grant even the most remorseful person a second chance," observed Joseph.

As I said previously, most of the enemies of Granada, and thereforemyself, were no longer a factor in my life, nor cause for concern. They were removed from the scene either by the natural course of events or as a result of my machinations. Even Mu'tadid, the rumors and spy reports told us, was on his deathbed. We have to await his successor to see what new threat, if any, will come from Seville.

My friends are secure. The Jewish communities of Granada and those in all of our territories are protected and thriving economically. I not only protected them, but I gave a significant portion of my annual income to support the poor of both the Jewish and Arab-Berber communities. I still considered the Jews a community of people chosen by Adonai to demonstrate to the world how to live moral, honest, caring, and useful lives. Over many years I encouraged and supported many poets and philosophers, both Jews and Gentiles. Most of them have thrived. My literary, philological, and religious books are read and held in highest esteem by people I respect and honor. I sometimes resent those whodislike my work and make their feelings public in their writings. In the case of my long dispute with Jonah ibn Jannah, there is an undercurrent of mutual respect and camaraderie. I actually enjoy my ongoing war of words with ibn Jannah, even the vitriol between us. He gets my juices flowing and makes my brain strive to answer his arguments.

Jonah ibnJannah and I grew up together in Cordoba. We shared some of the same teachers, but not all. As youths we both loved to debate,especially to debate each other. But the outcome of our debates rarely resulted in a clear winner. We both fled Cordoba about the same time and for the same reasons.Ibn Jannah wandered through Andalusia for several years before finally settling in Saragossa in the north. He makes his living as a physician and is, by all accounts, a very good one.

Unlike me, ibn Jannah has little talent for writing poetry and has not published any. The major thrust of his published works is concerned with philology. He feels strongly that "scripture can only be understood by the aid of philology."He repeats that statement many times in his various writings.

One of ibn Jannah's earliest books was titled *The Book of Criticism*. In this book, he made a vicious, and I felt, disrespectful, attack on one of my most beloved teachers, Rabbi Judah ben David Hayyudi.

After the publication of his critique of Rabbi Hayyudi, ibn Jannah welcomed into his home a man who happenedto be a mutual friend of ours. This common friend delivered a manuscript, written by me, that criticized Jannah's critique of Rabbi Hayyudi. Jannah replied to this by authoring another book, *The Book of Repute*. I countered with *The Epistles of the Companions*. The publication of *The Epistles* resulted in two more responses from ibn Jannah:*The Book of Sharing* and *The Book of Minute Research*. The last book was one of the earliest books written about Hebrew philology. In these works, Jannah slanderously identified me as an oaf, a freak, an idiot, and even a stammerer. During his career, ibn Jannah published six major works; a third of them were direct attacks on me.

Some of my responses to these attacks were published, but most were just delivered to ibn Jannah as written rebuttal. I think both of us were spurred on by the other to think and write more creatively. I believe each of us draws some measure of pleasure from our war of words. As a result of these exchanges, ibn Jannah will no doubt be remembered as one of the greatest Hebrew philologists of all time. I once told Joseph, "Joseph, ibn Jannah is now and will be long remembered for his knowledge and exposition of Hebrew grammar, usage, and the complex meaning of Hebrew words."

One of my protégés became well-known during my lifetime. I believe the fame his poetry achieved will live on through many generations. Solomon ben Yehuda ibn Gabirol was born in 1021 in Malaga. Ibn Gabirol was writing accomplished poetry by the time he was sixteen years old. He wrote and published some very important poems when he was only nineteen.

Unfortunately, ibn Gabirol was short and rotund, somewhat misshapen. He was also unhappily afflicted with dermal tuberculosis. That disease resulted in boils and an ugly, scarred face, as well as scarring on his arms, legs, and body. He mentions some of his deformities in his poetry. His mother died in 1045, and ibn Gabirol subsequently moved to Granada. I was familiar with his work and recognized his genius, so I sponsored and supported him for a time.

For two years ibn Gabirol lived in my household writing secular verse that frequently revealed his anger and his thwarted ambition. His stay with us ended after he insulted me. I have never spoken of what he wrote, not even to Joseph. I asked him to leave, and he did so. While he was with us, he also wrote several *piyyutim*, liturgical poems. Many of those *piyyutim*, and ones he authored after leaving our household, are included in *siddurim*, the prayer books used during our religious services. While in my house he also started work on a philosophical book that became a masterpiece. It isentitled *The Fountain of Life*.

After he left our house, ibn Gabirol claimed, in one of his poems, to have written twenty books on philosophical, linguistic, scientific, and religious topics. There is no doubt in my mind that his liturgical poetry will survive in our prayer books for centuries; they are brilliant.

Early each spring we invariably receive intelligence of an uprising, an invasion, raiding, or some sort of incident that demandsa military response. These crises require that I put on my armor and depart on a campaign. Sometimes circumstances dictate a large army, sometimes just a token force. In the spring of 1056, word arrived that in Linares, a town north of Jaen, one of my tax collectors had been murdered. One of the Zenata Berber tribes was responsible for the murder, and the same tribe was raiding the nearby villages of Carboneros and La Carolina. This was not a new scenario. It is often repeated, in different places, by different perpetrators, but it is not something that can be tolerated.

"You are fully capable of dealing with things here in Granada, Joseph. I will take a small force, maybe two companies of light cavalry, one of heavy, two units of mounted archers and slingers, and two units of infantry, and go deal with these rebels. Take care to keep our caliph happy while I'm gone."

"Of course, Papa, but there is no need for you to lead the force in person. You have more than one general capable of accomplishing the task."

"No, I must do this myself. The man who was murdered was a friend of long standing, Shlomo ben Yitzhak. Everyone knew he was my man, so this is meant to be a challenge to my authority. I will deal with it."

Colonel Samuel ben Yehuda, a Jew,commandeda company of heavy cavalry. He was another of Joseph's childhood friends. Ben Yehuda wasa full two meters tall, heavily muscled, and hadproven to be very brave and resourceful in battle. His men knewhe wasalways solicitous of their wellbeing but determined to do whatever wasnecessary to be victorious. He wasdestined to be a general. Joseph called on him in his home.

"I am worried about Ha Nagid," Joseph told him. "He is acting more and more like an old man, but he insists this most recent policing action is personal for him. I'm afraid he is planning to do something foolish. I think he intends to personally fight if the opportunity presents itself. Last night, I watched as he sharpened the blades of his sword and knives. He was reciting some of King David's poems as he worked. He inspected his own armor, and that of his horse, and contracted for the repair of some very minor weaknesses in the chaining. He is too old to be engaging in combat."

"Do not worry, Joseph. I will glue myself to his side. If there is any fighting, I will protect him. I know this Zenata Chief. He is a blowhard. If and when he sees our forces, he will either run to the mountains or surrender. In either case, he will beg your father for forgiveness with some lame excuse for what he has done."

"Thank you, Samuel. I will count on you to keep Ha Nagid safe. Also, please watch to make certain he does not tire himself and become ill again. He is not nearly asstrong as he once was."

"Of course. Please do not worry. I will make certain he returns home in better shape than when we leave. Time in the field, in the open air, will rejuvenate him."

We were gone for a little over two months and returned to Granada with only two wounded. I felt stronger and healthier than I had been for four years.

Colonel ben Yehuda and Joseph were strolling along a favorite path next to the river the day after we returned home. The day was clear, a few white clouds scuttling across the late morning sky. On that stretch of river, the water flows gently, and Joseph stopped to watch as a leaf got trapped in an eddy next to the bank.

"My father appears to be in much better health than when you left. He told me last night everything went well."

"Yes, being outside in the fresh air, and the healthy exercise, agreed with him. I don't know how he does it. After travelingall day, he stayed up almost all night studying his books or writing. Every day he sent a messenger loaded with documents to deliver back here to you, or to the palace, or to send on their way to the Diaspora. One or two messengers caught up with us with their dispatches every day. How many rabbis and officials do you think he communicates with?"

"I can't keep a count. The last time I tried to make a list, it was well over two dozen."

"He's a remarkable man, but I must tell you he gave me a huge scare."

"What did he do?"

"After two weeks, our scouts located their camp. We managed to get within a kilometer before they knew we were coming. They reacted quickly, grabbed what they could, armed themselves, and scrambled to saddle their horses and flee. Your father ordered me to attack immediately, then spurred his stallion, drawing his sword as he galloped toward the camp. I shouted to my captains to attack and gave chase, just managing to catch up to him as he encountered one of the rebels."

"I thought you were going to keep him out of danger."

"I'm sorry. I never expected him to rush in as he did. He was possessed. He was laughing as he shouted a prayer to God. I couldn't understand all of what he was shouting. He crashed into the first man he encountered, knocking him off his horse and slashing the man's sword arm. Then he jerked his horse to the side, attempting to engage a group of three. I managed to get between him and them, joined by six of my men. We wounded and captured ten and killed three before they scattered into the mountains. This happened in the foothills north of Navas de Tolosa. I split up our forces and we pursued their small bands, but only managed to find and capture another dozen before the rest of them crossed over into Castile-La Mancha. Ha Nagid didn't want to invade Christian territory with an armed force, so we turned back and spent time in La Carolina, Carboneros, El Altico, and Guarromain before going to Linares.

"In each of those places, your father held council with my officers and me. We selected two, sometime three platoons, with a lieutenant in charge. They were left as a garrison to prevent further raids. He also met with the leaders of each community and appointed new administrators to replace those killed by the rebels."

Joseph and Colonel ben Yehuda continued walking until they reached a bench under an overhanging weeping willow tree. Joseph nodded at the bench and they sat.

"Tell me more about my father's actions."

"We left two companies to garrison Linares, and your father made certain there was a fast response system in place with remount stations. He ordered that messengers must be able to get a fresh horse every ten kilometers, or less. He insisted that we be able to respond quickly to any future attacks or raiding parties. He also summoned my brother David to bring his family to Linares and assume a joint position as tax collector and subgovernor of the northern territories. He will report to the governor of Jaen province. All of this took the better part of a month in Linares alone."

"Do you think your brother will do well there?"

"He seems quite happy with the opportunity, although I think he will miss the interaction with family and the Jewish community here. Time will tell."

"His financial situation will certainly improve."

"Indeed."

* * *

Late that same fall, I again became ill and depressed. I rarely left my bed, not even to go to my study. I was content to lay propped up with many cushions while I read. I wasdisinclined to occupy my time with composing poetry. This morning Joseph sat at my bedside going over the tasks for the day. I handed him two folded sheets of paper.

"Keep these but do not read them until I am gone. I doubt I will last through this winter."

My complexion waspasty, my breathing labored. My right handshookslightly, and I had tohold it with my left hand to keep it steady. This morning I started coughing and was unable to speak for some minutes before I coughed up phlegm and clots of blood into a square of soft cotton cloth. Joseph took the fabric from me and handed me a clean cloth from a stack on the table next to my bed. I nodded thanks.

"This is not good, Papa. I am sending for your physicians. There must be something they can do."

"All three of them will be here this afternoon, Joseph, I agreed to that when they were here two days ago. They are giving me treatments for the congestion in my chest, but they tell me much of the pus is accumulating in my lungs. There is nothing to be done more than inhaling the steam fromthe eucalyptus oil that they treat me with."

"I will bring in some other physicians. They will have other treatments to try."

"No, Joseph, they will want to bleed me and do other invasive things to my old body. I am tired, and you are ready to take over. No more physicians, no more treatments. I have lived a long life, more years than I deserve. God has been my protector and my champion. It's enough."

* * *

Three weeks after that conversation, my father died in his sleep. The entire Jewish population of Granada and representatives from all of the communities capable of arriving within twenty-four hours of the news of his death attended his burial. The caliph came, bringing his entire family, including several concubines. All of the government officials and administrators, all of the generals and colonels of the army attended. We buried him in a plain, white cotton shroud in the Jewish cemetery just outside the Elvira gate to the city. Memorial services honoring him were conducted in every town with an organized Jewish community throughout Andalusia and in many other communities throughout the Diaspora.

All of the Jews who attended his burial wore white cotton cloaks, which they tore during the *keriah*. The family and visitors to our home crowded the meeting room and jammed the courtyard for each of the mandated seven days of the daily *Shiva* service. On the eighth day, alone and lonely in his study, I unfolded the two sheets of paper he gave me just before dying.

The first said:

I have not always been faithful to the one with whom you were conceived. Badis gave me a young Jewish maiden whom I loved in a way completely different from the way I loved your mother. For ten years I loved her, and then she died from the same pox that took your sister from us. This is a poem I wrote for her.

The poem brought tears to my eyes. It is too personal to share with anyone. The second sheet of paper held his final instructions to me.

When you deal with the caliph, you must use all of the wisdom and experience that the two of us together brought to him. You must convince him that all the ideas he embraces are, in actuality, his own. The largest threat to our Jewish community is disunity. I charge you with the responsibility and obligation to do everything necessary to protect our people and keep them united. When I am gone, dear Joseph, my son, you must take extraordinary care to avoid any action that might corrode your relationship with the caliph or with the Jewish community.

Twenty-Eight

THIS MORNING I received the following communication from the caliph:

My Dear Joseph ben Ishma'il ibn Nagrela,

Allow me again to offer condolences for the death of your beloved father. I believe I feel his loss as much as you. However, life goes on, and I require your services.

You will report to the palace tomorrow morning three hours after dawn to receive your official appointment as chief vizier and finance vizier. I know you have been fulfilling the duties of these offices for some time now, while under the supervision of the most revered and lamented Samuel ibn Nagrela, Ha Nagid.

Be prompt. You may bring along members of your immediate family to witness the ceremony if you wish.

It was signed, Badis, caliph.

* * *

Four years ago, my father died. It is hard to believe he has been dead that long. Last year we also lost my uncle, my mother's brother, Rabbi ben Judah. It was he who managed the family properties for so many years. His heart, weak for some time, stopped while he was sleeping. This has put additional family responsibilities on me and forced me to consider a serious consolidation of the family's resources. My brother Elyasaf is only eleven years old, eighteen years my junior. He is too young to assume the daily oversight of the family's resources, so I have that additional responsibility.

I sold all of our most distant properties and invested the capital from those sales in various business opportunities here in Granada. I offered David ben Abraham ownership of the two Ecija farms at a fair price with no down payment and no interest loans, to be paid off over time. He is very pleased. Three of the other properties were sold to the same managers who worked them profitably for many years, on equally generous terms.

My relationship with CaliphBadis is considerably more formal than the one my father had with him. Officially I am still his chief vizier as well as financial vizier, and he does listen when I have something he considers significant to contribute. I have not been able to maintain the numbers nor the reliability of the spy network my father constructed, but the information I do have access to regarding the actions and intentions of potential enemies is still significant. Some rivals for the caliph's ear are making inroads. I still have a strong hold on the finances of the kingdom, and Badis seems pleased with everything I continue to accomplish in that regard. The economy continues to grow, the treasury is adequate to meet all needs and his whims, and we maintain a strong military capable of responding to almost any threat.

I am happy to not be involved in the military adventures of the caliphate. Badis has at his disposal capable generals of proven ability who were educated and trained by my father. They conduct his military adventures for him. My father made it clear to Badis that I had no talent nor inclination to be a warrior. The caliph no longer takes the field himself. He is still much addicted to his cup.

Although I have considerable influence in the Jewish community of Granada, I am not able to exert the level of control over the ethical attitudes and practices that my father was. During the last three years, the economic situation continued to improve and the number of people moving into Granada multiplied. With the influx of population, many Jews have also arrived, with resources. They search out opportunities to invest capital in our robust economy. Some of these individuals have been loaning money at interest, to grow their capital. There has also been a large increase in the Arab and Berber populations, and this has attracted imams of less tolerant beliefs.

The result is inevitable. Borrowers default and lenders look for legal, and sometimes extralegal, activities to recoup their capital. The result is hard feelings, hard words, and an increase in anti-Jewish rhetoric and incidents. Last month, gangs of men beat up two Jews in the street, in broad daylight.Onlookers failed to intervene. Both of the men attacked were money lenders. I appealed to Badis, and he appointed one of his Zanhadja tribal chiefs to investigate, but there doesn't seem to have been a serious attempt to identify the perpetrators or bring them to justice. If this situation persists, I will be hard pressed to suggest a solution.

This morning I had a conversation with Amar, an Arab with whom I have been friends since we were children.

"My friend, I think something is happening that you need to be aware of," Amar said.

"Yes, what is it?"

"Last week I attended services at the new mosque built two streets away from my house, you know it?"

"Yes."

"The imam preached a sermon with the same old arguments about Infidels having power over True Believers. He did not name you, but it was clear from what he said that he is not happy that any of his followers are paying taxes to a Jew, or that one particular Jew has great power and influence in this taifa, as well as being very wealthy himself."

"This is a problem my father had to face all his life. I cannot respond to this imam's words, but perhaps I can make it known that if his words incite his followers to action, there will be consequences."

"What kind of consequences, and how would you prove he was responsible?"

"Ah, that is the problem I wrestle with, Amar. Thank you for telling me, though. I have always been thankful you are my friend."

My brother Elyasaf is making good progress in his studies. The whole family is looking forward to his barmitzvah. For his age, he is already a Talmudic scholar of significant accomplishment. He expresses much more interest in the Torah and Talmud than in government service. My son Azeriah is still much too young to start grooming for anything. I'm far from certain Elyasaf is interested in taking on the life's work my father chose for me.

My mother's health is still good, although she is now showing her age. I did not realize until recently how close she had been to her brother, ben Judah. I also long for his calm and steady personality and the efficiency with which he managed the family's wealth. This year we are in a drought, and the three farm properties we still own are all going to show a loss. I clearly remember my father discussing the uncertainty of agriculture. This year there was a general downturn in the economy, and the losses from the farms is more problematic because our other sources of income are also down. I am told that although the harvest will be much less than usual, the grape crop will likely result in a very high-quality wine, but that will not be realized for several years.

The caliph seems more and more remote. Following the example set by his father, Haddus, he has refused to name a successor from amongst his seven legal sons or the untold number of sons of concubines. The tribal chiefs are beginning to align themselves with the pretenders, and it seems clear that a civil war is in the offing when he dies, unless I can do something to prevent it. I have gone to Badis and told him of my concerns. I can repeat his responses verbatim:

"So, vizier, tell me which of my sons you are certain will make the best caliph, and once he is named, what will prevent him from getting rid of me to hasten his rise to power?"

"I'm afraid I haven't had the opportunity to get to know any of them well enough to make a choice, Sire."

"Well, their mothers are always nagging me to make a choice, inevitably each's eldest. I don't know any of them well enough to choose and prefer the company of my concubines to any of my wives. I consider the lot of them, mothers and sons, a pain in the ass. All the sons are spoiled by their mothers and ignorant of what a caliph's responsibilities and duties are."

"Do you think it might be wise to separate a few of them from their mothers and start grooming them for responsibility? Perhaps that would be a way you can identify those with the necessary level of ability. Have you talked with their teachers about their progress?"

"I have not. That would be an excellent task for you, Joseph. I hereby authorize you to hold discussions with their teachers and assess their learning, willingness to learn, and aptitude. Perhaps you can even develop an opinion. You can tell me about which of the worthies you would be willing to serve after I'm gone. Good idea. You do that,vizier, and report back to me in a month. Dismissed."

So, I have maneuvered myself into another task. I am to make recommendations about the successor to my caliph. The only possible way for this to turn out well is that one of the princeswill be so far superior to his brothers that the choice will be obvious. That is most unlikely to happen, but it's the only scenario I can think of that is likely to gain the support of the tribal chiefs, not to mention the caliph. I have, I fear, made the overall situation worse, especially for myself. My father would never have allowed himself to be trapped inthis position.

I spent the first days of my most recent assignment interviewing the tutors and former tutors of six of Badis's seven legal sons. The seventh is only four years old. Three of his sons are now in their twenties, and the reports concerning their intellectual achievements, filtered for the realities of life that their tutors live with, indicate the three are average, at best. All three we recently appointed as aides to different generals.

I summoned each of the teachers and generals to meet with me in my formal office in the alcazaba. This was not a good choice of a place to meet. Palaces have many ears, and nothing said in confidence is ever held secret for long.

I decided to invite, one at a time, the generals and the tutors of the three oldest sons to dine with me in my home. The results of these private conversations armed me with an improved idea about each of the three sons. All are laudatory about the achievements and character of their charges, but as I evaluate their expressions and body language, I am certain they are hiding their true opinions. Not at all surprising. None of the three sons is without serious flaws in hischaracter, but neither is my caliph.

I was summoned again into the caliph's presence. He wanted to learn the results of my inquiries. As much as I hoped for it, he did not forget my assignment.

"So, Joseph, what have you discovered? Whom do you want to be your next caliph?"

"As I am certain you are aware, Majesty, since nothing escapes your notice, I have limited serious consideration to your three eldest, Abu, Mohammad, and Abdallah. If you wish, I can investigate the qualifications of your younger sons, and perhaps you also have nephews whom you consider contenders. I generally believe it unwise to rush into anything, as you well know. My suggestion would be to assign each of your sons, and possibly some of your nephews, to work in the offices of your various viziers on a rotating basis. This will give all of us the opportunity to make an evaluation of their relative merits and suitability to be rulers."

"You prevaricate as much as me, Joseph. However, I like the idea. I plan to live at least another ten or twelve years, so we have time. I will order it."

I returned to my official office greatly relieved. Another crisis at least temporarily averted.

Twenty-Nine

SEVERAL JEWS WERE attacked in the streets this month. The frequency of attacks seems to be increasing, along with the severity, but so far nobody has been arrested. This morning, during my meeting with the caliph, I suggested he appoint someone new to lead the investigation. The Zanhadja chief in charge of investigating the attacks has yet to identify any perpetrators.

"Don't try my patience, Joseph. Concentrate on the duties for which you are responsible. None of your people have been killed, have they?"

"Does an innocent need to be killed before we put a stop to these attacks, Majesty?"

"Never mind. The people are angry. I rely on you, as I did on your father. You have my full support. You need to know, however, more and more people plead for me to rid myself and the caliphate of you. I ignore these strident voices. We both pay a price for my loyalty to you and to the memory of your father. A significant number of our population need a scapegoat to blame for their problems, especially now with the economy struggling. The Jews have historically been scapegoats. Why should now be any different? In any case, it is impossible for me to put a stop to it. Those wholend money at interest must know they will be resented; do you not agree? I know your father did not allow that practice."

"I am powerless to stop it, Majesty."

"I realize that, Joseph. For now, we must live with these attacks as best we can and pray nobody dies as a result. How goes the collection of taxes this month? The salaries of the mercenaries will be due in nine days. Will we have the necessary funds?"

"Yes, Majesty, there is enough in the treasury to cover those expenses for the next three months."

"Good. Anything else we need to discuss?"

"No, YourHighness."

I bowed my way out and retreated without turning my back to the caliph. I moved through the courtyard of an adjoining building then into the rooms that house my official offices. I passed through the waiting room ignoring the three supplicants hoping to gain my attention. I entered my outer office and closed the door behind me. Three clerks were busy writing. They all glanced up, saw it was me, and resumed their tasks. The fourth person in the room jumped to his feet. He was a full two inches taller than me, of light complexion, with strikingly blue-green eyes and light brown hair. His expression was inquisitive. This young man, Prince Abdallah, was in his early twenties. He was currently spending time in my offices learning, I hope, the intricacies of managing the caliph's finances as well as the twists and turns of diplomacy.

"Good morning,Vizier. May I have some time this morning to speak with you?"

"Of course, Prince Abdallah, please come in and have a seat."

He followed me into my office and closed the door after entering. I held out my arm, indicating the chair across from my desk. I remainedstanding until he was seated.

"What can I help you with?" I asked.

"I was wondering about the background of the large stack of documents relating to our current relationships with the caliph of Carmona. You gave them to me to read two days ago. I know some of the history we have with that taifa,but if I am to understand the realities of our relationship, I need more information."

I smiled inwardly. This young fellow actually shows some promise. He is interested in history, more than I could say about the other twoprincesI am evaluating for Badis. The other two lackcuriosity and demonstrateno initiative. They performthe tasks set for them without enthusiasm or interest. They are, fundamentally, uninterested in the details and importance of diplomacy, even less in financial record keeping.

"Good, Your Majesty. I am pleased you are interested in the history of our relationships with the other taifas. They have been and are complicated. The relationships depend a great deal on the personalities and aspirations of the rulers, their families, and the personalities and agendasof those whosurround them. I will instruct my secretary, Yacob, to give you full access to all our documents relating to any of the taifasyou develop an interest in. After you read the written records, please come to me and we will discuss your impressions and conclusions. I will be happy to address any questions you may have. I encourage you to write down questions as you go through the materials. I will do my best to answer them. As you know, I have, since I was quite young, been privy to my father's dealings with other countries, and I am happy to share with you any insights I have."

"Thank you, Vizier. I also have some questions about the rationale for the methods you use to collect taxes, and the reasoning behind your insistence on meticulous record keeping. Why is it necessary to know who paid an amount, when, and the method of payment? But that can wait, I suppose."

"Yes, let's defer the economics discussion until you have satisfied your curiosity about historical issues. Do you resent the bookkeeping tasks I have assigned, or do you understand my rationale for insisting you do that rather boring job?"

"The recordkeeping is quite tedious, Vizier, but I know if I am to understand the various systems you use, I must involve myself in the actual chores of keeping the records. I see there is no other way to learn the systems. So, no, I don't resent the work."

"Good. I am extremely pleased you see the benefits of learning the systems by working with them." I stood. "Come, I will accompany you to the library and have Yacob show you the filing system we use so you can find the documents either by the taifa with whom the events took place, the date when the records were made, or the names of the principals with whom we negotiated."

This one, at least, shows promise. I will keep close watch on his progress in the office and his activities away from the office.

I spent the rest of the day reviewing documents relating to our ongoing negotiations with three other taifas. I also talked to several men with information about various ongoing investigations and projects. I checkedthe current status of our state resources and the logistics of delivering payment to our troops. Finally, I gaveinstructions to bring in the three petitioners who hadbeen waiting impatiently in my anteroom, one at a time, in the order of their arrival. They hadbreathed the air in my waiting room long enough. The first two voicedheartfelt pleas to reduce their taxes. The first man I interviewedmadea good case for the downturn in his situation and finances, with supporting documentation.I grantedhim a reprieve. The second man lackeda convincing argument and wasdenied. Another enemy made.

The third man wasAbu Ishak, an Arab from Elvira. He washoping, because of his learning and recognition as a scholar and intellectual, to obtain a position at court. I knewhe made a direct appeal to Caliph Badis, in writing, but hadnot received a response, not even an acknowledgement of his request. His goal wasto gain me as an advocate. He triedto impress me with his intellectual credits and accomplishments. He wasoverbearing and strident. After a half hour, I managedto get rid of him with a vague promise to mention him to the caliph at my first opportunity.

Today wasa good day. I thank God for it. I spentthe morning with the students in my yeshiva, our discussion of Talmud uplifting. Most of my students are actively involved and thinking. They think in innovative and creative ways, about both the obvious and the hidden meanings of the words. My heart soars; my brain smiles.

Granada has been calm the last few months. The number of incidents of Jews being attacked on the streets has diminished. The army was deployed three times to answer occasional raids by Arab and Berber tribes with no hope or thought of conquest. We have been able to reduce the numbers of employed mercenaries, since the threat of war with our neighbors has lessened. The economy of the caliphate is in the process of recovering. Tax revenues are up as a result. I cope, on a daily basis, with the details of keeping our complex government and economy operating smoothly. I am fortunate in being able to recruit bright, intelligent assistants who are willing to take on responsibility and reduce my workload.

Lately I meet with the caliph only once a week, unless there is something that specifically requires his approval or attention. He seems content with this arrangement. I am told his drinking has slacked, and although he partakes every day, he is less often incapacitated.

Prince Abdallah finished his apprenticeship in my offices but still shows up on a regular basis to inhabit the library, poringover historical documents. Lately he requested access to current documents dealing with ongoing negotiations and intrigues. Occasionally he comes to me with specific questions or asks for some background information. I do my best to give him what he asks for and more, when possible.

Prince Abdallah is also spending time honing his warrior and command skills while serving as an aid to General Abu ibn Mohammad. I invited the generalto my home,and over a leisurely dinner I managed to extract the information that he is pleased with Abdallah's progress and grasp of military tactics and strategy. General ibn Mohammadwas one of my father's favorites. He understands, and puts into practice, all my father taught him.

"Vizier, I honor the memory of Ha Nagid when I am frank and honest with you. I believe Prince Abdallah should be named successor to our caliph. However, my opinion and fervent wishes must be limited to you. For obvious political reasons, I cannot afford to promote any one prince over another."

"I fully understand. I have the same issues."

"As you know, we recently returned from an excursion to put down a minor insurrection in a small town near Jaen. The princeconducted himself with considerable bravery and skill. He clearly has won the admiration and loyalty of the troops he commands."

Whenever the opportunity presents, I mention Abdallah's progress and aptitude to Badis. He takes the information in but does not indicate interest or pleasure. I never press the issue.

Abu Ishak of Elvira has become more and more of a pest. After asking for my frank opinion of the man, Badis refuses to grant him an audience. Abu Ishak has taken up permanent residence in the city. He is being supported by several wealthy Arabs as an intellectual and teacher. He also serves as tutor to the children of several of the Berber tribal chiefs who have never been thrilled with the fact that my father, and now I, had greater power than they do. Abu Ishak speaks out against me whenever the opportunity arises. Based on the reports I receive about his activities,he seems to be quite eloquent as well as insidious.

Thirty

THIS MONTH IS historic for Granada. Badis officially named Prince Abdallah as his successor. I am pleased and relieved. Prince Abdallah continues to come to me with questions and to ask for guidance as he grooms himself to assume responsibility for the caliphate. I am vindicated.

I am not yet thirty years old. Unfortunately, I feel more and more like an old man. I sneeze often during the day and night; my nose runs almost constantly; I have fits of coughing. I have trouble sleeping because of this annoying illness, and the result is that I am easily distracted. My father's physicians, now mine, tell me there is nothing seriously wrong with my health. They say because I have no fever, I haveno infection. They claim the symptoms I exhibit are a result of pollen from flowering trees and shrubs.

"Ha Nagid suffered from the same cause each year at this time," they all explain, and I must agree.

The incidents of anti-Jewish rhetoric and physical attacks are increasing again, and I am frustrated. Every attempt I make to lessen these outrages proves ineffective.

My inability to affectchange in the Jewish community is also frustrating. I do not have the influence over the community that my father enjoyed. Actually, he demanded that influence and received it. Most of the Jews in Granada who enjoy some measure of authority were given their positions and power by my father. They feel little allegiance or loyalty to me. My proposed solutionsto lessen the anti-Jewish attacks by encouraging stricter adherence to the Torah, particularly with reference to the lending of money for gain, are met with derision. I have spent considerable effort trying to convince the money lenders to stop charging interest, or at least to charge only minimally. They ignore my logic despite the danger to themselves.

Badis is still content to leave all the details of operating the government in my hands. The demands on my time, and the complicated decisions that must be made, weigh heavily on me. I often wonder how my father managed to do this job so successfully for so long. I feel inadequate, and now, with my uncle gone, there is nobody with whom I can let off frustration by talking through the problems I am struggling with. I know I served that purpose for my father. My son Azeriah is too young to understand. My wife Sarah, bless her, is a woman concerned only with problems women face.

A few weeks ago, I was desperate. I tried to unburden myself by sharing some of my concerns with Sarah. I know she is intelligent and capable of analyzing. I sometimes talk with her about the various interpretations of the intellectuals about points raised in the Talmud. She learned much about these matters from her father, my teacher. She is not ignorant and far from stupid. This morning I tried again. She stared at me, her face shrouded. She seems unable to understand what I want or need.

We sat in silence, our knees touching. The lavender scent she uses in her hair assaulted my olfactory senses, causing me to sneeze repeatedly. I sniffed and fumbled for the piece of linen in my pocket that I use to wipe my nose.

"I don't know what it is you want me to do or say, Joseph. Your nose is running."

* * *

The situation for Jews in Granada is deteriorating. Badis assigned bodyguards for me, one unit of infantry to guard my home day and night. Another unit accompanies me back and forth to the alcazaba. Theincreased level of anti-Jewish sentiment appears to have been incited by the writings of the troublemaker, Abu Ishak. He is determined. He never ceases in his efforts to castigate me and my people. A copy of his most recent effort was brought to me by one of my clerks this morning. It reads:

> *Do not consider it a breach of faith to kill them, the breach of faith would be to let them carry on.*
>
> *They have violated our covenant with them, so how can you be held guilty against the violators?*
>
> *How can they have any pact when we are obscure and they are prominent?*
>
> *Now we are humble, beside them, as if we were wrong and they were right!*

This morning on my way to my offices, a crowd of people followed us, shouting for the soldiers to leave me so they could give the dirty Jew what he deserves. Fortunately, the soldiers ignoredthe taunts and didtheir job. However, they are stoic; I cannot determine if they harbor the same feelings of resentment toward me or not.

* * *

The general situation worsens, but I was not harassed on the way to the alcazaba this morning, a departure from what happened all last week. Nonetheless, I could hear the shouting and screams of pain from the direction of the Jewish quarter of the city. My bodyguards hustled me along while glancing nervously over their shoulders. I wasunable to determine if they, the guards, weremore concerned for my safety or for the danger to themselves.

As soon as I entered my offices in the alcazaba, my guards all disappeared. I called out to my clerks.

"Go see if I can have an audience with the caliph."

The clerk who did so returned within a few minutes.

"I am sorry, Vizier. The caliph is away, at one of his horse farms. He is not expected to return for several days."

I sent my apprehensive clerks out to discern which, if any, generals were in the alcazaba. They all returned to report none of the generals were expected to be at the palace today. Then I sent word requesting that the commander of the alcazaba guard to come to my office.

After about twenty minutes, the man sauntered in. He is a man I know well, the chief of the Lambuni Zanhadja tribe. His name is Yahya ibn Umar al-Lambuni. He and I have crossed verbal swords on several occasions. I know he speaks ill of me to Caliph Badis.

"*Salem al echem*, sir," I greeted him.

"*Salem al echem*, Vizier. What can I do for you this morning?"

"I am wondering what the situation is in the Jewish quarter, and what, if anything, you are doing to gain control of the situation. On my way in this morning, it was obvious rioting is occurring and people are being injured."

"I was not aware there is a situation in the Jewish quarter, Vizier. Do you have specific information about what is happening?"

"Nothing specific. I know that the mood of the population of Granada is increasingly anti-Jewish. This morning on the way to the palace, I could clearly hear evidence of unrest and violence emanating from the Jewish quarter."

"Really . . . I am not aware of this. I will send some people to investigate. However, perhaps your people have brought this on themselves with their superior attitude and stiff-necked insistence on exercising power and control over my people."

I did not respond but stared at him, waiting.

"Oh, very well, I will look into this for you, Vizier, and see what can be done."

"Thank you, Yahya ibn Umar."

He stared at me for a moment then turned and left, but not in a great hurry. Forty minutes later I could hear a crowd approaching the building. Somehow, they had gained entrance into the alcazaba and were gathering outside our building. Soon the shouting began:

"Kill the Jew, kill all Jews." The chant was repeated over and over, gaining in strength and volume.

* * *

As I write this, I'm sitting at my desk, my clerks are huddled on the floor of my private office. Outside the office, the sounds of a confrontation are clearly heard. A strong voice with a Nubian accent orders the crowd to disperse. There is angry shouting interrupted by the rhythmic thumping of swords against shields and the sound of marching leather-soled sandals on the pavement.There is the cacophony of shouted commands, screamed invectives,and dull thuds as objects, clubs and perhaps swords, strike shields, helmets, and unprotected body parts. There is a scream as someone iswounded, then fading shouts from the crowd as they retreat.

The door to the outer office opens, and I hear the Nubian commander order the door shut and barricaded. Then a knocking at the closed door to my office.

"Vizier, it is Captain Appou ibn Naojil. I served your father, Ha Nagid. Do you remember me?"

"Yes, Captain, I remember you very well. Please come in, I am very happy you have arrived."

A tall ebony man opens the door, his glittering white teeth seem to burst from his mouth in a wide smile.

"I have only twelve men with me, but we are resolute. We will defend you and your clerks for all you, and your father, have done for us. The situation is not good. The mob outside is huge, and it will be impossible for us to force our way through it to bring you to safety. Unfortunately, some of the Berber soldiers are joining the rioters. We will do the best we can."

"I understand, Appou ibn Naojil, and I am extremely grateful for your support."

* * *

Today is 9 Tevet 4816 (December 1066). I have done my best to fill Ha Nagid's shoes for ten years. As I write this, a mob numbering hundreds is storming my offices in the alcazaba. Captain Appou ibn Naojil and his twelve Nubian infantrymen cut and slash, fighting valiantly. The mob presses ever forward. They step on and jump over their wounded and slain comrades. They force my Nubian defenders back and gain entry to my outer office. They take advantage of the close quarters. Many infuriated men are jammed into the small space. The Nubians, despite their skill, training, and discipline, are unable to maneuver and fight with efficiency. They are smothered by the overwhelming number of men who are crazed by the wounding and death of their comrades. They keep pressing into the office, slipping on the blood and bodies of the slain, but pressing, pressing forward until the last Nubian is unconscious, or dead, on the floor. The blood of my defenders is mixed with the blood and severed body parts of the mob.

I followed the instructions of Appou ibn Naojil and barricaded myself and my clerks in my private office. There are no more sounds of fighting. I hear shouted instructions to rip out the doorjamb of my outer office.It is being used as a battering ram.

I stand in front of my desk. My clerks cower on the floor behind the desk. I hold the sword given to me by Appou ibn Naojil in my right hand and a dull ceremonial knife in my left. I am driven by fear, frustration, and rage as I stab and slash.

I repeat over and over again, in Hebrew:

"Blessed are you, our God, King of the universe. Make me as strong as Sampson."

Epilogue

JOSEPH MANAGED TO inflict superficial wounds on three attackers, but using clubs and weapons taken from the fallen Nubians, they beat him to the floor and continued striking him until he was unconscious.

They drug him into the courtyard, where three beams from the now destroyed outer office were fashioned into a large tripod, the ends of all three beams resting on the pavement stones. Two of the beams formed an X-shaped cross, while the third beam held the cross upright at a twenty-degree angle. From an unknown source, spikes and a hammer were produced. They stripped Joseph naked, nailed him to the beams, then stabbed him with knives in the abdomen and chest, leaving him to die slowly.

Before crucifying Joseph, the mob beat all of his clerks until they were dead. While Joseph's murder was taking place, other mobs, incited by rabid imams and disenfranchised Arabs and Berbers, rampaged through the Jewish quarter of Granada. They murdered an estimated four thousand Jews while destroying homes, shops, and a synagogue. In front of the synagogue, the mob ignited a bonfire of religious scrolls and books. No troops were dispatched to control the mob or to deter them.

Joseph's wife Sarah managed to flee the city with their son Azariah. Mother and son arrived safely at Lucena, where they were taken in and protected by the Jewish community of that city. Azariah died of an unknown illness before his bar mitzvah.

There is no written record of Caliph Badis's or Prince Abdallah's response to Joseph's death. Badis continued to rule Granada until his death in 1073. Abdallah inherited the caliphate and ruled from 1073 to 1090.

References

Cole, Peter. 1996. *The Selected Poems of Shmuel Ha Nagid.* Princeton: Princeton University Press.

Gravett, Cristopher, and Christa Hook. 1993. *Norman Knight, 950–1204 AD, Weapons, Armour, Tactics.*Oxford: Osprey Publishing.

Heath, Ian. 1976. *Armies of the Dark Ages, 600–1066.* Sussex: REG Games Ltd. (Wargames Research Group) and Heritage Models Inc.

Kaufman, J. E., and H. W. Kaufman. 2001. *The Medieval Fortress, Castles, Forts, and Walled Cities of the Middle Ages.*Illustrated by Robert M. Jurga. Da Capo Press.

Mahr,Aryeh, and Esteve Polls. 2006.*Shmuel Ha Nagid: A Tale of the Golden Age.*Jerusalem: Mahrwood Press.

Menocal, Maria Rosa. 2002. *Ornament of the World: How Muslims, Jews, and Christians Created a Culture of Tolerance in Medieval Spain.* New York: Back Bay Books; Little, Brown and Company; and Hachette Book Group.

Robert Irwin. 2004. *The Alhambra.*London: Profile Books.

Scheindlin, Raymond P. 1986. *Wine, Women and Death: Medieval Hebrew Poems on the Good Life.* New York/Oxford: Oxford University Press.

———. 1991. *The Gazelle: Medieval Hebrew Poems on God, Israel, and the Soul.*New York/Oxford: Oxford University Press.

Weinberger,Leon J. 1873. *Jewish Prince in Muslim Spain: Selected Poems of Samuel ibn Nagrela.* Tuscaloosa, AL: University of Alabama Press.

Al Andalus, https://en.wikipedia.org/wiki/Al-Andalus

malagahistoria.com/malagahistoria/alcazaba.html

Slavs in Andalusia, https://www.britannica.com/topic/Slav

Slaves in Andalusia, https:en.wikipedia.org/wiki/Slavery_in_Spain

Arabic and Hebrew Language and Poetry, https://brill.com/viw/ title/15760.lang=en

Caliphical Civilization, https://en.wikipedia.org/wiki/Caliphate

City/States of Andalusia, https://en.wikipedia.org/wiki/Al-Andalus

Difference between Arab and Berber, www.differencebetween.net/ micellaneous/culture.../difference-between-Arab-and-Berber

Ibn Nagrela, https://www.encyclopedia.com/religion/ encyclopediasl-almanac.../ibn-janah-jonah

Samuel ha'Nagid-https://www.jewishvirtuallibrary.org/ Samuel_ha-rsquo_nagid

Feud with Jonah ibn Janah, https://en.wikipedia.org/wiki/ Johah_ibn_Janah

Malaga, https://malagahistoriacom/malagahistoria/alcazaba.html

Hammudites, https://fr.wikipedia.org/wiki/Hammudites

Umayyad, https://en.wikipedia.org/wiki/ Umayyad_conquest_of_Hispania

History of Islam in Andalusia, www.bbc.uk/religion/religions/islam/ history/spain_1.shtml

Jews in Andulus,https://en.wikipedia.org/wiki/Golden_Age-of- jewish-culture -in-Spain

Nagrela, Man of Letters, https://sourcebooks.Fordam.edu/source/ha- nagid.asp

Nigrella the Author, kehillastisrael.net.docs/learning/Sephardic_ poetry.html

ibn Nagrela, https://sites.google.com/site/samuelibnnagrela

ibn Nagrela, https://en.wikipedia.org/wiki/Samuel-ibn-Naghrilla

Samuel Ha Nagid, https://www.britannica.com/biography/ Samuel-ha-Nagid

Umyyads, https://www.metmuseum.org/learn/educator/ curriculum.../the-spanish-umyyads

Caliphs of Cordoba, https://wikipedia.or/wiki/caliphate_of_cordoba

Ottoman Court Positions, https://en.wikipedia.org/wiki/ Ottoman_court

Umayyad Caliphate, https:en.wikipedia.org/wiki/ Umayyad_Caliphate

Battle of Alfuente, journeysendessays, blogspot.com/20101..battle-of- alfuente.html

Samuel ibn Nagrela, https://sites.google.com/site/samuel ibn nagrela

Cuisine of the Sephardic Jews, https://wikipedia,org/wiki/ cuisine-of-the-sephardic-jews

History of Seville, https://en.wikipedia.org/wiki/History_of_Seville

The Sanhaja, https://en.wikipedia.org/wiki/Sanhaja

Young Ha Nagid in Malaga, https://pen.org/ shmuel-hanagid-993-1056/

The Zenata, https://en.wikipedia.org/wiki/Zenata

Nagid's war poems, https://www.jstor.org/stable/1486304

Samuel Ha Nagid, https://www.jewishvirtuallibrary.org/ samuel_ha_rsquo-nagid

Cuisine of Al-Andalus, https://archive.aramoworld.com/issue/19805/ the cuisine of al-andalus.htm

1066 Granada Massacre, https://en.wikipedia.org/ wiki/1066_Granada_masacre

Almanzora River, https://en.wikipedia.org/wiki/Almanzora_(river)

Andarax River, https://en.wikipedia.org/wiki/Andarax

Guadalhorce River, https://en.wikipedia.org/wiki/Guadalhorce

Guadalmedina River, https://en.wikipedia.org/wiki/Guadalmedina

Guadalfeo River, https://en.wikipedia.org.wiki/Guadalfeo

Gualdalquivir River, https://en.wikipedia.org/wiki/Gualdalquivir

Rio Darro, https://en.wikipedia.org/wiki/Darro_(river)

Rio Genil, https://en.wikipedia.org/wiki/Genil

www.ingramcontent.com/pod-product-compliance
Lightning Source LLC
Chambersburg PA
CBHW061612100726
47898CB00002B/630